Praise for *The Last Kind Words Saloon*

'Larry McMurtry possesses one of the most engaging, tempting-to-imitate voices in contemporary American fiction, a voice so smooth and mellow you can almost hear the ice clink against the glass as he talks'   Max Byrd, *New York Times Book Review*

'Those who enjoy McMurtry's rueful humor and understated tone of elegiac melancholy will devour the book in one setting'
                                        Michael Lindgren, *Washington Post*

'A deftly narrated, often comically subversive work of fiction . . . If *Lonesome Dove* is a chronicle of the cattle-driving West that contains within its vast, broad ranges a small but heartrending intimate tragedy of paternal neglect, *The Last Kind Words Saloon* is a dark postmodernist modernist comedy'
                                        Joyce Carol Oates, *New York Review of Books*

'By turns droll, stark, wry, or raunchy, this peripatetic novel . . . will satisfy many readers who long for more from literary icon McMurtry'
                                        Keddy Ann Outlaw, *Library Journal*

'[*The Last Kind Words Saloon*] is never dull, and it's also very funny. As always, McMurtry's characters are plain-spoken but subtle and full of dry humour . . . Moseying along with McMurtry is always worthwhile'   Adam Wong, *Seattle Times*

'In this "ballad in prose", as McMurtry describes his latest book, he paints the familiar historical characters in unfamiliar ways . . . lovely'   Richard Eisenberg, *People*

Praise for *Dead Man's Walk*

'McMurtry has crafted a tale of love, fear and sacrifice in the face of Wild West adversity. With his vibrant, dynamic landscapes and language that springs from the page, this book captures the heart until the last word'
The Times

'A well-told novel, undemonstrative in its depiction of violence, and it offers a fascinating lesson on the realities of life in the mythical Wild West'
Sunday Times

'In *Dead Man's Walk*, McMurtry uses a simple, wry, immensely accessible storyteller's voice to ponder the same questions that Melville and Conrad did. This is a great book . . . Larry McMurtry, at his best here, is one of the finest American novelists, ever'
Los Angeles Times

'Succeeds marvellously . . . resurrecting two brilliantly conceived characters and delivering a rousing tale of the Wild West'
San Francisco Chronicle

'Gee-haw! Larry McMurtry is back in the yarn-slinging business – with a vengeance . . . Readers will gobble up *Dead Man's Walk* – a wild and woolly read – from cover to cover'
Denver Post

'McMurtry spins some scary, bloodthirsty tall tales and peoples them with remarkably vivid characters'
New York Daily News

'McMurtry remains a good storyteller, and he remains a master of dialogue, doing a sort of frontier version of Oscar Wilde'
Washington Post

Praise for *Comanche Moon*

'McMurtry's revisionist vision of frontier life is always compelling'
Booklist

'The [frontier] myth is intact, if a tad tattered by McMurtry's darkly comedic touch and sly debunking of chivalric conventions. But at its core are McMurtry's respect and gift for exaggerated and fanciful pageantry and heroic form'   *New York Daily News*

'A sprawling, picaresque novel'   *New York Times Book Review*

'[A] fine tableau of western life, full of imaginative exploits, convincing historical background, and characters who are alive'
Kirkus Reviews

'A monumental work that has few equals in current literature'
Library Journal

'*Comanche Moon* has its considerable pleasures . . . a singular treat'
San Francisco Chronicle

'McMurtry is one of our finest storytellers, and he's at his best here'
People

'Consistently entertaining'   *Entertainment Weekly*

'Almost impossible to put down . . . McMurtry knows how to deploy his most suspenseful episodes for maximum effect. He treats his large cast of characters with humour and respect'   *Boston Herald*

Praise for *Lonesome Dove*

'With prose as smooth as worn saddle leather . . . McMurtry gives the reader the cattle drive and the Old West in a way it has never been done'

USA Today

'Highly visual, almost cinematic . . . original . . . deeply affecting . . . As for action, *Lonesome Dove* has it all and then some'

New York Times

'A marvellous novel . . . moves with joyous energy . . . amply imagined and crisply, lovingly written. I haven't enjoyed a book more this year'

Newsweek

'Larry McMurtry tops them all with his long-awaited epic, *Lonesome Dove* . . . McCrae and Call are seasoned frontiersmen and ferocious Indian fighters . . . Throughout *Lonesome Dove*, McMurtry examines their bond – an unspoken and hardly understood friendship. In western fiction, a like relationship seldom has been more finely crafted . . . And the women! If there is a contemporary male novelist blessed with keener insight, I'd like to know about it . . . What McMurtry has created is nothing less than a masterful odyssey, and an enduring addition to the lore of Western Americana'

Los Angeles Daily News

'*Lonesome Dove* is anything but predictable . . . skilfully drawn characters crop up at nearly every turn . . . Mr McMurtry knows the easy camaraderie that develops among cowboys on the trail. He knows the depth of the devotion that men in that part of the country have for their women. He knows about rattlesnakes and sandstorms and stinging scorpions and runaways. In Mr McMurtry's hands, the trail drive becomes a way of examining some fundamental questions. Is it the way we live that matters? Or is it what we accomplish that's really important? . . . Splendid'

Wall Street Journal

Praise for *Streets of Laredo*

'McMurtry has written a sad, funny elegy not only for his characters' pasts, but for the waning of the American West'   *New York Times*

'One of McMurtry's most powerful and moving achievements'
Los Angeles Times

'Larry McMurtry remains a genius at dialogue. The scene where the seven whores start reminiscing about the first men in their lives is wonderful'   *New York Times Book Review*

'*Streets of Laredo* is a splendid addition to the literary portrait of McMurtry's native Texas and the West that he has been creating for three decades. It's also one of his most affectingly melancholic books ... The characters are as finely etched as any McMurtry has ever minted'   *Newsweek*

'A marvellous novel in its own right, and in every way a worthy successor to *Lonesome Dove*'   *Chicago Tribune*

'Gorgeous ... violent, funny, achingly sad, filled with heroism and regret ... If you can put *Streets of Laredo* down, I'll eat my ten-gallon hat'   *Cosmopolitan*

'The winding down of a grand American legend offers a vision of dust and death through a golden haze'   *Time*

'Those who have been waiting ... for an appropriate sequel to the memorable and Pulitzer-winning *Lonesome Dove* can take heart. *Streets of Laredo* continues that epic of the waning years of the Texas Rangers with all the narrative drive and elegiac passion of its forerunner'   *Publishers Weekly*

ALL MY FRIENDS ARE
GOING TO BE STRANGERS

Larry McMurtry is the author of more than thirty novels, including the Pulitzer Prize-winning *Lonesome Dove*. He has also written memoirs and essays, and received an Academy Award for Best Adapted Screenplay for his work on *Brokeback Mountain*. The cinematic treatment of *Terms of Endearment* swept the boards at the 1984 Academy Awards, winning Oscars in several categories, including Best Picture. He lives in Archer City, Texas.

By Larry McMurtry and published by Pan Macmillan

Larry McMurtry

ALL MY FRIENDS ARE GOING TO BE STRANGERS

PICADOR

First published 1972 by Simon & Schuster, Inc., New York

First published in the UK 1994 by Phoenix

First published by Picador 2015
an imprint of Pan Macmillan
20 New Wharf Road, London N1 9RR
Associated companies throughout the world
www.panmacmillan.com

ISBN 978-1-4472-7460-5

1 3 5 7 9 8 6 4 2

A CIP catalogue record for this book is available from the British Library.

Typeset by Ellipsis Digital Limited, Glasgow
Printed and bound by CPI Group (UK) Ltd, Croydon, CR0 4YY

Visit www.picador.com to read more about all our books
and to buy them. You will also find features, author interviews and
news of any author events, and you can sign up for e-newsletters
so that you're always first to hear about our new releases.

For Marcia

PREFACE

I wrote this novel very rapidly; in a sense, I exhaled it. Another way to put it is that *Moving On*, written just previously, expelled it, as a kind of afterbirth.

Moving On was a long effort, twenty-five hundred pages in manuscript, at least in the initial draft. As I approached the end I felt tired but also exhilarated; some energy remained beneath the fatigue, and a momentum that I didn't want to lose. Indeed, within the fatigue itself there was a kind of high.

Moving On, of course, could not be prolonged just because I was high and still eager to write. Its final sentence duly arrived, and that was that; but the sense of momentum remained. I felt that if I just had another novel to write I could probably race through it before my energies subsided and I sank into creative sleep.

Danny Deck was the perfect point-of-view character for a novelist in such a situation. He wasn't me, but there was no large gap between his sensibility and my own; I became comfortable with his voice at once and liked his quirks and his mainly sad appreciation of the absurd.

Better yet, his dilemma was one most artists face and struggle with at some point, usually as inconclusively as Danny himself does: whether art can be persuaded to allow its artists a little of normal life and common happiness and yet permit them to create.

Danny's bleak conclusion is that art won't be persuaded—not really; not "normal" life, as exemplified for him by Emma Horton and her solidly normal kitchen.

That sort of mundane happiness, he recognizes, he's probably just not going to have. This recognition is the more wrenching because Danny's just written one slight book and is far from convinced that the level of art he's likely to produce will be worth the loss. What if, torn forever from the warmth of Emma's kitchen, he only writes bad books, or, at best, minor books?

Though young, Danny has already read a lot, and is realist enough to realize that most writers, whatever they give up and however hard they strive, are still only able to be minor. Is the sacrifice of common happiness worth it if one is only going to be minor? That's one of the animating questions the book asks. Is Danny correct in his judgment that it is art that's distancing him from happiness? That's another.

These dilemmas are intensified for him by his loss not only of the warm, normal Emma but the not so warm, but brilliant, stimulating, unignorable artist-woman, Jill Peel, a girl as fascinating to him as she is elusive.

In the end Danny comes to believe that he can expect nothing of life except pages and words; this stirs in him a kind of fury against art, as well as personal despair, and he attempts to drown his hated second novel in the Rio Grande.

The lady-or-the-tiger ending, with Danny standing dejected in the middle of the Rio Grande, not dead but not eager to live, has irked many readers. On the whole, Danny Deck has been far more successful at getting loved by readers than he ever was at getting loved by the women in his life. I am constantly being asked whether he's dead or alive, and, if alive, whether he will ever reappear.

For the benefit of those hopeful readers, I can now assert that Danny lives. It's been sixteen years since I last laid eyes on him, but he's phoned in several times lately and seems determined to come back and speak his middle-aged mind on a variety of subjects; his many old friends can expect to be seeing him shortly in a novel called *My Girlfriend's Boyfriends*.

—Larry McMurtry
1989

1.

I THINK I fell in love with Sally while she was eating breakfast, the first morning we were together. Either I did it then or I did it a little earlier the same morning, watching her stretch. I had gone up to Austin to waste time and eat Mexican food and ended up getting invited to a party at a professor's house. He was a dapper little English sociologist with a great lust for students—he referred to girls as fuckists, a term I had never heard. Several times during the evening he came over to me and pointed at a girl and said, "There's a great little fuckist for you, my boy."

Later on in the evening I think he made a pass at me, but I could have been wrong. He was very tipsy and it could have been just drunken friendliness. His name was Godwin Lloyd-Jons. Sally had been his fuckist for several months, but at the time I didn't realize that. I got drunk enough that driving back to Houston didn't seem like a good idea, so I spent the night on Godwin's living room floor, alongside several other young drunks.

Sometime during the night Sally and Godwin had a big fight—I have a vague memory of hearing doors banging. He kicked her all the way out to the street, but she had no money at all so she walked around the block until she figured Godwin had had time to pass out and then came in and got a sheet and pillow and spent the night on the floor, next to me. I hadn't even seen her at the party—I think she was upstairs getting ready for the fight. When I woke up she was right there beside me, yawning and stretching. Sunlight filled the living room, but we were the only two people awake. "Let's go eat breakfast," I said immediately, before somebody else could wake up and ask her. I had never seen such a beautiful long-bodied girl in my life. My immediate thought was how wonderful it would be to wake up beside her every morning and watch her stretch. Her face looked soft. She was a little surprised by my invitation and looked me over for about two seconds before she accepted. I stood up and reached out my hand to her, thinking she might let me help her up. She looked at me for another two seconds and didn't take my hand. She got up by herself and stretched again. As we were walking down the shady sidewalk she finally let me take her hand. She also smoothed my hair, which was extremely uncombed. We both felt shy because we were holding hands, and I felt even shyer because Sally was three inches taller than me. All I knew was that I had suddenly found someone new that I liked, and it was a deep enjoyment. She was wearing a loose blue dress.

We walked all the way to Guadalupe Street and ate a huge breakfast in a little cafe—ham and eggs and toast and most of the grape jelly they had. Sally was very quiet, but I talked constantly. I was trying to conceal, at least for an hour or two, that I already didn't want to leave her. As we were walking back to Godwin's we both got a little nervous. Neither of us knew what we were going to do. All I knew was that I wanted to prolong knowing her. I stopped talking and we walked along silently, holding hands. A block or two from Godwin's we came to where my green Chevy was parked, and we stopped and sat on the fender for a while. I kissed her twice, but she was too preoccupied with her problems to be really interested in kissing. "I have to decide if I'm going to go back to him," she said. "If I don't I guess I have to go to my parents, in Lake Charles."

"Why'd he kick you out?"

Sally looked annoyed. "He wanted me to give him a blow job," she said. "I didn't feel like it. Then he said I was frigid."

"Let me drive you to Lake Charles," I said. "I've never been in Louisiana."

She looked at me for several seconds. She looked so vulnerable that I felt I had to try very hard to be trustworthy. "Okay," she said. We kissed again and she was more interested. I felt very shy. Then an old lady and a basset came walking along and we got off the car and went on to Godwin's. He was sitting on the front steps, wearing red Bermuda shorts and no shirt. He was rubbing some kind of salve onto his chest, and he didn't look very dapper.

"I'm glad you're back," he said to Sally. "Awful pain. I was looking for you in the garden and a bee stung me. Never even saw the little bugger. I'm all swollen. First bee sting of my life."

Sally looked remote. "Danny's going to take me to Lake Charles," she said. "I just want to get my dresses and my radio."

She walked up the steps and into the house. Godwin put the lid on the bottle of salve he was using. "This bloody stuff doesn't work," he said.

"Wet baking soda's supposed to be good," I said.

Godwin sighed. "I love her and you're taking her away," he said. "Not ethical. You were my guest—now you're robbing me. No ethical code advocates robbing one's host."

I was embarrassed. I hadn't expected him to say he loved her.

"You have some grace," he said. "You know it's wrong, what you're doing. Go away before she comes out and I shall always respect you."

"I don't think she loves you," I said.

"A fact that alters nothing," Godwin said. "I love her. Please leave. You're obviously a promising young man. I've heard you're the best young writer in the state. A theft of this nature will only drag you down. Go away and write. I need Sally."

I felt very defensive. "You don't treat her well," I said.

It made him furious. "Oh, bugger you!" he said. "Pretentious young bastard. How could you write? What do you know? I *don't* treat her well, as it happens, but it's fucking none of your business. I love her, however I treat her. Losing her will cost me a bloody whole year of pain. Bugger you! You'll treat her too bloody well and make her miserable too. Fucking little thief! Please. Don't do it. Go away before she comes out."

"Look," I said. "She doesn't want to stay here. If I don't steal her somebody else will."

The temper went out of him. "You admit it's a crime, but you're still going to do it," he said. "There's no salvation for you. Only a bloody writer would be that unscrupulous."

[3]

"I've only published two stories," I said. "What does my being a writer have to do with it?"

"I do not propose to explain it," he said. "My bee sting hurts. Take Sally then. You shan't have her long. Robbery breeds robbery. Somebody will take her from you as easily as you're taking her from me. I might have held her, given a bloody break or two, but you'll make her fucking unholdable forever. Then I suppose you'll go away and write about it."

"Do you dislike all writers?"

"Every bloody one," he said. "They ought to be imprisoned. They're all thieves."

"I didn't plan this," I said.

That made him mad again. "Oh, fuck off, for God's sake," he said. "Who cares what you didn't plan?"

Sally came out then. She had her clothes in a blue suitcase and carried a radio under one arm. She sat them down on the steps a minute, to readjust her hold. Godwin took a can of beer from between his ankles and sipped it.

"Love, don't leave me," he said. "He's utterly bloody wrong for you. I know I was a brute last night, but I was really quite drunk. Can't I be forgiven? I'm only that awful when I'm drunk."

"I forgive you," Sally said. "That wasn't even it. I just don't want to stay."

"What was *it*?" Godwin asked.

"Geoffrey told me he went to bed with you," Sally said. "He said you wanted him to move in and stay in the room next to mine. I guess I'm just too simple a girl for that."

"Oh, bugger!" Godwin said, leaping to his feet. He grabbed Sally's radio and threw it all the way out into the middle of the street—it busted to smithereens when it hit the pavement. He kicked her suitcase down the steps but I caught it and it wasn't hurt. Sally ran down where I was. Godwin was purple in the face he was so mad.

"Get out of here!" he yelled. "Go have a simple straight-A fuck somewhere, that's what you need. You goddamn well don't need an odd fucker like me in your life!"

"I just said I was simple," Sally said.

"And so you are, my dear," he yelled. "A simple, stupid, frigid

[4]

young bitch! God spare me from your kind! God spare me! I'd rather fuck turtles, if turtles can be fucked, than to touch you again! Get away from my house. I'm sorry I ever knew you." He was trembling like he was about to collapse.

"You shut up!" Sally said. "What's so bad about being simple?"

"*I'm* not simple," Godwin said. "God spare me from simple little American beauties like you. Your simpleness is the bloody most destructive force on the fucking planet! I hope I never meet anyone under forty again."

Then he sat down on the steps and began to sob. We didn't know what to say. Finally I picked up Sally's suitcase and we walked away, leaving the busted radio in the street. Before we got half a block Godwin began to follow us, waving his beer can and crying for Sally to come back. He followed us all the way to my car and stood on the sidewalk crying. His chest was white with salve and his tears were making it messy.

"Love, don't leave me," he said. "Geoffrey meant nothing to me. I would never have let him move in. You know I love you most dearly."

Sally looked exasperated. "Oh, Godwin, go wash off your bee sting," she said.

It switched him once more from tears to anger. He flung his beer can at us but it missed the car and landed in the street. It was almost empty anyway. Godwin suddenly rushed at the car and began to shove it, trying as hard as he could to turn it over.

"Cunt!" he yelled. "Selfish young cunt! Cunt! Cunt!"

He was really yelling and the Chevy was really rocking. Sally scooted over next to me.

"Let's go," she said.

Just as I was about to start the car Godwin quit shoving and rushed around to the front end. Suddenly he disappeared from view. He was obviously doing something in front of the car, but we couldn't see what.

"What now?" I asked. Sally looked disgusted. I left my motor running and got out to look. Godwin had his arms wrapped around the front bumper and his feet braced against the car in front of me. He looked grimly determined.

"You shan't take her," he said. "I shall hang on till death. You'll have to crush me."

I checked the rear and saw I could back out with no trouble. Godwin's jaw was set and his feet still braced. He had a death grip on the bumper.

"Look," I said. "We really are leaving. It's just inevitable."

"I've challenged the inevitable before and beaten it," he said. "We have nothing to discuss."

I got in next to Sally. "We can back out," I said. "How long do you think he'll hang on?"

"Not long," she said. "He's not very stubborn."

I backed out quite slowly and without speeding up much eased backward down the street. It was a wide, quiet residential street near the university. Sally was right. After I had backed past two houses Godwin appeared in front of us, sitting in the road.

"See," she said.

I drove up beside him, but kept far enough away that he couldn't rush us. He stood up just as I pulled beside him and actually grinned at me. Somehow he had become composed and dapper again.

"Well, fun and games," he said. "It's not worth the skin off my ass. You're bloody gutsy. I could have scared most kids off. Merry fucking and may you rot in hell."

He bent and looked in the window at Sally. "Bye, love," he said, his voice dropping. He thrust his head in, past me, and kissed her cheek.

"Bye, Godwin," she said. "You better not let Geoffrey in or you'll really be screwed."

Godwin shrugged, as if it were a matter of no moment. He smiled a dapper smile, but only with his mouth. His eyes were wet. He strolled to the sidewalk and we drove on, past the university, out 19th Street, out of Austin. It was mid-July and the highway shimmered with heat.

"I have to admire his temper," I said.

Sally sniffed. "I don't," she said. "He yells a lot, but he sure can't fuck very well."

2.

FORTUNATELY discontentment doesn't affect my appetite. Sally had just walked out the door, mad, which made me very discontent, but just before she left she had fried a whole chicken and I sat at the ironing board and ate the half of it that was rightfully mine. The ironing board was what we were using for a kitchen table.

Sally hadn't really wanted to go to Lake Charles, when she left Godwin. I was completely in love with her, so I took her to Houston with me and a week later we got married. I wouldn't have minded living in sin for a while, but Sally was scared of her parents. Lake Charles wasn't very far away and she was afraid they would get wind of things, in which case her father would come up and kill us. I was just as glad to get married, but I was surprised at how often Sally got mad at me, afterward. We had only been married three weeks and she had already walked out in high dudgeon five or six times. I could never understand what I did to put her in high dudgeon, but whatever it was I always felt utterly to blame.

It was a hot, muggy Houston dusk, and big Gulf Coast mosquitoes flitted against the window screen while I ate my chicken. The fact that Sally had gone away mad preyed on my mind and made me indecisive. It took me five minutes to decide whether to put her half of the chicken in the oven or in the icebox. Finally I put it in the oven, and just as I did someone knocked at the door. My immediate thought was that it must be Mrs. Salomea, a formidable lady whose backyard we walked through in order to get to our apartment. Just

[7]

that morning I had done something absolutely inexcusable and I was sure Mrs. Salomea was coming to accost me about it.

I think having Sally to sleep with had given me the confidence to do what I did. I had been wanting to for months, before she came, and hadn't had the nerve. Mrs. Salomea had a terrific old tree in her backyard. Its top branches must have been two hundred feet above the ground, and it was always full of squirrels. I had a little single-shot .22—it had been the only gun I could afford all through my childhood, when hunting had been an obsession with me. I thought I had outgrown the obsession, but Mrs. Salomea's tree full of squirrels made it come back on me. All the time I was writing my novel I could see the squirrels out the window and I kept wanting to go out and shoot one. Sometimes in the morning, before I started writing, I would sit with the .22 and shoot eight or ten squirrels in my imagination, always aiming at the ones on the highest branches. That morning, in a moment of complete happiness, I had actually shot one.

Sally was the reason I was so happy. We meant to make love when we went to bed, but for some reason I got to talking and we didn't. I guess we slept all night feeling sexy, because about dawn we woke up doing it. We had just sort of rolled together. I went right back to sleep and when I woke up again, about seven, I felt wonderful. Sally was still asleep. A crease in the sheet had made a crease on one side of her face. I felt clear and dry and hungry, and extremely like working. Out the window I could see the squirrels in Mrs. Salomea's tree. I felt that I had lived a routine life long enough. I would have taken a parachute jump, if one had been offered me just then. It was obvious to me that I could do much more than I had been doing. I put on some Levi's and got my .22 and one shell and went outside. The thick St. Augustine grass in the Salomeas' yard was wet with dew. Pale-yellow shafts of sunlight slanted down through the leaves of the great tree. I was only going to shoot a running squirrel, not one that was sitting. Finally a brown squirrel ran along a branch very high up, eighty-five feet I'm sure, maybe a hundred, just a movement on the branch with the sun flickering through the leaves right above him. I swung and shot and he dropped straight down all those feet of air, as if a string had been stretched from where I hit him straight to the ground. It was a perfect shot. He was dead before he left the branch. His beautiful brown coat had beads of dew on it when I picked him up. I know I should have left him alive, but I couldn't have, not that morning. I'm afraid I was his fate—otherwise I couldn't have hit him at that distance, with him running and the sun in my eyes. I hadn't shot a gun in seven or eight years, either; but that is not to say it was a lucky shot. It was perfect, not lucky. I was frying him when Sally woke up.

"What have you done now?" she said. She was standing in the kitchen doorway, holding her clothes over her arm.

"I can still shoot," I said.

Sally was horrified. "We have cereal we can eat!" she said, pointing at it. "Wheat germ is perfectly healthy. I wouldn't have married you if I'd known you were going to kill animals."

She wouldn't touch the squirrel—I had to eat it all myself. "Squirrels are in no danger of extinction," I said. "Animals would drive us off the earth if a few weren't killed now and then."

My reasonableness didn't placate her. I apologized several times during the day, but it did no good. There was no knowing if she would ever forgive me for killing the squirrel—or for anything else I did that she didn't like. Forgiveness was not the kind of act Sally was prone to. By her own admission she had never been heartbroken in her life.

She liked to eat meat, too. It just never occurs to her while she's eating it that an animal has been killed. She looked at me all morning like I was the Butcher of Dachau. Finally it bugged me.

"People with appetites like yours shouldn't be so idealistic," I said. "How would you like to live on kelp for the rest of your life?"

Maybe my saying that was why she walked off mad, six hours later. She has delayed reactions. Sure enough, it was Mrs. Salomea who had knocked at the door.

"Danny?" she said. I began to try to think of a defense, and also to look for an apron. It was very hot and I was only wearing my underwear.

"Yes ma'am," I said. I found a big dish towel. Sally didn't have any aprons.

"I'll be right there," I said. "I'm not fully dressed."

"I'll let myself in," she said. I heard the door shut. Mrs. Salomea neither wasted time nor stood on formalities.

Somehow the dish towel I found made me look even less dressed than I was. I really felt indecent, but I knew I couldn't stall much longer, indecent or not. Mrs. Salomea was noted all over Houston for her impatience. She was the wife of a very well-to-do decorator—I guess he could be described as locally prominent. His name was Sammy Salomea and he decorated mansions. It was generally agreed that Mrs. Salomea was eating him alive, one joint at a time. I think she had him eaten about up to the hips. She was thirty-eight or so, but very trim. In the days before I got married the Salomeas would sometimes invite me into their yard in the late afternoons to be a fourth at badminton. They were free with their liquor and I always managed to get drunk on those occasions. Those were the only times I ever got to drink good liquor. Mrs. Salomea's first name was Jenny. She and I always teamed against Sammy and some guest or other and we always slaughtered them. We were both extremely good bad-minton players and could have slaughtered almost anyone we were put up against. Up to a certain point I'm a very well-coordinated drunk and I hit some terrific smashes. Sammy Salomea was slightly in awe of me, but Mrs. Salomea wasn't in awe of me at all. I was slightly in awe of her. I always stayed as late as I could, drinking their liquor and watching her eat her husband. I told myself I was gather-ing material for a book I meant to write, to be called "Cannibalism in Texas," but I was really just fascinated by Jenny Salomea. She was the scariest woman I had ever known, and God only knew what she was going to have to say about my shooting that squirrel. I finally tucked the dish towel into my shorts and straggled into the other room, feeling sheepish and quite apprehensive. I don't think she approved of Sally, either. She was standing by our bookcase in her tennis outfit, a drink in one hand.

"Hi," she said. "I wanted to ask you something. Does your wife like cunnilingus?"

The question completely disoriented me. I had been about to try and explain that shooting the squirrel had been a rare, isolated act, one that could never possibly repeat itself.

"Beg pardon?" I said.

"I think that's the way you pronounce it," she said. "Cunnilingus."

"That's the way I've always heard it pronounced," I said, though truthfully I don't think I'd ever heard it pronounced before at all.

"Does Sally like it?"

"I don't know," I said. "We've only been married a week."

"You better hurry up and try it. A girl that pretty's not going to stay around very long if she gets bored. I saw her walking down the sidewalk and she looked pretty bored."

"She's not bored," I said. "We just got married. How come you asked me that?"

"I've never done it," she said. "I lead a pretty routine life. I thought maybe you could show me about it while your wife's taking a walk."

I'd been horny for her the whole two years I'd lived in the apartment, and she'd never so much as given me a look. Now I was married and there she was. There was no bull about her, either. She was obviously ready to peel off her tennis shorts. Nothing ever happens conveniently for me.

"I'm just a student," I said. "How about Sammy?"

"Oh, come on," she said, indignant that I would even suggest it. "Sammy's not going to root around like that. He doesn't like to expose himself to germs—his mother scared the shit out of him when he was a kid."

"I meant where is he," I said, though I hadn't. Sammy was very fastidious. I had forgotten that.

"He's in Ecuador. He has a client with a ranch there."

"I don't understand why you came here now," I said.

"I told you in plain English," Mrs. Salomea said. It was obvious her patience was being strained.

"If you don't think you know how say so and I'll go home and get drunk," she said. "You're not as *macho* about sex as you are about badminton, are you?"

Her manner was awfully irritating. "I know how," I said. "I just got married, remember?"

"Big deal," she said. "I bet she was desperate to get away from somebody or she wouldn't have taken up with you."

Oddly, I had come to the same conclusion. It made me furious, that Jenny Salomea could figure it out so easily.

"Go to hell!" I said. "I didn't even invite you in."

"Why don't you just admit you don't know how? You don't have to get vulgar. I know you're just a kid. You're so sloppy you look like you'd be good at it—that's why I asked. Also, we're handy to one another."

"We've been handy to one another for *two years*," I said.

"Yeah, but you weren't sexy then. You looked too studious. You even looked studious when you were drunk. Maybe it took a little sex to make you sexy. They say it works that way. Makes the feathers shine."

"I just fell in love," I said. "Didn't you notice that?"

"Sure," she said. "I wouldn't have come here when you weren't in love even if I *had* thought you were sexy. You don't think I want you in love with me, do you? You'd be harder to keep out than the god-damn mosquitoes. I don't like love anyway. I was just hoping for a little cunnilingus."

"It's the wrong time of day," I said. "Sally was probably just going around the block."

"That's a bunch of horseshit," Jenny said. "I know her type. She'll be gone for hours. We could have already done it if you weren't so slow off the mark."

Just then there was a knock on the door. I was very grateful for the interruption. It was a man from Western Union.

"Daniel Deck?" he said. He looked taken aback to see me in the dish towel. I admit it made me look awfully sleazy.

"Yes?"

"Telegram."

"My goodness," I said. "I've never gotten a telegram in my life."

He handed it to me anyway. "Could be a mistake," he said. "I've never delivered one to anybody who looked like you." He was a middle-aged guy who seemed bored with his profession.

The telegram was really for me. I could hardly believe it. I walked back to where Jenny Salomea was, trying to believe it. It was from an editor at Random House, for whom I had revised my first novel:

DEAR DANNY. REVISION EXCELLENT. NOVEL ACCEPTED.
CONGRATULATIONS. YOU DID GOOD. LETTER AND

CONTRACT WILL FOLLOW. I GOT YOURS ABOUT MARRIAGE.
CONGRATULATIONS ON THAT TOO. KISS SALLY FOR ME. ALSO
PROSPECTS GOOD FOR AN IMMEDIATE MOVIE SALE. COLUMBIA
VERY EXCITED. HOW WOULD 30,000 STRIKE YOU? OR MORE.
YOURS. BRUCE.

"Jesus Christ," I said. "I sold my novel. It's going to be published."

"Yeah?" Mrs. Salomea said. "Somebody told me you were writing a book. What you gonna do now?"

"I don't know," I said. "I can't believe it." I really couldn't. I kept looking at the telegram to make it seem real. Things were swirling. I never expect most of my dreams to come true, even though I keep dreaming them, and when one does come true I don't know how to handle the feelings I have. I felt very odd—I was glad and excited and curious and a lot of things. I became instantly giddy, and within the giddiness was a kind of fear. I had got one dream but something felt wrong in the pit of my stomach. Maybe some other dream was being taken away from me forever. Maybe I wanted that one more. I didn't know, and at the same time I felt dizzy with relief. It was actually going to be published.

"Well, I guess that leaves getting drunk," Jenny said. "Put some pants on and come up to the house. We got some champagne. Do you have any dirty books?"

I was looking at the telegram again. I had just really noticed about the movie. Thirty thousand must mean dollars. "What?" I said.

"I was going to borrow a dirty book, if you've got one," she said. "You're not going to be much help."

"I've only got *Tropic of Capricorn*," I said. I had stolen it from the library.

"I wouldn't know one from another," she said. "Lend it to me."

I found the book for her and got some clothes on and we went to her house. I had never been in her house before, only in the yard. The house was full of terrible art, but I was feeling very happy and would have forgiven Jenny or almost anybody worse art than that. My stomach had quit hurting and I had the telegram in my hip pocket. Jenny really began to impress me. She gallantly put aside her personal desires and helped me celebrate. Not only was she not totally

[13]

selfish; in some way she was lavishly generous. They had champagne all right, but only in jeroboams. I couldn't believe it.

"Oh, Sammy likes to think big," Jenny said. "He never buys anything small." She insisted that we open one. "Sure," she said. "You must have some friends somewhere who'll want to celebrate too."

I could barely carry the bottle, it was so heavy. We opened it in Jenny's kitchen, which was easily a hundred times the size of ours. In the center of the kitchen was the biggest butcher's block I'd ever seen. It was a whole section of a redwood tree.

"That's magnificent," I said. "You could butcher an ox on that thing."

"That's an idea," she said. "Sammy bought it in San Francisco. It weighs over a thousand pounds."

We opened the huge bottle and drank about a quart each, in almost no time. I couldn't stay off the woodblock. It was irresistible. I helped Jenny up and we danced—it was the only way I could keep her from reading the Henry Miller book. The Salomeas had a terrific hi-fi system. I began to feel drunk, but it was one of my better-coordinated drunks. We danced for twenty minutes and neither of us fell off the woodblock. Jenny was a well-coordinated drinker too. The woodblock was just the right size for cha-chas.

"You're a sexy kid," she said, as we were sidling around one another. "I can't stand your wife."

"I don't know her very well," I said. I didn't want to argue. Jenny Salomea was a sexy lady. She kept lifting my T-shirt and counting my ribs, as we danced. I hadn't been to the barbershop in a couple of months and my hair was almost as long as hers. It seemed to amuse her. Also the woodblock was affecting. I've never seen a sexier object. The name Sally began to blink in my brain. Fortunately the phone rang. It was Jenny's sister—she was divorcing somebody in Galveston and wanted to talk about it. I got clear of the woodblock. Western Union and Southwestern Bell had combined to keep me faithful, at least for one evening. As soon as Jenny got off the phone I said I had to go.

"Run mouse run," she said, not particularly angry. She lifted up my T-shirt and counted my ribs again.

"I love Sally," I said. "I better give monogamy a chance."

"I took that attitude once," she said, holding out her champagne glass. "Now I'd rather give cunnilingus a chance."

I felt apologetic, but she was very pleasant. We went in and threw our champagne glasses in her huge fireplace, though neither of us could remember precisely what tradition that went with. I had taken a liking to Jenny and had mixed feelings. She insisted I take the jeroboam with me—it still had an awful lot of champagne in it.

"If you're too drunk to walk you can borrow my car," she said, as I staggered out the door with the big bottle.

"I can make it to the library," I said. "There's probably somebody there to drink it with."

"Okay."

She walked through her yard with me, rubbing my back. "As soon as your wife leaves we'll play some badminton," she said. I had both arms around the bottle of champagne. Jenny kept sniffing me in various places—apparently she liked how I smelled. It was too much. I had a warm impulse and turned and kissed her. She was nothing loath, but kissing merely seemed to amuse her.

"You'll never learn," she said, chuckling.

"Why not?"

"You just won't," she said. "Not you." She said it fondly, though, and she gave me a little shove, to get me started.

3.

I HAD almost more liquor than I could carry, inside and out, but fortunately I didn't have far to carry it. Rice University was just across the street. I staggered along, hugging the jeroboam and feeling slightly guilty. It was obvious to me that if the phone hadn't rung Jenny Salomea and I would have done something adulterous on her woodblock. I have no real resistance to temptation, drunk or sober. Very few attractive temptations come my way and when they do I almost always yield to them. I can't smash them away like they were badminton birdies. I just don't have any moral coordination, as Jenny Salomea well knew.

On the formal quadrangle in front of the library I ran into Sally. She was riding a bicycle. A tall math major I knew slightly was riding another bicycle, right beside her. He was a campus genius, and very smug about it. I had never liked him and I liked him even less when it dawned on me that he was taking a bike ride with Sally. His name was Rick Leonard.

"Hi," I said. "Where'd you get the bike?"

"Borrowed it," Sally said. She looked like she was enjoying herself. I really didn't like the tone of things. My stomach was getting bad signals again. I tried to set the jeroboam on one of the hedges that filled the quadrangle, but it didn't work. The bottle sank into the hedge.

"What's in the bottle?" Rick asked.

"Champagne."

"How come?" Sally asked.

"Mrs. Salomea gave it to me. She's not so bad. It's to celebrate selling my novel. I just got a telegram."

I handed it to her and she sat on the bicycle and read it. She could sit on the seat and reach the ground with both legs. Her legs were remarkably long and remarkably shapely. I loved to watch her stand that way, although I was generally in a disapproving mood.

"Gee, that's nice," she said, a little speculatively. Rick did not pretend to be delighted with my success. When the news got out I would be a campus genius too. Actually it griped him that Sally had to break off the bike ride.

I was an honors student and had a key to the library. Rick had one too, but he declined to come to my celebration. He didn't deign to make an excuse. The library was the usual madhouse. It had supersilent floors that had to be waxed every night in order to remain supersilent. The waxing staff was hard at it, riding their giant waxers around the huge rooms. I had one friend on the staff, a happy-go-lucky little Mexican named Petey Ximenes. Petey was not important enough to merit a giant waxer, but he didn't care. He had a middle-sized waxer and spent his evenings smoking marijuana while he followed his waxer in and out of the fifth-floor stacks. He loved to get high and follow his waxer around. The other concern of his life was fourteen-year-old girls. He spent his afternoons hanging around a Mexican junior high on the North Side, picking up fourteen-year-olds. Usually he bribed them with lemon drops and screwed them. He had very trusting eyes.

"Hey, guy," he said, when he saw us come out of the elevator. He immediately took a comb out of his pocket and began to comb his ducktail. They had been out of fashion for several years, even among Mexicans, but Petey hadn't kept up. When he began combing his hair his waxer went swooshing on down an aisle.

"You better turn that off," Sally said sternly. For some reason Petey disgusted her. He looked at her humbly with his trusting eyes, but it didn't make her any friendlier. The huge bottle didn't surprise him— he had long ago concluded that I didn't lead a normal life.

"I sold my novel," I said.

"Good deal—you gonna be famous," Petey said. "Lots of money, lots of ass." Then he realized that was a mistake. He hadn't adjusted to my being married. Sally gave him such a hostile look that he didn't open his mouth the rest of the night.

We went downstairs and found Henry, another friend of mine. Henry was an executive-level janitor. As usual, he was at the main desk, making phone calls to Hollywood. His aspiration was to be a screenwriter. Once in the twenties he had somehow met Darryl F. Zanuck, and Zanuck had told him that if he ever wanted to get in pictures he had only to give him a call. Henry had been wanting to get in pictures for about fifteen years, and had taken to calling Zanuck almost every night. He never got past the outermost answering service, but he was convinced it was because Zanuck was so busy. He had written eight strange screenplays, all of them involving the Seventh Cavalry—in the most bizarre of them the Seventh Cavalry only barely managed to keep the Flathead Indians from razing San Francisco, which Henry had resituated somewhere near Portland, to save shooting costs, he said. Since I was a fellow writer he let me read his scripts and make criticisms. I thought the scripts were hilarious and encouraged him to write more, which was probably bad.

Henry thought my novel was hopelessly dull and kept trying to get me to put the Seventh Cavalry in it somewhere. He was a gaunt man who smoked a very heavy pipe and had a drooping lower lip as a consequence.

"Don't that beat all?" he said, when I told him I had sold my book. It was his one comment. While we waited for him to finish trying to reach Darryl Zanuck a crowd of students gathered around us, drawn by the champagne bottle. Most of them were history graduate students, a perennially horny lot. They were indifferent to my success but they certainly weren't indifferent to Sally. They didn't bother to conceal their lust.

The only person in the crowd that I liked was Flap Horton, an undergraduate like myself. He was wavering between history and English—I was wavering between English and nothing. Flap had only been married six months himself. His wife Emma was chubby and loved to drink. We all drank together when we could afford to. Flap had looked sheepish ever since he got married. He seemed to get skinnier as Emma got more chubby.

When Henry finally got off the phone we went down to the basement and drank the rest of the champagne out of paper cups from the janitor's water cooler. Petey was insecure amid so many Anglos. He chewed his hangnail. Despite Sally's order he hadn't turned off his waxer—it was somewhere on the fifth floor, still swooshing around. The history majors talked incessantly, trying to impress Sally with their erudition. Their effort was a big flop, as I could have told them it would be. Nothing bores Sally like erudition. She looked bored and remote, and she can bring off remote looks better than any woman I know, partly because she's so tall and beautiful, and partly, I guess, because she *is* remote. She has very high cheekbones.

Only Flap was really happy about my success. He generously got drunk with me—otherwise the celebration was a dud. Henry spent twenty minutes lighting his pipe. The history majors even bored *me*. Sally didn't utter a word—she obviously wished she had gone on with her bike ride. We didn't seem very married. I would really have rather finished the champagne with Jenny Salomea, even if it had led to adultery. I longed for Emma Horton to be there. She was my fan and was always pleased when I did something successful. I tried to hold onto a little enthusiasm, but I needed more help than I was getting.

"Why do you always put the Seventh Cavalry in your screen-plays?" I asked Henry.

"Well, ain't that the stuff of life?" he said. No one was listening. Getting a novel published was no way to start a drinking party, evidently. I had worked on the novel for over a year and suddenly I felt very strange about it. I was not certain that I liked it, or even wanted it to be published. Maybe it was really a terrible book. I felt flatter and flatter. Sally was glad when we finally left the library. I gave Flap the big, empty bottle—he said Emma might want to plant a vine in it. The night was warm and sticky and still full of mosquitoes.

"I knew you'd make it if anybody did," Flap said as he walked away.

"Why?" I asked. People were always saying things like that to me and I couldn't understand it. I lived in constant doubt about myself, and never expected anything I did to come out right.

"Well, you've got discipline," he said. He was carrying the bottle over one shoulder, like a huge club.

Sally and I walked on home. It was true that I got up and wrote for a couple of hours every morning, but I had never thought of that as discipline, particularly. I just happened not to mind getting up early. In fact, I liked to get up early. I liked writing too—at least I usually liked it.

Our apartment was about a foot below ground, not so good a thing in a place as swampy as Houston. The mats I used for carpeting were soggy, and the whole place smelled like wet straw. It was hot inside. The minute we got in Sally pulled off the T-shirt she was wearing. She had a beautiful long torso—even watching her back made me feel sexy. I got the carbon of my novel out of the box, to see if anything about it looked good, and I found I couldn't read it. I just couldn't focus on it. Sally had been thinking she might read it, but she hadn't gotten around to it. I put my novel back under the bed and got out Paul Horgan's *Great River*, which I was reading for the fifth or sixth time. I can always lose myself in books about rivers—I had read every book I could find about the Nile and the Ganges and the Amazon and every other big river. Sally lay on the bed beside me while I read. She was tying knots in the cord of the apartment's one Venetian blind.

"I'll be glad when you turn the light out," she said. "It's drawing bugs."

It was drawing a few small bugs. "I left your chicken in the oven," I said. "It was great. You can really cook."

"I don't need compliments," she said. "I know I can cook."

I looked at her and got a cool look back. It was just beginning to dawn on me that she hated for me to read. No one close to me had ever liked it that I read a lot—I thought surely Sally would. If I was going to have to feel guilty about reading I didn't see how marriage could be worth it.

"Are you going to eat your chicken?" I asked.

"No," she said. "Rick bought me a cheeseburger and a malt."

Rick was wealthy, too. We had never been able to stand one another. I closed the book and watched the bugs swarm around the light. The screens in the apartment were terrible. When I turned off the light the bugs all came to the bed.

"I guess I'll be getting some money," I said. "We could even have a baby."

"Good-o," she said. I thought that would please her. A baby seemed to be what she wanted out of marriage. She had already mentioned it several times.

"Why did you want to read when we could be fucking?" she asked.

I hadn't been doing things in any particular order of precedence, but I guess from Sally's point of view that was wrong. She certainly had an order of precedence. I couldn't understand why Godwin thought she was frigid. I had never slept with a quicker comer—a man would have had to be awfully premature to get there ahead of Sally. I couldn't believe my good luck. I had never really expected to get married at all, and I certainly never dreamed I'd get someone who was so beautiful, and such a joy to sleep with.

A few small bugs got squashed between us, while we were making love. Afterward we sat up in bed and picked them off one another's bellies. We were very sweaty. The window was open and we sat and watched cars go by on the street while we dried off. Then unfortunately a car turned in. It was our landlord, Mr. Fitzherbert.

"Thank God we finished," I said, lying back down. "Just keep still."

"It's our apartment," Sally said. "We can fuck in it if we want to."

Unfortunately our apartment was tacked onto Mr. Fitzherbert's garage. He was a large, aging oilman who lived with his ancient mother and three even more ancient aunts. I don't know what his problems were, but he handled them by getting really drunk every night. He drove a Chrysler Imperial and usually came roaring into the garage about midnight. Our apartment was extremely flimsy and when he entered the garage the left wheels of the Chrysler passed within about two feet of our heads. It had been in my mind for two years that if he ever got really drunk and drove into the apartment instead of the garage I would be done for. Now there was Sally to think about, and the physical danger was only part of it. Mr. Fitzherbert didn't like us sleeping together. He had thrown a fit one night just from hearing our bed squeak, and we were only turning over.

When he drove in and killed his motor I lay very still. Sally sat very still. But Mr. Fitzherbert was cagy. He opened the car door—it bumped against our wall—but then he too became very still. He was listening for us. For about two minutes things were very silent—all that could be heard was an occasional bug, hitting the window screen. It was a war of nerves. I could imagine Mr. Fitzherbert, sitting in the Chrysler. He was listening for the least sound of movement.

Wars of nerves don't interest Sally long. Suddenly she bounced on the bed with her behind. It made an awful squeak. Apparently Mr. Fitzherbert was stunned. No sound came from the Chrysler. Before I could stop her, Sally did it again. She bounced three times and made three really loud squeaks. Anybody could have told it was just someone bouncing on a bed, not two people making love, but apparently Mr. Fitzherbert was in no mood to make distinctions. He came out of the Chrysler roaring and began to kick our wall.

"No fucking!" he yelled. "No fucking, you hear!"

We didn't say anything. The war of nerves was over and Sally had stopped bouncing. But Mr. Fitzherbert was just warming up.

"You hear me in there?" he yelled. "You hear? Cut out the fucking! Hear me? Dirty little students! Fuck all the time. *No respect for property!*"

He screamed the last, and then was silent. I guess he was listening to hear if we were listening. I was ready to strangle Sally if she bounced again, but the damage was already done. Mr. Fitzherbert was going into a fit.

"Come out and fight!" he yelled. "Stand up and fight! No more of that shit on my property! None of that while I'm around."

Then he began to bang the wall of the apartment with the door of the Chrysler. That's what I'd been afraid he would do—he had done it the other time too. Bang bang bang bang! Things began to shake. It was a heavy door and a very light wall. Books began to fall out of the bookcases. Sally began to bounce again, out of bravura, I think. I just sat. Her bouncing was nothing compared to the beating Mr. Fitzherbert was giving the wall. My one picture, which was of an uncle of mine, fell off its hook—I heard the glass break when it hit my typewriter. I was afraid the door might bust through the wall, which meant that Mr. Fitzherbert might also bust through the wall.

If he saw us both naked there was no telling what he might do. The reading lamp fell on the bed, and books kept thumping to the floor. Sally quit bouncing. It was such a flimsy apartment that it was possible to imagine the whole thing falling in on us, if Mr. Fitzherbert didn't stop. I think that's what we both did imagine. Of course the car door was hitting the wall about two feet from where we sat, but we could hear things falling in the kitchen too. And the shower suddenly started running—it had a hair-trigger mechanism, on hot, at least—and was a good place to get scalded. Mr. Fitzherbert went back to a four-beat rhythm and I could barely think. Sally hugged her knees.

Suddenly he stopped. He leaned against the wall, right behind our bed. We could hear him panting. "Jesus," he said, in an unhappy voice. In a minute he said, "Jesus Christ," and stumbled out of the garage. We saw him angle across the driveway toward his house. After so much noise, things seemed very quiet.

"He didn't shut his car door," I said. "I better go shut it for him."

I put on some pants and went and shut it. When I came back in I turned on the light a minute, to survey the damage. Sally was still picking bugs off her belly. I inched into the bathroom and managed to turn off the shower without getting scalded. Steam was drifting into the bedroom.

"You could have turned that off first," Sally said. "The car door could have waited." She flicked away a gnat and gave me one of her cool looks.

"You could have sat still, too," I said. "What's the point of provoking Mr. Fitzherbert? He's a nice man. I doubt if he ever gets laid. It's no trouble to sit still for five minutes."

She wouldn't argue with me—it was one of the most maddening things about her. She just ignored my reply. I picked up the picture that had fallen and broken, a picture of my Uncle Laredo riding the beautiful gray studhorse that he had called El Caballo. Only the glass that covered the picture had broken, but it still annoyed me. I felt very out of sorts with Sally. Making love hadn't done us any good at all. I was as tense as could be. Her cool looks affected me strangely. One minute I felt like hitting her and the next minute I just felt small. I knelt on the floor and picked up the books that had fallen out of the bookcase. Most of them were Signet paperbacks, including several issues of *New World Writing*. My real ambition was to get something published in *New World Writing*—getting a whole book published was not so much a real ambition as a fantasy. As soon as the steam cleared out of the bathroom Sally got up and went to the John.

"I guess when the advance money comes we ought to get a bigger apartment," I said, when she came back. "We'll have to get a bigger place anyway, if we have a baby."

"Good-o," she said. She sat on the bed and ruffled my hair with one foot. Obviously she no longer considered that we were at odds. She never really got tense, so it was easy for her to stop being at odds. She stretched out her legs and put the soles of her feet against my shoulders. It was clear from the way she did it that she was interested in screwing some more, but I didn't respond to the invitation. I had stopped feeling tense, but I felt extremely wan. The evening had taken something out of me. I don't think Sally ever felt wan in her life and I didn't think she'd understand it if I tried to talk about it. For some reason my spirits were sinking straight down to zero. Marriage was beginning to look awfully complicated. I really sort of felt like being alone.

Sally shook her legs free and made a beautiful V with them, for my benefit. She kicked herself a few times, with her heels, and rubbed herself casually with one finger. When she saw I wasn't going to leap up and screw her her face became petulant. One of the things I had already learned about her was that she wasn't at all patient.

"I wish you weren't so clean-cut," she said. "You're nothing at all like Godwin."

"I'm not clean-cut," I said. "What made you say that?"

"Because you are. Just because you haven't been to the barbershop lately doesn't mean you aren't clean-cut."

The remark really made me mad. "Don't be so arbitrary," I said. "Just because I don't feel like screwing again right now doesn't mean I'm clean-cut. I'm not clean-cut at all. If you think I am you ought to explain what you mean. I'd like to argue about it."

But Sally was never interested enough in any argument to stay with it for more than two sentences. Arguments didn't really involve her. Her face became utterly expressionless and her eyes stopped taking me in. Not only was she not interested in pursuing the argument, she no longer cared to believe I was there. My spirits came rushing back, but they were very hostile spirits. I started putting on my sneakers. I wasn't just about to spend the night with somebody who didn't believe I was there.

Sally got up and went into the kitchen. I grabbed a shirt and started to leave, but I looked in the kitchen to see what she was doing. There was no light in the kitchen except the light from inside the icebox. Sally was leaning on the icebox door, eating a piece of chicken. I was choking with things I wanted to say to her, but they were all jammed together in my throat. I left, got halfway down the driveway, and then came back in and got my novel out from under the bed. I might want to read it before I came back. I looked in the kitchen again. Sally was still leaning on the icebox, finishing off the chicken. She didn't say a word and I didn't either. I felt like yanking all the shelves out of the icebox and shoving her in for a while. Nobody but her could give total silence quite such an uncomfortable quality. The few sentences she uttered were like eternal judgments. I stood in the door a whole minute, hoping she would say something so I could yell and scream at her, but she could have leaned on the icebox door until daybreak without uttering a sound. She was eating a drumstick when I left.

As I was walking across the library parking lot, carrying my novel, I saw an odd thing. A man in a green filling-station attendant's uniform was bouncing a golf ball on the parking lot. He was fantastic. He must have been the world's greatest golf ball bouncer. He leaped in the air, to get his weight behind the ball, and flung it against the asphalt of the parking lot with all his strength. I would never have imagined that a golf ball could bounce so high. It went up and up, out of sight in the darkness, higher than the library, and came down and bounced back up fifty feet and came down again in diminishing bounces until the guy finally caught it. He instantly leaped in the air and flung it again. It was drizzling slightly. The parking lot was lit and shone with rain. I watched for a good ten minutes, trying to understand what the guy's motive was. It was one o'clock in the morning. He was smiling and his hair was wet and hanging down in his face, and a terrific passion came into it when he leaped and flung the golf ball, as if each time he was going for the world's record bounce. I put the box my novel was in on my head and used it for an umbrella while I watched. Finally the man stopped for a breather. He was a friendly guy. "It keeps you on your toes," he said.

I sloshed on into the library and slept on a couch. Henry was at the front desk, writing a screenplay. In my mind I was still arguing with Sally about whether or not I was clean-cut. I kept arguing with her for a long time—the waxing people were coiling the long black cords of their waxers when I finally relaxed and shut my eyes.

4.

DAME JULIANA woke me up. She was a short, robust redhead whose real name was Mrs. Norwich. Flap Horton had nicknamed her Dame Juliana. She had never much fancied me, but she ran the library and I did my best to coexist with her. She was the only bosomy librarian I had ever known. In horny periods I had fantasies about her in which I generously gave her not only much better legs than she really had but a far more loving disposition too.

The couch I had gone to sleep on was in the PR section, which was English literature. A thirty-nine-volume set of John Ruskin was shelved just at my feet. I had often meant to dip into it, but when I sacked out in the library I was almost never sober enough to read.

"I thought you got married," Dame Juliana said. "Even if you're as smart as people say you are I don't see that it's our place to provide you a bed."

"No ma'am," I said. "I guess I just read too late and fell asleep."

"Nobody could get that scruffy reading," she said. I might be clean-cut to Sally, but I was anything but to Mrs. Norwich.

"I sold my novel last night," I said. "We had a little celebration."

"What kind of publisher would wait until after dark to buy a book?" she asked. "Your feet stink, you know?"

"I was just going home to wash."

"Your wife must have something wrong with her nose, otherwise she couldn't live with you," she said, hurrying off to wake up other couch-rats who hadn't made it home the night before. People were always flaking out on those couches and waking up with Dame

Juliana's indignant bosom hanging over them. The history graduate students were always plotting ways to get her into the library at night, so they could gang-rape her, but nothing ever came of their plots. The gang-rape of Dame Juliana was just their collective fantasy. It kept them going year after year, while the microfilm machines destroyed their vision. Some of them already had to grope their way to the couches after a hard day in the cubbyholes.

Walking home, I felt very good. My novel was going to be published and Sally was probably still in bed, all warm and sleepy. I wasn't mad at her anymore—on such a nice morning it was hard to remember what I had been so mad about. Beyond the trees of Rice, huge white Gulf clouds were rolling into one another—tremendous clouds. They only meant it would rain and make the floor mats soggier, but I liked to watch them anyway.

When I got to the apartment there was no Sally. The bed was empty. It upset me badly. I had expected her to be there and was all ready to crawl right in bed with her and make love before getting back to work on my second novel. Now that the first one had sold I really had to go ahead and finish the second. At the moment it was only forty-five pages long.

But Sally was gone and there was no note. Her things were still there, though. At least she hadn't left me. I went outside and tried to decide where to look for her. I had an awful feeling in my stomach. Of course she could just have gone for a walk. Sometimes she took walks at funny times.

Then I noticed Jenny Salomea. She was sitting in her yard with her back against the big tree. She had on a red bathrobe and was hugging her knees with her arms.

"Good morning," I said, walking over.

"Your wife left with a gentleman," she said. "I told you last night you were boring her."

She looked at me a little too triumphantly. I felt as un-triumphant as I have ever felt. I also felt a little weak in the legs, so I sat down near Jenny in the dewy grass.

"I guess you do love her," she said. "What made you think she loved you?"

"I don't know," I said. "I guess she was grateful to me for about a week, for taking her away from a guy in Austin."

"You should have just screwed around awhile," Jenny said. "You didn't have to marry her just because she acted fond of you for a couple of days. But that's you, right?"

"I don't know what's me," I said.

Jenny yawned. "I read that book you loaned me," she said. "All that sounds like fun to me."

I had gone from feeling horny to feeling very unhorny. Jenny was so sure Sally didn't love me that I was convinced. I was not really in the habit of having somebody love me, but believing that Sally did had felt wonderful for about three weeks. Realizing that she didn't took a lot of the fun out of life. She was probably off screwing Rick Leonard, at that very moment. I didn't dare ask what the gentleman looked like. The real complication was that I loved her. I had given myself over and had no mechanism for taking myself back. Despite her problems—I guess they were problems—she wasn't very hard to love. Jenny Salomea held my hand for a while. She could tell I was in no mood for sexual novelties.

"Don't look so blue," she said. "Maybe he was her brother. Anyway, you sold your book. You'll probably be famous."

I shook my head. "That won't make her love me," I said.

Jenny looked disgusted. "You better learn to call a bitch a bitch," she said. "Otherwise you're going to lead a dog's life, like Sammy has."

"I don't want to call anyone a bitch," I said.

Jenny was getting angry. She stood up and tugged at my hand. "Okay, Danny," she said. "That's enough of that. Don't sit there looking like an only child. Come on upstairs and let's do something. I can't stand a man who gets depressed over nothing."

"It's not nothing," I said. "It's my marriage."

"Your marriage is nothing, okay," she said. "It's not worth an ounce of pigshit. I can tell what kind of girl she is, even if you can't. You married a bitch and she doesn't love you and she won't stay put. So what? I married a queer. He hates the way I smell, even. Tough luck for both of us. It happens to a million people a day. I'm not going to sit in the yard and mope about it all day. Come on upstairs and help me have a little fun. I need a little fun. I never have—much fun."

She saw I wasn't coming, and turned and went to her house. The seat of her red bathrobe was wet, from the dewy grass. What she had said made plenty of sense. There was no point in avoiding anything. I got my bike and pedaled over to Rick Leonard's apartment, about six blocks away. I don't know what I expected to do, except not avoid anything, but it didn't matter. Sally wasn't there. Rick was playing chess when I knocked. He played chess by mail, with a man who lived in Norway. He was as surprised to see me as I was not to find Sally.

"I can hardly wait for your reviews," he said as I was leaving. He gave me an arch look and went back to his chessboard. He was almost as good at arch looks as Sally was—I suppose that's why I thought they would be together. If she hadn't married me they could have got married and spent their lives giving the world arch looks.

It occurred to me that Flap Horton might have come by to see me and then asked Sally to go walking with him, or something. He was turned on by her, as he was by almost all pretty girls, but it didn't worry me. It was only fair: I had been turned on by Emma ever since I'd known them, and Flap knew it, more or less. It was nothing that was ever going to get out of hand. I pedaled over to West Main, where the Hortons lived, thinking Sally might be eating breakfast with them. They had a great four-room garage apartment, far and away the best apartment of any student couple I knew. It was twice as cool as my place. Occasionally, if we were involved in a late carouse, I stayed and sacked out on their couch. It was a Salvation Army store couch and not as comfortable as the ones in the library, but eating breakfast with Emma and Flap was a lot more fun than being awakened by Dame Juliana.

Sally wasn't at their place, either. Flap was still asleep and Emma had just washed her hair. "Great news," she said, beaming at me when I came in. "I knew you'd sell it. Can I hug you to celebrate?

"Oh, you look so successful," she said, after we had hugged. She had become shy about hugging me since I married, but she was really glad about my novel. She was always begging me to let her read it, but I wouldn't. I didn't want anybody to read it unless it got published. Emma was my only true, wholehearted fan. She wound a blue towel around her wet hair and went in and made me some pancakes while we waited for Flap to wake up.

"I guess you could read it now, if you still want to," I said. The huge champagne bottle was sitting by her stove. It was too bad she had missed the celebration. She was one of the roundest girls I had ever known. There wasn't a flat plane on her body. Her shoulders were round, her calves were round, even her feet. Her features were rounded too. Most people would have put her down as chubby, but for me it all worked. Every part of Emma turned. I liked to watch her pad about the kitchen making pancakes. Her cheeks were pink and she was glad I was successful.

She was such a fan of mine that she had tried gallantly to make friends with Sally, but I guess they were antipathetic types. Emma was a lot more talkative.

"I guess I'll have to quit writing now," she said. She wrote short stories from time to time. So did Flap. He and I sent our short stories to *New World Writing* and they all came right back. Emma never sent hers out at all—or if she did she never told anyone about it. In paranoid moments Flap and I suspected her of sending them out secretly. She wouldn't let us read them, either, so for all we knew she was a secret genius. If she had suddenly got a story accepted I don't know how we would have lived with it. It was a petty paranoia, unfair to Emma. She was happy as a lark when the *Texas Quarterly* accepted two of my stories. It wasn't that she was competitive, it was just that Flap and I were insecure.

I heard her say that she would have to quit writing, but I didn't answer her for a while. I was leaning back against the wall, a little mesmerized by the quiet of the kitchen. Emma's kitchen was easily the most restful place I ever went. The sun was shining through the window, and Emma kept walking back and forth through the big sunny spot in front of the stove. From time to time she stopped making pancakes long enough to rub her wet blond hair with the towel. I liked her calves, chubby though they were. When she stood in the patch of sunlight they were golden as well as round. I wondered, for a moment, how it would have been to marry her instead of Sally, but it was only a passing thought. I was really thinking about my second novel. That was one of the things I loved about Emma's kitchen—it was a place where I could muse.

Mostly I mused about scenes, or the things my characters said to one another. I saw their faces and heard the way they spoke. Emma knew all about my musing and sometimes snuck up and put a cold washrag on my forehead when she saw me looking vague, but I don't think she really cared. Maybe she really liked having me there writing. It was a pleasant thing to do in a sunny kitchen.

"Why should you quit?" I asked.

"Because you're a real writer now," she said. "I'll never be a real writer. I ought to concentrate on making pancakes. When I get kids I won't have time to do anything but cook, anyway."

"Come on," I said. "Lots of mothers write books."

Emma looked at me solemnly, as if I had hurt her. "I wouldn't want to do it that way," she said. "I don't want to write tacky little books. Even if they were clever they wouldn't really be good. If I was going to do it I'd have to do it the way you do it, and I can't."

"There's nothing holy about the way I do it," I said.

"No, but nobody but you could do what you do," she said. "Lots of mothers could do what I'd do."

I let it drop. There was no real reason why I should try to persuade Emma to keep writing. What she said about babies reminded me that Sally was planning to get pregnant. If she really didn't love me it might not be a good idea to let her, but talking her out of it after I had said she could wasn't going to be simple. I felt really mixed up and tried to forget about it all by eating a lot of pancakes. Flap came in while I was on my second plateful. He had a fit of sneezing just as he sat down.

"Did you take your sinus pills?" Emma asked. Flap stared at his plate as if he hadn't heard the question, and she went to the bathroom and got him his pills. His nose looked swollen. He took his pills meekly enough, but he didn't look really alive until he had eaten several pancakes.

"Any more good news?" he asked.

"I've just been awarded the Prix de Houston," I said. "The mayor's on his way over with a mariachi band."

"I think you ought to go to a doctor," Emma said to Flap. "You wheezed half the night."

"I only slept half the night."

"It kept me awake," she said, holding up a couple of pancakes so I could see if I wanted them. I nodded and she put them on my plate.

"You're just jealous because you didn't get any champagne," Flap said. "If you'd got drunk you wouldn't have heard me wheeze. I only do it when the weather's muggy."

"I guess if you don't want to go to a doctor we could move to Tucson," she said. "It's not very muggy there."

Flap yawned and snapped his fingers. "Pancakes," he said. "No medical advice."

It was easy to imagine children in their kitchen. I could imagine five or six little boys, sitting around on the floor like puppies, some with brown hair and some with blond. Emma would have to step over them when she cooked. I thanked her for the pancakes and told Flap to keep taking his pills and got my bike and pedaled home. I was very worried that Sally might not be back from wherever she had gone, but fortunately she was. She was lying on the bed tying knots in the venetian-blind cord. She looked quite cheerful.

"You could use a shave," she said when I came in.

"I want to grow a beard," I said. "I'm bored with shaving." Since she was cheerful there was no point in reminding her that just last night she had told me I was too clean-cut.

"All right," she said agreeably. "You grow a beard and I'll have a baby."

The two things didn't seem quite on the same scale, but I didn't say so. I wasn't even sure I wanted to grow a beard—the statement had just popped out of my mouth. Shaving was a bore, but a beard might turn out to have its drawbacks too. I felt deeply equivocal about everything. I sat down at my writing desk and tried to write, while Sally tied knots, but I had already missed the best hours for writing, and I was as equivocal about writing as I was about everything else. I wasn't sure my first novel was any good, and I wasn't sure my second novel was going to be any better. I looked at the paragraphs I had written the day before and they seemed pretty ordinary. I doubted that anyone could have distinguished them from the paragraphs of a hundred other writers. When I got people talking I was okay, but my descriptive prose didn't seem to me to be particularly worth reading.

I wrote a page or two, but I didn't really make much progress. In my mind I wasn't writing at all—I was trying to think of a way to get

Sally to tell me where she'd been without sounding paranoid about it. The two pages I wrote had no clarity and I knew even as I wrote them that I would write them over the next day. Sally kept tying knots.

"I think you're a frustrated boy scout," I said. "Want a bacon sandwich?"

She didn't, so I made one for myself and came back and sat on the bed to eat it. "I came by early to apologize," I said. "Where'd you go?"

"I had a visitor," she said. "Godwin's in town. He took me to breakfast."

"What'd he want?"

"Geoffrey's left Austin," she said. "Godwin's got nobody to live with him. He looks like he's going crazy. He said he'd buy me a motorcycle if I'd come back."

"I didn't know owning a motorcycle was one of your ambitions," I said.

"I've wanted one for years," she said, yawning. "He asked us to a party tonight, too. He knows a professor here who has a pool."

She turned on her side and went to sleep and I sat beside her for an hour and a half, rereading *Great River* and brooding about Godwin, Sally, babies, novels and other problems. I read and brooded until I slid into a stupor and fell asleep. After a while it got too hot to sleep and we both woke up and took off our sweaty clothes. We went to the kitchen and drank several glasses of ice water apiece. Both of us felt sort of sluggishly sexy—we fiddled around a little, standing by the icebox. The heat gave a kind of vegetable quality to everything. Sally and I leaned together like too heavy, slightly damp plants. I was sensate but torpid. When we grew tired of standing we sprinkled water on the hot sheets and spread out on the bed. We had a sense of sex but no great urge for movement. The damp, sexy torpor was pleasant in itself. I felt like I had suddenly been switched into slow motion. I kept feeling her and she kept feeling me and finally, after about half an hour, we evolved from our plantlike state back into agile animals. We fucked awhile, as Godwin would say. Or as Sally might say. Or Jenny. I don't know what I would have said—I have some oddly decorous habits of speech.

I had poured down too much ice water just before becoming an animal and it joggled in my stomach and slowed me down a little. Still, there's nothing that can be done in the middle of the afternoon that quite competes with sex, ice water or no ice water, and whatever the nomenclature you adopt. As we were resting, all soaked and slushy, I had a fantasy of us doing it in an icebox—not ours but a great big icebox with no shelves in it, very white and cold. We could leave the door open. I thought about it awhile and decided I hadn't had enough, even though we were on a sweat-soaked bed instead of in an icebox. Sally was just as happy to continue—she was really sort of unfinishable. We kept on screwing until I got sore, but somehow it didn't get us to where I wanted us to be. I just wanted us to be finished so that we were close to each other and not excited, and I couldn't make it happen. Sally could have six orgasms and still keep herself, somehow, whereas I couldn't even kiss her and keep myself. She thought it was nice of me to make it possible for her to come a lot, but that was about all she felt. When I finally quit she got up and took a shower. I grew unhappy, lying in the messy bed. I felt as though nothing in my life would ever be complete, not even for five minutes. Sally came out of the shower with a towel in one hand, a beautiful five-foot-ten-and-a-half inches of girl. Water dripped down her long legs and onto the floor mats and she was as far away and as much on my mind as if I hadn't just been screwing her off and on for an hour. All the screwing should have changed something, or made some fundamental difference. It shouldn't have left things just the same.

"Let's go to the party," Sally said. "I want to swim."

I wasn't crazy about going someplace Godwin was going to be, but it was the only invitation on our calendar and if we didn't go we'd just sit around the hot apartment all evening, not knowing what to do with each other. I would brood about one novel or the other, and Sally would tie a thousand knots in the venetian-blind cord.

"Okay," I said.

"I can wear my red bikini," she said. It was the only garment she owned that she really seemed to like.

"It'll drive Godwin wild with passion," I said.

Sally was drying her legs—she looked up for a moment and made an amused face. "He's already wild," she said.

5.

THE ABRUPTNESS with which major changes can occur in life was something I had never really experienced until I met Sally. I went through three years of college and no changes of significance occurred at all. I read books and wrote my novel and got drunk frequently. That was about all that happened. Existence really held no wild surprises—or wild surmises, either. Sally was my first wild surmise. I woke up on Godwin's floor and looked at her and almost immediately my life began to veer crazily one way and then another, like a car being driven by W. C. Fields. Around any corner might be a drawbridge, a vegetable cart, or a brick wall—and I wasn't driving. I was being zoomed. If I had been alert I wouldn't have gotten in the car in the first place, but I hadn't been alert and it was too late to jump out.

Not asking where the party was before I agreed to go is a perfect example of my general lack of alertness. Once I had agreed to go there was no way I could back out. Sally was looking forward to wearing her red bikini. The professor who was giving the party was named Razzy Hutton—Razzy was short for Erasmus. He was English, like Godwin, and was what he called a lineal descendant of Erasmus Darwin. His specialty was protozoa and he wore white trousers the year round. Of course in Houston it's summer most of the year round, so the wearing of white trousers didn't really class him as a great eccentric. It was just one of the many little things I held against him.

All he had to hold against me was the suspected theft of an octopus. One had disappeared from the zoology lab while I was taking

Razzy's course in protozoa. I *did* steal the octopus, actually, but Razzy had no way of knowing that. His case against me was built entirely on prejudice, just like my case against him. We brought out all each other's instinctive prejudices. He was tall, thin, and blond and should have worn a monocle. If he had worn a monocle I would have hated him even more.

Razzy was quite social, and a darling of the Houston rich. Three of Houston's more prominent Lesbians were sitting by his pool when we walked in. They were drinking vodka and orange juice and baiting Godwin, who looked pale and slightly crazed. I guess the Lesbians were scaring him. The three of them glanced at me as if I were some kind of unattractive dog, but when Sally came out in her red bikini they all but slavered. I expected steam to come out from under their skirts. None of them was attractive enough to show herself in a bathing suit.

"She's precious," the fattest one said hungrily. Her girl friend took offense at the remark and went off to get more vodka, watching Sally over her shoulder. Sally dove in and got wet. The Lesbians began to drink faster and I started drinking from scratch, meaning to catch up if I could. Godwin was pacing back and forth near the diving board. Finally he came over and shook my hand.

"You're looking bloody well," he said.

"The patina of success," Razzy said. "He rather glows with it." He was drinking extremely dry martinis, and his tone carried the perfect degree of chill, like his martini glass.

"Ah yes," Godwin said. "You sold your book. Now you have a license to steal any bloody thing you happen to want."

"Hopefully he'll start with a change of linen," Razzy said. "Do swim as soon as possible, will you? You have a body odor."

I drank my glass of vodka and orange juice in about three swallows. It had just hit me what a mistake it had been to come. Sally was floating on her back, her bosom and belly shining with water. The three Lesbians were watching her. Godwin seemed almost friendly, but Razzy Hutton exuded a rare quality of nastiness. He obviously meant to insult me in every way possible.

"We're all corporeal beings," he said, "but very few of us allow ourselves to smell. Very few of us gulp our drinks, either. If you propose to walk among us as an equal you must begin to cultivate one or two of the more basic of the civilized graces."

"That's fucking nonsense," Godwin said. "The boy's a frontier genius, don't you know? The fact that he farts in public is part of his appeal."

"I don't fart all that often," I said defensively.

"Come, don't apologize," Godwin said. "Genius need never apologize for itself. I didn't even fart in private until I was thirty years old." He said it sadly, as if it were something he had often regretted.

"Really?" Razzy said. "What a titillating detail."

"Those three women you invited scare me fucking green," Godwin said. "I think I'll go in with Sally."

He went in to get his bathing suit. The three Lesbians got up and came over and Razzy introduced me to them. He managed to do it without moving his lips. I felt like I was in the middle of a school of piranha fish, and I tried to look humble and unappetizing.

"You write, or something?" one asked. Her name was Sybil. She had red hair, protruding teeth, and two large jewels.

"Yes ma'am," I said.

"Do you write with a pencil or a fountain pen?" the fat one asked, handing Razzy her glass.

"On a typewriter."

"Oh, like a journalist," she said, reaching for the fresh drink Razzy had instantly provided.

"I've read one or two of Daniel's effusions," Razzy said. "He's far from being a master of English syntax."

"I can't read the young," the fat one said. Her name was Lorena.

"Why not?" I asked. I was feeling a great dislike of them all. Beyond us, Godwin tiptoed out in a blue bathing suit and snuck into the pool. He went right under water, like a frogman in some kind of spy movie.

"Oh, there's such a crudity of sentiment in the young," Lorena said. "They've known no heartbreak."

"Precisely," Razzy said.

The skinniest of the Lesbians maintained a total and very sinister silence. She had straight black hair.

"You look like a workman," Sybil said. "Are you salaried?"

"I'm just a student," I said. "I work on weekends for a termite exterminator. It's simple work."

"Do you like Lawrence?" Lorena asked. "I knew Lawrence. I know Frieda. I knew Mabel Dodge Luhan. Dorothy Brett is a good friend of mine."

"I like him a lot," I said.

"He was a silly ass," Razzy said. "He's the best argument I know against educating the working classes. He should have been kept in the mines."

Lorena was drunker than she looked. "I once measured the penis of Tony Luhan's brother," she said.

We all looked blasé. So far as I could tell, Godwin had never come up. I was vaguely worried about him.

"I can't remember how long it was," Lorena said. "It was at a party in Taos. We measured the penises of all the men. His was much the longest. I remember that much."

Godwin finally surfaced, in the vicinity of where Sally was float- ing, and all three women turned and went to the edge of the pool. I don't know what they had against him. They stared at him. Sally swam over to the edge of the pool and got out and began to sun her- self in what little was left of the sun. Godwin looked forlorn, treading water all by himself. I was through with my second drink. I got a third and sat down by the pool. Godwin had begun to swim laps. He was not in very good shape. Once he paused near where I was sitting. "In my youth I trained to swim the Channel," he said.

Soon he swam away. I didn't feel like swimming. I became drunk. Razzy put a Fats Domino record on the phonograph. He must have asked Sally to dance, because I noticed them dancing. The Lesbians were chain-smoking as they watched. No one else had come to the party. Godwin looked waterlogged, but he kept swimming, doggedly. Sally danced in her red bikini. It grew dark as I drank, as Godwin swam, as Sally danced. Razzy Hutton was apparently only jointed at the hips. He never bent his arms or legs. When I was drunk I decided that if he insulted me once more I would hit him. I never wanted to be at a place where he was again, even if it meant leaving Rice with no degree. He kept playing Fats Domino records. I went over and stood by the phonograph. After a while he came over to change the record.

"An extraordinary nigger," Razzy said. "A primitive genius."

"I don't ever want to be a master of English syntax, Dr. Hutton," I said.

"Well, you bloody well aren't," he said. "You don't hold liquor well, either. Watch you don't bump the phonograph."

"I'd rather you didn't dance with my wife," I said.

Razzy looked amused. He walked back to Sally and I followed him.

"You're a beautiful child," Sybil was saying.

Sally shrugged and walked over to watch Godwin swim. It was hard to tell whether he was swimming or drowning. I could tell that Sally was bored with things. "You have interesting parties, Razzy," Lorena said thickly. She was as drunk as I was.

"Someone ought to propose a toast," Sybil said. "We've had no toasts tonight."

I felt giddy and strange. Razzy was insulting me silently, somehow. I had a sense of fat being in the fire, of bridges about to be burned. Sally was trying to drag Godwin out of the swimming pool.

"I think our young author should propose one," Razzy said, deftly putting me on the spot.

But I felt reckless, the way I had when I shot the squirrel out of Jenny Salomea's tree.

"To the penis of Tony Luhan," I said. "However long it was. Or was it his brother's?" I added, remembering the story better.

"You crude little beast," the sinister black-haired one said. Lorena slapped me and almost knocked me down. I wasn't standing very steadily. Sally started laughing, I think at Godwin—he was beached like a small dying whale on the poolside. Razzy stood before me ramrod straight. All he needed was a monocle.

"We might excuse your odor," he said, "but your conduct is quite unforgivable. Leave this company at once!"

I punched him in the stomach. He took three steps backward, gasping. His mouth was open—I think it was the first time he'd opened it wide enough for me to see his teeth. It wasn't as hard a punch as I meant it to be. I don't know how to punch. I think it was the insult that left him breathless.

"You'll never—" he croaked. "You'll never—"

"You'll never get your octopus back, either!" I yelled. "It's a wonderful pet. I confess my theft!"

"He's always stealing," Godwin said, staggering into our midst. "Who's he stealing now? What's wrong Razzy? You look like you swallowed an ice cube."

"I hit him," I said. "I also stole his octopus. A specialist in protozoa doesn't need an octopus. We play sex games with it. It's our bed toy."

Sally walked past us and went in to get dressed. She didn't take the scene seriously. The Lesbians decided to mother Razzy. While they were fanning him back to health Godwin took me aside.

"I'm leaving with you," he said. "You came under my auspices. They'll all blame me for your behavior. I admire you. I've wanted to hit that fucker for years. I'll buy you and your lovely wife the best dinner in Houston. My wedding gift to the two of you."

"Maybe in a minute," I said. I expected Razzy to attack me as soon as he recovered himself. I was wrong, however. He strode into his apartment without saying a word. Perhaps he had decided not to soil his hands with me. Or perhaps he had gone to look for the sword-cane I imagined him having. He might emerge and run me through. Godwin went in to dress. Recklessly I walked over to the Lesbians. They looked sullen. We stared at one another. It was another war of nerves.

"Who do you read?" I asked, addressing myself to Lorena.

"You're looking to get slugged again, kiddo," she said.

"No ma'am," I said. "I just wondered who you read."

"The masters," she said huskily. "Gide. Mann. Colette."

"I was just curious," I said.

The sinister one stepped forward, her hot little eyes shining with hatred.

"I have powers," she said. "I now put a curse upon you. Your keys will no longer fit in locks. No door you really wish to enter will open for you again. From now on you will be thirsty. Water will stop running from your faucets. No one will give you presents. People will not like your clothes. Your stomach will be unsettled and you will belch all day. There will be sand in your beds. You will be constipated often. Those whom you remember will not remember you. You will have a rash between your legs."

The hairs on the back of my neck were standing up. I had never had a curse put on me before. She was matter-of-fact about it, and very convincing.

"Soon a pane of glass will drop between you and your wife," she said. "You will be able to see her, you will be able to hear her, you will be able to want her, but the pane of glass will always separate you. You will not be able to touch her. The pane of glass will enclose you like a cylinder, separating you from all women. You will want many women, but nothing will ever shatter the pane of glass."

She stopped talking and stepped back to light a cigarette. No wonder Godwin was afraid of them. I turned and went right in to find Sally. She was letting Razzy Hutton help her zip her dress. I don't know why she needed help. It upset me badly.

Godwin came out of the bathroom with his shirt unbuttoned. He had a coat and tie in his hand. "Danny and Sally are dining with me," he said to Razzy. "You must make our apologies to the company."

Razzy merely smiled. He had become inscrutable. I was thinking of hitting him again, but Godwin gave me no chance. He whisked us out and half an hour later we were drinking champagne at an intimidating French restaurant. It didn't intimidate Godwin, of course. He spoke French fluently, and probably well. After the champagne we had a rack of lamb and three bottles of a wonderful red wine. I was far too drunk to talk. Even Sally was drunk—the color in her cheeks was almost as deep as the color of the wine. I remembered, in my drunkenness, that a bridge had been burned. I didn't want to stay at Rice. I wanted to leave Houston, and the sooner the better. I didn't want dawn to find me in the city. The one thing I knew clearly was that life had changed, and we were leaving as soon as we finished dinner.

"We have to be gone by morning," I kept saying as I ate the excellent food and drank the wine.

Sally got bored with hearing me. "Quit saying that," she said. "Nobody's arguing. I'm bored with this place, too."

Godwin squinted at his wine glass. "I can't forget those women," he said. "Hideous women."

"They acted like dykes," Sally said cheerfully. Eating made her look happy. She was oblivious of the fact that the juicy slice of lamb she was eating had once been a live sheep.

"It isn't because of Razzy," I said. It really wasn't, but I was too drunk to try to explain why I wanted to leave. I had been there for three years and had made myself a place and suddenly I didn't fit it anymore. All the furniture of my life had been changed around. Sally was there, the apartment was too small, I couldn't see much of the Hortons, I had sold my novel, I didn't want to study anymore, Jenny wanted me, Godwin was around—it was all too much. Without wanting it to happen, I had let myself be dislodged. Dislodged was exactly how I felt.

It was an enormous restaurant bill, but Godwin paid it with a smile. I remember his smile as he paid it. When I'm drunk, things swirl. Once in a while they stop and I notice something before the next swirl begins. I have the ability to drive when drunk, but once I stop driving I have no ability at all. I drove us home and went to the John and puked. When I came out of the John I noticed that Godwin and Sally were sitting on the bed necking. I yanked Sally up and hit Godwin. He hit me back. It was much too small a place to fight in. Godwin went into one of his purple rages.

"I'll have my revenge," he said. He picked up my typewriter and went into the bathroom with it.

"Why were you kissing him?" I asked Sally. I had forgotten Godwin. "Why were you kissing him?"

"He just wanted to," she said, making a face at me. She was very irritated.

There was a screech from Godwin. We went to see. He had put my typewriter in the bathtub, meaning to run water over it, and had started the shower instead. Naturally he had scalded himself.

"Very well then, if I'm not wanted I'll sleep in your car," he said. He was drunk but dignified and his suit was wet. He went off to sleep in the car.

"You could be a little nicer to him," Sally said.

"I hate your red bikini," I said. "I knew it would make trouble."

I started packing my things and she started packing her things. It sobered us a little. Sally began looking through one of her high school yearbooks. Fortunately we had few clothes. Mr. Fitzherbert came driving in as we were packing, and I went out to tell him I was leaving. He was standing in the driveway in a rumpled business suit, looking at Godwin's feet, which stuck out of the back window of my Chevy.

"Aw no," he said unhappily when I told him. He shook his head. "You're not really going, are you? Momma's gonna skin me alive when she hears I let you get away. You're the only good renter we ever had."

For once he was not very drunk. "Now how am I gonna tell Momma about this?" he asked sadly, putting a hand on my shoulder. I asked him to give whatever we left to the Salvation Army, and he said he would.

"Maybe I'll tell her your folks needed you to help 'em with the place," he said worriedly. "Otherwise she'll think I scared you off with my drinking. That ain't it, is it?"

"No sir," I said. "I drink too."

"Son, don't get in the habit," he said. "Take care of your body, whatever you do."

He was about fifty-five years old. We shook hands and he went in. He was a decent man. I felt choked up. I liked Mr. Fitzherbert. I liked my apartment. I liked the table where my typewriter sat. It was only an ordinary brown table, but it was just the right height. I enjoyed sitting at it and writing every morning, through the years. I even liked the smell of the damp floor mats. The apartment and I had seemed to belong together, from the first, but I'm that way about all the places I stay. Without meaning to, I begin to love them, and then I sort of adhere to them, physically. Leaving is like tearing off skin—also it jumbled my insides. I felt like feeling snug, and I no longer felt snug. I couldn't remember why I had decided to leave, but we were already half-packed. We didn't own very much. Sally had gone to sleep on the floor, reading her annual. I wrapped my type-writer in a quilt and put it in the trunk of the car. If Godwin hadn't been in the back seat I might have fitted the table in, but I didn't feel up to dragging him out.

I put a pillow under Sally's head and managed to make all my paperbacks fit neatly into two boxes. There were fourteen library books that had to be taken back. I took off my party clothes and put on my Levi's and sneakers and went over to the library to return the books. It was about two o'clock in the morning and the man with the golf ball wasn't in the parking lot.

Petey Ximenes was waxing the main reference room, under the watchful eye of the two white supervisors. He looked sulky and his ducktail was unkempt. On the fifth floor he could wax at his own pace, but apparently someone had decided his pace wasn't fast enough. They brought him down where they could watch him. I had never seen him in such a foul humor—I think he was contemplating charging the two men with his waxer. I told him I was leaving, but I don't think my words registered. He shook my hand absently when I told him goodbye. He didn't even look at me. I couldn't find Henry, so I left my library key on the circulation desk.

It was odd, going out the door and knowing I couldn't just turn and go back in, if I thought of a book I wanted to read. The door clicked and I was really out. I could see Petey through the big window, still waxing. The quadrangle was full of soft, mushy summer mist. Somewhere above the mist I could hear an airplane. I walked over to Main Street and sat on the curb for a while, watching cars go by. The mist made the streetlights look faintly orange. I didn't feel one bit drunk, anymore. I got up and walked eight or ten blocks down the orange, misty street and turned off into the darker streets and walked another hour or so.

Houston was my companion on the walk. She had been my mistress, but after a thousand nights together, just the two of us, we were calling it off. It was a warm, moist, mushy, smelly night, the way her best nights were. The things most people hated about her were the things I loved: her heat, her dampness, her sumpy smells. She wasn't beautiful, but neither was I. I liked her heat and her looseness and her smells. Those things were her substance, and if she had been cool and dry and odorless I wouldn't have cared to live with her three years. We were calling it off, but I could still love her. She still reached me, when I went walking with her. Her mists were always a little sexy. I felt, in leaving her, the kind of fond gentleness you're supposed to feel after passion. It was the kind of gentleness I never got to feel with Sally. Its expression might be stroking a shoulder, or something. I had had such good of Houston, she had dealt so generously with me, always, that I walked and stroked her shoulder for an hour or two, in the night. Then, when she was really sleeping, I went home. I wanted to be gone when she woke up.

Almost at once Sally and I got into it. We finished packing in no time. She just had two suitcases full, and I had about as much. When I turned out the lights and shut the door to the apartment I noticed her trying to stuff Godwin's feet inside the car.

"Where's he staying?" I asked. "We can drop him off."

"He's going with us," she said. "Didn't you hear him at dinner? That was all he talked about."

"I didn't hear him say a word about it."

"So what? You were blind drunk."

"I must have been deaf drunk," I said. "Anyway, he's not going. We're married now. We haven't even decided where to go."

"I thought we were going to California."

It was the only place we had really mentioned, but I didn't think we had made a firm decision.

"That doesn't have a thing to do with Godwin."

"Sure it does. He knows people there. You don't know a soul. He can help us get settled."

"We're grown," I said. "We can get settled ourselves. Godwin can stay in the apartment tonight. Mr. Fitzherbert won't mind."

"No," Sally said, getting angry. "You don't know how he is when he wakes up from a drunk. He'll be crazy at first. He loves me and if he comes-to drunk and finds me gone he'll kill himself."

"Let him," I said. "You married me. He has to stop loving you sometime."

"He doesn't have to stop tonight," she said sullenly.

"I don't have to take him anywhere, either," I said. "I don't want him loving you. I love you, remember?"

"Don't say stupid things like that," she said. "You're so fucking jealous you can't see straight." She kept trying to get his feet in the car, but his knees wouldn't bend. I felt feverish, as if I were getting drunk again. I remembered they had been kissing and I went over and tried to make her let go of his feet. It infuriated her and she jabbed me suddenly with her elbow and hurt my ribs. I smacked her cheek, but it had no effect on her at all except to make her stop believing in my existence again. She neither spoke nor looked at me after I hit her, but she managed to get Godwin's feet in the car. I felt guilty and at a loss. I wasn't mad enough to drag him out. I went back in the dark apartment and sat on my table awhile. I had begun to long to stay in the apartment. Jenny Salomea was just across the yard, in the big, empty house. I felt I ought to say goodbye to her, but I didn't see how I could. I felt as if I were running out on her and Mr. Fitzherbert. But I had to go. After I thought a little I stopped worrying about Godwin. There were thousands of miles of desert between us and California. I could run off and leave him at a filling station if I needed to. He had plenty of money. He wouldn't suffer.

Outside, it was just graying. I went out and got in the car. Sally ignored my existence.

"You needn't think I'm taking him all the way," I said.

She was completely silent. She sat combing her hair.

As we were driving past Rice Godwin suddenly burst awake. Before I knew what was happening he was trying to claw his way out a car window. Characteristically, he was purple in the face, and he seemed to be frightened out of his mind. When he couldn't get out the window he tried to come over the seat.

"Bloody kidnapers," he yelled. "Let me out! Don't you know it's a capital crime?"

I had to stop in the middle of the street. For about ten seconds Godwin was demonic. "Kidnap! Kidnap!" he yelled. No one was around. Sally screamed at him and I stiff-armed him two or three times, until he fell back panting amid our clothes.

"Fucking white slavers," he yelled. "Why have you drugged me? Is this the Ivory Coast?"

Sally knew how to handle him. She pressed her hands over his eyes. "Calm down, Godwin," she said. "You'll be all right. It's just us."

He panted for a while and then grew calm. "Head's splitting," he said. "Frightful dream. I was in a brothel. Arabs were abusing me."

"We're going to California," Sally said.

"You're not," I said to Godwin, so there would be no doubt about my position. But he was in no state to be talked to.

"It seems an abrupt departure, if I might say so," he said, his voice growing softer. "My dear children. Splitting head." Then he went back to sleep.

I drove out South Main for two or three miles and then remembered the Hortons. I couldn't leave without telling them that I was leaving. Flap might think it was just part of my discipline, but Emma would be hurt. I turned around and started back.

Sally gave me a questioning look. She was still combing her hair.

"I forgot the Hortons," I said. "I have to say goodbye to them."

Sally looked disgusted. "I don't see why we have to go all the way back, just for them," she said. "They won't even be awake."

I decided not to answer. If she could be silent, so could I. I just drove. The streetlights were on but it was light enough that they looked odd. Rice slept under its light sheet of mist.

"I'm not coming in," Sally said, when I stopped at the curb in front of the Hortons'.

I got out without looking at her and went to their door. Silence was not so hard to manage. But I felt bad in my stomach and had a hard time knocking on the door. I felt strange about leaving, again. It was not Houston I had to leave now, it was my friends. I knocked several times. Emma was hard to wake up, and Flap was harder. I could see Sally sitting in the car examining her hair. Finally Emma came to the door, a little bleary, in her white bathrobe. A troubled look came over her face when she saw me. Perhaps a troubled look was in mine.

"Come in," she said, holding open the screen.

"Can't," I said. "Could you wake up Flap?"

"Did someone die?" she asked.

"No," I said.

"Please come in," she said.

I shook my head. I didn't want to go into the kitchen. It would be harder to leave than my apartment and my table. They would try to make me eat breakfast. Emma frowned and went and got Flap. She must have impressed something on him, because he looked awake when he came to the door. His hair was down in his eyes.

"I'm going to California," I told them. "I'm quitting school."

They looked at me solemnly. I had meant to go into an explanation involving Razzy Hutton and one thing and another, but it didn't come out. I couldn't have stated the real reason—I felt too emotional. The Hortons were beautifully reticent. They left their questions in the same place I left my explanations. Emma's round face changed as she watched me. Tactfully they didn't ask me one thing. They accepted it as being a necessity of mine, something I might explain some other time.

"Tell Sally goodbye for us," Emma said, barely audibly. She was struggling to do her duty. They could see Sally sitting in the car.

"Well," Flap said. "Who will we drink with now?"

"I decided last night," I said, by way of explanation.

I couldn't think of another remark, one to leave on. As I was trying, Emma slowly started crying. Suddenly she yanked open the door and hugged me, sobbing.

"You shouldn't," she said. "You can't take care of yourself. You just look like you can." Then she rushed back into Flap's arms. As usual Flap looked sheepish. He rubbed Emma's back.

"She won't be good to you," Emma said, crying. "I know she won't! She won't be good to him—I know she won't!"

"I promise I'll write you," I said.

At the car I waved and they waved. Sally still looked disgusted. I drove on out of Houston, thinking of Emma and feeling very down. I had nothing snug left. When I noticed things again we were in the gray grasslands beyond Rosenberg. Houston was somewhere behind, beneath great white banks of Gulf clouds. Sally was idly nibbling her nicely combed hair. We were both silence experts. She had always been one, and I had just become one. Godwin Lloyd-Jons' pleasant snoring was the only human sound in the car.

6.

WHEN GODWIN woke up, one hundred and fifty miles later, he immediately began to talk about Stendhal. Unlike Sally and me, he seemed to feel wonderful. He lay back comfortably amid our clothes and talked almost without interruption for two hours. He was really conning me, like Scheherazade conned the Sultan—he knew I was itching to kick him out, and his talk was just a stall. But it was a brilliant stall, and anyway my spirit was at a low ebb. I let myself be conned. Sally was as silent as Stonehenge.

From Stendhal Godwin went to Alexander Herzen, whose memoirs he had just read. From Alexander Herzen he went to literary hoaxes, and from literary hoaxes he went to the Portuguese epic. From the Portuguese epic he went to pornography and from pornography he went to Lady Murasaki. It was at Lady Murasaki that I began to suspect a con, but Godwin didn't stop talking just because I was suspicious. From Lady Murasaki he went to Baron Corvo, from Baron Corvo he went to skaldic verse, and from skaldic verse he went to Ezra Pound. He even seemed to have read Sara Teasdale. He was only a sociologist, but the literatures of the world seemed to be at his fingertips. It was a virtuoso performance, two hours long. He told us all about the Angry Young Men, reviewed the life and works of John Stuart Mill and ended up discoursing on Uruguayan fiction. I admire virtuoso performances, and was an ideal audience. I listened and kept driving westward, through towns where the name of Stendhal had probably never been uttered. Sally was not so appreciative. I doubt she even realized it was a virtuoso performance, but if she had it wouldn't have mattered. Godwin should have known better than to bore her, but he was intent on his performance. At Uruguayan fiction her gorge apparently rose.

"Oh, shut up, Godwin," she said. "Nobody wants to hear about all that stuff. I wish this car had a radio."

"It has one," I said. "It's just broken."

"Big deal," she said. She was not in a friendly mood. Determined as I was to get rid of Godwin, I was almost grateful for him. He absorbed part of her unfriendliness.

"Sorry, love," he said.

We stopped and ate in Del Rio. It was an overcast day and the barren country looked dismal. The fat carhop who served us looked dismal, and the three of us looked dismal too. None of us had cleaned up before setting out for the West. Godwin had monologued himself into a state of hoarseness.

"I say," he croaked, "did the three of us strike one another during the night? I believe we were all outrageously drunk. Wasn't there some kind of row?"

"Yeah," Sally said. "You kissed me and Danny behaved like a horse's ass."

"I just behaved like a husband," I said. "What did you expect me to do?"

"It was none of your business," she said. "I always kiss people when I'm drunk."

"Now, now, now, now," Godwin said. "Really, now."

"Have you actually read skaldic verse?" I asked.

"I read the *Times Literary Supplement* regularly," he said.

"I don't want to talk about reading," Sally said. "You two should have got married. You both know too much about books."

I decided I had better remind Godwin he couldn't go all the way with us. I didn't want him to think I was a fool—or a marshmallow.

"You have to get a bus back to Austin," I said. "We can't take you to California with us."

Sally looked at me as if I had said something very inhuman, but Godwin didn't seem surprised. "You won't abandon me here, will you?" he asked, looking out at Del Rio as if he expected to see vultures circling in the sky. I couldn't really blame him. It was bleak country.

"No," I said. "You can ride with us to Junction and get a bus straight back to Austin."

"Righto," he said gamely.

But he was sly. We hadn't driven twenty miles before he began to get sick. I knew immediately that it was just another performance, but this time it was the kind of virtuoso performance that Sally was susceptible to. Godwin was clever. He pretended he was trying to be stoic. Now and then he would groan, making it sound as if the groan had been wrenched from him inadvertently. Sally asked him what was the matter.

"Don't know," he said. "Could have been the hot dog."

Slyly, he had eaten a hot dog, whereas Sally and I had eaten cheeseburgers. I had no way of disproving that he had been poisoned. The drive-in had been pretty fly-blown. Godwin became limper and limper and made himself look sicker and sicker. The country we were going through was dippy and he pretended the dipping gave him great pain.

"Vile place," he said. "I shall have a colon spasm if I'm not lucky."

"I'm worried about him," Sally said. "Maybe he's got ptomaine."

All I was worried about was how to get him out of the car, once we came to Junction. The clouds seemed to be coming lower. "We might be going to have a flash flood," I said. "I hope he can swim."

They both looked at me as if I were crazy. "Are you nuts?" Sally said. "This is the desert. There's no water in miles of here."

Less than fifteen minutes later Godwin was over his illness and he and Sally had both come to realize that deserts are very good places for flash floods. The heavens had simply opened. Heavy drops of rain were followed by heavy sheets of rain. In no time, maybe three minutes, the road was covered. The dips began to fill. In ten minutes the highway, at its levelest, had a foot of water on it. In the dips it was halfway up our fenders. We could hardly see anything. We might as well have been under a waterfall. I slowed to two miles an hour. Sally looked scared. The rain beat so loudly on the roof of the car that none of us could think. I went into a dip and water sloshed over the fenders. There was a strong current pushing across the road, making the car hard to hold. We were in a narrow arroyo and almost didn't get across, but we inched on in low and gradually began to climb the next rise.

"Look," Godwin said, "I can swim, you remember that. The question is, What does one swim for? I can't see a bloody thing."

Neither could I, but I could tell we were going up instead of down. The water got shallower. The minute I felt us going down again I stopped. We were on top of a dip.

"I don't know why I married you," Sally said. "I bet we all drown."

She began to cry, but neither Godwin nor I had time for her. The water was getting deeper, outside the car. I backed up until I judged us to be right on top of the high place between dips. It was a little better than bumper deep.

Despite having predicted that there would be one, I really knew nothing about flash floods. I had no idea how deep it might get. I set the emergency brake. Sheets of water were still slapping against the windshield. Our breath had caused the windows to fog over, making it still more difficult to see.

"I guess we ought to get on top of the car," I said. "I don't know if it will wash away, but I don't want to be in it if it does."

"I have been watching the countryside," Godwin said. "There's not a bloody fucking thing out there. It must be miles to a house. There aren't even trees."

"There are barbed-wire fences," I said. The car was rocking and we all felt claustrophobic. I wanted out. So did Godwin. We counted three and I jumped out in the rain. Water was almost to my knees. Godwin got out too. We practically had to pull Sally out. It soaked us instantly, but once we got soaked it wasn't quite so terrifying. It was a very hard rainstorm though. Streams of water ran off the car, as well as under it. Godwin slipped and fell down. After that he clung to one of the door handles. He was terrified of being swept away into endless miles of West Texas. I managed to get Sally up on the rear end, but that was as high as any of us got. She sat there, trying not to drown, and Godwin clung grimly to the door handle. I simply stood by the car, water swirling around my legs, trying to hit on a plan. Undoubtedly the barbed-wire fences were under water, so there was no point in trying to swim to one of them. They would probably just cut us to shreds. My wet hair was in my eyes and I couldn't have seen any distance at all even if it hadn't been, so it was very hard for me to make a good plan. I held Sally's hand, so we wouldn't get separated. Not getting separated from her was the chief element of my plan.

Fortunately, the flood began to end. The water was only three inches above my knees. The rain began to ease up, so that we could see one another better. Then it slacked enough so that we could see across the road. At about that point we began to hear screaming. I guess the rain had been drowning it out. It was Mexican screaming and it wasn't far away. I remembered we had passed an old bus of some kind, just as the flood hit. Godwin let go the door handle and came back where I was, to listen.

"Those are sounds of distress," he said.

"You two stay here," Sally said. She held my hand with both of hers. Godwin waded a few steps back of the car, peering into the rain. It was definitely stopping, but Sally didn't realize it. The screams seemed mostly to be the names of saints.

"My God," Godwin said. Then he began to wave his hands. "Here, here!" he yelled. "Don't give up! We're coming!" I still couldn't see whatever it was he saw, but it was obvious he was about to do something impulsive. He began to strip, yelling, "Here! Here! Don't give up!" as he did. He flung his shirt behind him, then his pants. They immediately washed away. I don't know if they were ever seen again. I could see some kind of bus, down in the dip where the water was really deep, and I shook free of Sally and waded toward Godwin. He had somehow managed to get his pants off without removing but one shoe, and he was standing on one foot in the current and struggling with the other shoe. When he got it off he dropped it in the water and immediately splashed down the little slope and dove into the brown water.

It struck me as madness, but the rain grew light enough that I could at least see what had prompted him to do it. From where I stood it looked like a Mexican village was drowning. The old bus I had passed was drowned out almost at the bottom of the dip in the road, where the water was at least six or eight feet deep by this time. The bus had contained numerous Mexicans, either a small village or a very large family. Several soaked Mexican kids were sitting on top of the bus and others were trying to clamber up. One goat was on top of the bus and three or four more were swimming unhappily around it, making goat noises. Three very wet dogs were swimming around with the goats, looking as if their hour had come. Several squawking chickens, their feet tied together, were in the process of washing away, and a very fat Mexican woman who clung to the door of the bus kept yelling about the chickens and calling out the names of saints. She saw Godwin, who was swimming toward them in a classic crawl, and it merely seemed to alarm her the more. Two tiny Mexican men were vainly trying to break her hold on the door and hoist her onto the bus. A young woman began to crawl out one window of the bus, a baby in her hands. She slipped and dropped the baby, which splashed into the brown water. I began to take off my shirt. Godwin looked up and saw the baby fall and quickly redoubled his efforts. They were not necessary though. The young woman didn't seem to be flustered. The baby bobbed up and she reached down, picked it out of the water and handed it up to a kid on the roof of the bus. It began to squall. The tiny men had broken the fat woman's hold on the door. It seemed for a moment that they too would be swept away, but the current was sweeping them against the bus instead of around it. Godwin arrived at that time, to everyone's consternation. The fat woman screamed. One of the dogs immediately swam toward him, menacingly. Godwin lost his nerve and swam back a little way, pursued by the sinister wet dog. The goats didn't like him, either. He began to swim after the drowning chickens, but the chickens were long gone. One tiny man got on top of the bus and pulled at the fat woman's hand, while the other stayed in the water and pushed on her ass. The young woman had managed to get on top of the bus and was nursing her baby. The clouds broke open at that moment and the bright West Texas sun shone over the desert. The water where I stood was receding and it was obvious there was no longer a real need to get the fat woman onto the bus, but the Mexicans didn't notice. The one in the water was near to drowning and couldn't be blamed for not noticing that the danger had passed. Godwin was no help at all. He was swimming forlornly in a wide circle around the bus, followed by a goat and the mean brown dog, who yapped at him from time to time. Finally, by a great team effort, the two Mexicans hoisted the fat woman to safety amid the children. One child dove in for a swim. Sally realized that the danger was over and waded out to where I was watching. The water in the dip was still quite deep, but the sun had split the clouds for good. The young woman still nursed the baby, and the fat woman chattered at the men, who chattered at Godwin, whose strength was ebbing. His gallant rescue attempt was either going to get him dog-bit or drowned—or maybe both. I wanted to throw a rock at the dog, but I couldn't find one. A goat clambered up on the hood of the bus, giving Godwin an idea. He swam to the hood and pulled himself up beside the goat. Apparently the current had sucked away his underpants, because he was naked. Back down the road I could see other cars stranded on other humps. The young woman giggled at Godwin and the old fat woman scowled at him and made furious sounds of outrage. Perhaps she hadn't realized he had been coming to help. Godwin kept the brown dog at bay by splashing water in its face. This made the dog furious, but there was nothing it could do about it. The kid who had gone swimming grabbed the tail of a goat and let the goat tow him. Godwin looked sheepish and kept his legs crossed. Several of the kids sat looking at him. He smiled appealingly at the woman who was nursing the baby.

"Look at him," Sally said. "He's already thinking about screwing her. Let's go off and leave him."

It had just occurred to me that I ought to go off and leave him. It would be the perfect way to get rid of him. If I let him ride to Junction he would con me into letting him ride to El Paso. He would feign illness, or do something equally sly. If he had only kept his clothes on I could have gone off and left him in no time and never given it a thought. The Mexicans could haul him to Junction. But his clothes and all his money had washed away. He was naked and not among friends. West Texans were not apt to take kindly to a naked Englishman. His best chance lay with the Mexicans, but the matriarch of the bus didn't seem to like his looks.

When I heard Sally suggest it, I knew I couldn't do it. I felt tired of things. The flood had been almost fun—the Mexican kids were having a jolly time in what was left of it. But Sally shouldn't have suggested going off and leaving Godwin. It made everything seem wrong. She was the one who was supposed to have loyalties to him. I didn't like being put in the position of having to be loyal to my worst rival.

"We can't go off and leave him," I said. "His clothes have washed away."

"Big deal," she said. "He goes around naked half the time anyway."

"Not in the middle of the desert, he doesn't," I said.

"I thought you wanted to get rid of him," she said, looking at me closely. She had a genius for making me feel on the spot. Even in the aftermath of a real flood I felt on the spot.

"I do," I said, "but look at him. He's naked, he's broke, and he's among strangers. We can't go off and leave him that way."

"I could," Sally said. "I'll be glad when I get a baby." She looked darkly at the young Mexican woman on top of the bus. Then she went to the car and changed her wet clothes. I waved for Godwin to swim back.

"Just catching my breath," he yelled. The brown dog had lost interest. I think Godwin really was intrigued by the young woman, and I couldn't blame him. She was smiling and one of her lovely breasts was bare. But it looked hopeless: to get to her he would have had to plow through a crowd of goats, kids, and little brown men. After some more grinning back and forth he slid into the water and swam to our side of the dip.

"I liked Texas from the first," he said, looking across the desert. It was by then a desert full of water puddles, with a bright sun shining on them.

"Why?"

"Oh, you know, surprises," he said. "Something happening all the time." He managed to find one shoe.

When we got to the car Sally was just struggling into some dry blue jeans. I gave Godwin a shirt and some pants, but he seemed in no great hurry to get dressed. The swim had invigorated him.

"Quite an adventure," he said. "Travel never fails to bring home to me what a fucking bore the university is. This is country a man can pit himself against. All it needs is a few bloody Arabs and it could be North Africa. I was there, you know, in the last days of the Raj. Wonderful times. Spit and polish such as will never be seen again."

"You know good and well why you liked it," Sally said. "There were lots of little brown boys for you to screw."

Godwin was just putting on the shirt I had given him. He was highly insulted. "I'll ask you to apologize for that, love," he said. "I have never, as you put it, screwed a boy in my life."

"Oh yeah?" Sally said.

"Apologize!" he shouted suddenly. "I'm no bloody pederast. I loathe pederasts! They're the scum of the earth. Apologize!"

"Fuck you," Sally said. "I wouldn't apologize to you if you were the last man alive. Put your pants on so we can go."

Godwin had just stepped into his pants, but what she said made him insane with rage. He sloshed around the car, furious, and grabbed Sally by her long wet hair and started trying to drag her out the car window.

"You fucking little whore, I'll drown you," he said. "I've never committed pederasty in my life." He was really tugging on her hair and Sally was yelling. I was inside the car, holding onto her, but I decided I would have to get out and fight Godwin off. Her hair was long enough that he had wrapped it around one hand. He couldn't really get her out, but neither of us could break his hold. Sally's arms and shoulders were out and Godwin seemed to be getting madder.

"You abominable little bitch," he said. "You're the fucking destroyer of innocents! Geoffrey knew nothing of women until you got your whory little hands on him. I'll drown you in the nearest ditch, you evil slut."

I got out of the car as quickly as I could and was running around it to tackle him when I noticed that all the Mexicans were standing on their bus, watching the fight. Just as I looked off, Godwin screamed horribly. He fell backward in the mud. He had gone into the fray with his pants unzipped and Sally had reached down and zipped him. I don't know precisely what got caught in the zipper, but it was something tender. Sally calmly rolled the car window up and locked her door. Godwin got up and ran spraddle-legged down the road for several steps and then stopped and extricated himself, yelling curses and making sounds of great pain. He was as wet as if he hadn't just changed.

"It was a good try, it was a good try," he said, looking around at me wildly. "Thank God it was only a zipper."

"She saw you looking at that girl on the bus," I said.

Godwin looked around and was a little unnerved to see all the Mexicans standing on the bus watching the show. It brought him out of his fit. The young woman had tucked her breast back into her bodice.

"I do like the looks of that child," Godwin said, waving heartily at the Mexicans. "Look, perhaps I'll just ride on with them. They're poor folk. They'll not turn me down."

"Big Momma may sic the dogs on you," I said.

"Nonsense. The woman was hysterical with fear."

I more or less agreed. The Mexicans would take him in. He clapped me on the shoulder and held out his hand. I shook it.

"You're something of a gentleman," he said. "Allow me to give you some advice. Stop in the next town and divorce Sally. I never dreamed you'd marry her or I would have strangled her for you at once, out of simple kindness. As soon as you're divorced, give up writing. Do those two things at once and you've at least a chance for happiness."

"But I just got a book accepted," I said. "I'm writing another one. Why should I give it up now?"

Godwin was straightening his shirt collar. He was in the process of assuming a dapper appearance, and bedraggled as he was, he looked rather happy.

"Wait much longer and it may be too late," he said. "There are no writers in heaven, you know. They don't even know how to enjoy the bloody earth. Will you say goodbye to Sally for me? I shan't be seeing her for a while."

I felt odd. Godwin looked like he wanted to be going, and I had a strange desire to continue the conversation. I felt like I was about to learn something I needed to know.

"Why do you keep wanting her?" I asked.

He smiled coyly. "Some of us have to court the destructive element," he said. "Otherwise you bloody writers wouldn't know anything about it. Besides, she's nice to fuck."

"That's not the point," I said. "You love her."

"It's a good thing she thought to zip my cock," he said. "Otherwise I'd have drowned her. I'm afraid you'll never learn."

He started wading out to the bus. The sky had become absolutely cloudless and blue, and West Texas stretched away, a hundred miles to the Pecos, four hundred to the Pass of the North.

"You don't have any money," I said. "I could lend you a buck or two."

"Thanks awfully," he said. "I won't need it." He waved, squinting a little in the sun. The water was only a little above his waist. The Mexicans let him on top of the bus and in no time at all he had made friends with them. I got in the car, and as I was about to drive on I looked in the rear-view mirror and saw that Godwin was talking merrily to the young woman. She was sitting next to him. I tooted my horn in farewell and drove down into the next dip. Sally was combing her wet hair, and the inside of the car smelled of wet clothes.

That night we parked beside Highway 90, near the town of Valentine. We had all our blankets with us, so we didn't get cold. At three I woke up and drove on, with Sally asleep in the back seat. There was a very white moon, high over the Davis Mountains. When I went through the town of Van Horn I thought of my Uncle Laredo, who lived on a ranch forty-seven miles off the paved road. I ought to have visited him, but I didn't feel up to driving forty-seven miles on a dirt road. I would visit him if I ever came back.

At dawn we went through El Paso. It was strange, leaving Texas. I had had no plans to leave it, and didn't know how I felt. I drove on into New Mexico, Sally still asleep. Then I really felt Texas. It was all behind me, north to south, not lying there exactly, but more like looming there over the car, not a state or a stretch of land but some giant, some genie, some god, towering over the road. I really felt it. Its vengeance might fall on me from behind. I had left without asking permission, or earning my freedom. Texas let me go, ominously quiet. It hadn't gone away. It was there behind me.

From Highway 80 I could look south and see the Rio Grande, cutting through the desert toward El Paso, the Big Bend, the Valley, and the Gulf. I rolled the car window down—the air was cool and the desert had a fresh, pleasant smell. The sage was still dewy. Sally woke about that time, lovely as ever. She sat up, the blankets around her, yawning. She smelled like a girl and looked like she had looked the morning I had fallen in love with her—young, open, soft. She looked that way every morning. One thing I had been right about was that it would always be pleasant to wake up beside her. For Sally sleep canceled everything. Her face held no memory, her body had no past.

"What's the next town?" she asked.

"Las Cruces. Hungry?"

"Boy," she said, yawning again.

7.

UNTIL WE MOVED to California, I hadn't met many writers. Emma and Flap and various other people I knew played around with writing, but it was pretty doubtful that they were real writers. I knew a couple of journalists who planned to knock off and write novels some day, but I couldn't count them as real writers either. Aside from professors, the only person I knew who had actually published anything was an old man named Sickles who had written a booklet on driver training. One of the reasons I couldn't tell whether I was a real writer or not was because I had no one authentic to compare myself to.

California changed all that. I met young writers everywhere. They lined the streets. There was one in every bookshop. I would hear them talking about poetry in Chinese grocery stores. Fifty lived in the basement of the City Lights Bookshop. For a week or two it was very exciting, meeting writers. Just meeting them made me feel like I *was* one, after all. But pretty soon I began to feel depressed about it all. I didn't feel much kinship with any of the writers I met, but that wasn't what depressed me. What depressed me was that there were so many of them. None of them became my friends, or stayed in my life more than a day or two, but once I became aware of how many writers there were I could never stop being aware of it. I would go down in the basement of the City Lights Bookshop and look at the scores of little magazines they had there and it always depressed me terribly. Even if I was a real writer, what was the point? There were hundreds of others, maybe thousands. We couldn't all be good enough to count. Most of us were undoubtedly mediocre—in thinking we were better we were just deceiving ourselves. I had a feeling I was deceiving myself. I kept writing pages and looking at them later and it seemed to me I was going to have to get ten times as good as I was. I didn't know if I could get even twice as good. I wished I had stayed in Texas, so I could have postponed realizing how likely it was that I was only mediocre.

Also, I was terribly homesick. It was supposed to be summer, but San Francisco was cold and foggy. When we got there we were both anxious to get settled, and since we didn't know the city at all, we figured one place was probably about as good as another. All I knew was that I wanted to be somewhere near North Beach, where the Beat Generation lived. Of course most of them had stopped living there years before, but in my mind that was where they lived when they were not in Denver, or on the road, and when I walked the streets I always half expected to come around a corner and see Jack Kerouac or Allen Ginsberg. It never happened, but as long as I lived in San Francisco I continued to expect it.

In order to make it more likely, we took a little two-room apartment on Jones Street, overlooking Alcatraz. It didn't have much heat, and I was always cold. Finally I went down to an army surplus store and bought a huge green parka, meant for use above the Arctic Circle. I took up residence in my parka and seldom left it. Sally was never cold, that I could tell, and it soon turned out that the apartment was really hers, so it was fortunate that I had my parka to live in. We went down to the St. Vincent de Paul store on Mission Street and bought a mattress and an old table and four chairs, all for about twelve dollars. We didn't really need to live quite so starkly, because the second week we were there I got three thousand dollars as an advance on my novel, but we were in the process of adjusting to California and didn't have time to adjust to money too. My brown typing table was only one of the many things I missed about Houston. In the cold, gloomy late afternoons I invariably grew depressed and sat at the window for hours. I huddled in my parka, watched the gray fog envelop Alcatraz and thought wistfully of how hot and muggy it must be in Houston. The things I missed most about Texas were the Hortons' kitchen, my typing table, and the sun.

Sally was much happier than I was. She bought a black sweater and wore it everywhere. Her hair got longer and she learned to tie it in a knot. She made friends with a young couple who lived on the ground floor of our building. We lived on the third floor. They had lots of room and we had lots of view. They were the Beaches, Willis and Andrea. Andrea was a skinny girl from Michigan; for some reason she distrusted me to such an extent that I never really got to make friends with them. Willis was blind but very well adjusted. Andrea worked for IBM and made lots of money and Willis stayed home and listened to classical music. He had an FM radio and sixteen hundred classical record albums. In the afternoons he practiced the cello. He was very good at it and Andrea was very good at whatever she did for IBM. Willis was very fat, probably because he sat around all day and ate cheese and drank wine while he listened to his records, but he was nice enough and he didn't seem to mind being blind. The Beaches' mutual competence turned me off a little. I would have thought it would turn Sally off, but it didn't. She became their friend. She went down to visit Willis from time to time and on weekends took long walks with Andrea.

My friend in the building was a writer named Wu. Wu was from mainland China and was writing a novel about conditions there. He was standing in the doorway of his apartment when I carried my typewriter into ours, and the first words he said to me were "I'm glad you are an author, too." He always referred to us as authors. He was very dignified in manner, but the effect was spoiled by the horrible gray clothes he always wore. They made him look like a Korean refugee, whereas in reality he was a refugee from somewhere deep in China. He talked about China constantly—like Texas, it was apparently a hard place to leave behind. Sally thought Wu was about on par with Petey Ximenes. She begrudged him air space in our apartment. Wu was prone to long Oriental silences when she was around, and Sally matched him with long Sallyesque silences. Anything I said at such times sounded silly, but I talked anyway.

Wu let me read his novel, which at the time of my arrival had reached a length of eighteen hundred pages. Wu was almost fifty years old and had been working on the novel for the entire nineteen years he had been in America. He was a great believer in revision and revised each section of the novel six or eight times before he went on to the next one. The novel was a kind of literary Great Wall. It filled all the shelves of Wu's pantry. Its bulk really awed me — my first novel was only three hundred and eighteen pages in manuscript. Wu's was nearly six times as long and it wasn't even finished. Every time I went to visit him I carried home a hundred pages or so to read. It was called "The Hotbed of Life." In many respects it reminded me of Henry's screenplays, though I don't believe the Seventh Cavalry ever appeared in it. It was full of the wildest improbabilities, some of which were never explained. In one sentence the story might leap thirty years ahead, and then in the next leap sideways two thousand miles across China. I didn't believe a word of it, but I loved to read it. It was obvious to me that it could never be published in America, and probably not in China either. Wu was tranquil about it. It was his life work. He was studying English literature at San Francisco State College and he spent a lot of time reading the metaphysical poets.

Also, he liked to play ping-pong. I liked to too. In no time at all it became one of the props of my life in California. We played at a Chinese ping-pong club on Grant Street. There were twenty tables in one room, all constantly being used by intent Chinese ping-pong players. All the members seemed to play with maniacal frenzy and earnestness. It was like being in a room where twenty small-scale wars were going on. I expected a lot of courtliness and bowing, but instead there were screams of vexation and what I guess were Chinese curses. The racket of twenty balls constantly hitting tables and paddles would have driven any non-devotee mad, but oddly the ping-pong club was one of the few places in San Francisco where I felt at peace. For me it was the California equivalent of Emma's kitchen — not as nice as Emma's kitchen but the best I could do. I could even muse sometimes while playing ping-pong.

For a fifty-year-old man, Wu was a whiz of a ping-pong player. Sometimes I won, but usually I didn't. Wu was all defense. He never hit a slam in all our games together. He just hit my slams back. I hit better slams at ping-pong than I did at badminton, but nine times out of ten Wu hit them back and sooner or later I'd miss. I didn't care. I liked hearing all the balls. I liked being among the darting Chinese. It freed my spirit for an hour or two, and my spirit needed all the relief it could get. I bought a very good nine-ply paddle, and Wu and I played every day. After drinking iced tea all my life I found I liked hot tea, so when we came home from our daily ping-pong game, if Sally wasn't there, I made some hot tea and Wu would peer into my paperbacks as if they contained the secret of America. He was poor and owned only anthologies himself. I don't know why he chose English literature to study. He talked mostly about the wars he had seen and the frustrations of his life. He had had much difficulty at borders.

"War is not so bad," he said pleasantly, sipping tea. "If war is over here, I go over there. If war is over there, I go over here. Always can move faster than war unless there is a border. But getting across border is where the trouble starts."

Wu was very eager to read anything I wrote, and because I was eager to have him as a friend, I usually let him. The problem was that I wasn't writing much. The move had disoriented me as a writer. I no longer had my writing table to sit at and a tree full of squirrels to watch. In San Francisco I didn't even like to get up early. Looking out at the cold fog only depressed me and made me want to go back to bed. Often I did go back to bed. In Texas I had been a student. I had classes to go to at nine thirty. If I wanted to write I had to get up and hit it before the day got out of hand.

Some days I was sorry my novel had been accepted. If it hadn't been I could have given up on writing and gone out and gotten a job. I was an experienced termite exterminator and could probably have gotten a job. If not, I could have gone back to school. Some days I had a great yen to read literary history, and reading literary history almost always made me yearn to be a scholar. Whatever candle of talent I had had seemed about to flicker out, and it seemed to me it would be much cozier, much more comfortable, just to be a scholar. I could sit among my books and read to my heart's content, and be a scholar, like George Saintsbury, or C. S. Lewis. I sipped hot tea and encouraged the fantasy of myself among my books, but the only books I had were paperbacks and even as I was encouraging the fantasy I knew what was wrong with it. I loved to read and probably would love to sit among books, but I hated to write about what I read. I hated writing themes and term papers and would probably hate writing scholarship just as much. Besides, George Saintsbury and C. S. Lewis were so good at it that there was no need for me. I wouldn't count as a scholar, any more than I counted as a novelist. I was just an apprentice, and might not ever get to be a journeyman, much less a master.

For the first few weeks I was no match for the cold gray weight of San Francisco. On the few days when the sun shone I could see how the city might be beautiful, as beautiful as everyone else seemed to think it was, but despite those days and despite what everyone else thought, I couldn't really feel it as beautiful. It made me too chilly, and let me sit home too much.

Also, since I wasn't in school, I had no real way to make friends. I was too pinched by the newness of things just to go out on the street and seize people and make them my friends. I got by on ping-pong and my parka and Wu and Market Street. On Market Street there were numerous three-feature movie houses. They were full of winos and thugs and snoring bums and they stank horribly and were over-crowded and overheated and usually showed terrible movies, but I didn't care. They were there, and when I gave up on my novel for the day I could drift down to Market Street and pick out a couple of movies and forget things for a while. I can watch any movie, and I averaged one or two a day all the time I was in San Francisco. The hot, smelly movie houses were my Houston surrogate. I never went to the art films that were always being shown—I only went to the third-rate movies on Market Street. I didn't want to see films that reminded me about life—I wanted to see films that bore little relation to it: Italian spectacles, horror movies, comedies, anything unreal. I was escaping from reality for a couple of hours, and wanted the escape to be as pure and complete as possible. I could always have reality—it was all around me. It was much like fog. I wanted to see Steve Reeves, in bright Technicolor, wrestling elephants with his bare hands. In one movie I saw, Steve Reeves apparently killed an elephant by twisting its foreleg. He lifted the leg and twisted it, he grunted a few times, the elephant fell dead; a beautiful Roman matron, her bosom shaking, ran out of a villa and gave Steve Reeves a hug. That was the kind of thing I wanted to see.

Wu was not a very good novelist, but he was a smart man. He knew that I was homesick and depressed and he tried, in his way, to help me. Sometimes, in the manner of Confucius, he gave me advice, but more often his approach was gently Socratic. I puzzled him even more than I puzzled myself, and he loved to try to figure me out.

"You do not leave Texas for any reason," he said one day. "So. If a man leaves a place for no reason, he is not needing any reasons to go back. Is this not true?"

"I guess," I said. We were sitting in his place, sipping Turkish coffee, which he loved. He had a parrot named Andrew, after Andrew Marvell, his favorite poet.

"Then you are going back?"

"No," I said. "I have to stay here until I finish my novel."

"This is a matter of pride," Wu said. "You are ashamed to go back to your friends. If you go back, then they are thinking you a coward. Is this true?"

I had stopped trying to understand my own motives, and couldn't really say if it was true or not. Wu always nodded when I spoke, no matter what I said.

"Maybe," I said.

"You are knowing 'To His Coy Mistress'?" Wu asked. "Very great poem? Is this true?"

We discussed "To His Coy Mistress" about every third day, so I merely nodded. It was Wu's favorite poem. He could not get enough of talking about it. His asking if I had read it was merely a rhetorical opener.

"Is not world enough and time," Wu said patiently. "This is very clear. Nice times are so good to have. If there is no reason, you should be going to Texas and having nice times."

I agreed, but secretly. I wasn't about to be coward enough to leave Texas and then go running right back. I was giving Wu a runaround. I hated Turkish coffee and much preferred drinking tea in our apartment, but it happened that Sally was there, and anyhow Wu's sense of hospitality demanded that he serve me Turkish coffee once or twice a week. My runaround didn't fool him and he looked a little sad when I stood up to go home. He really liked me and was always hoping he could persuade me to profit from his experience.

"I was leaving China for many years," he said. "Very hard country to leave. Then I was wanting to go back. But America is interesting country too. I have not been going to Texas so far. I would be going with you, if you are ever needing me to.

"Of course Sally would not be needing me to," he added, remembering her. It was undeniable. She would not be needing him to. His English was a little strange, but his points were not hard to get.

Wu wrinkled his yellow brow when he said good night. Sally wrinkled her white one when I walked into our apartment, my ping-pong paddle sticking out of the pocket of my parka. She was learning to make onion soup.

"You didn't bring any wine," she said. "You're so busy trying to be the ping-pong champion of Chinatown that you can't even remember wine. It's a wonder you can find your way home."

"I agree," I said. "It's a wonder." I liked the smell of onion soup, but it wasn't enough. I looked at her and she was smiling quietly. She had forgotten I was there; she had even forgotten I had forgotten the wine. The fog was in and the apartment was cold. I sat down at the typewriter meaning to write while the soup cooked, but all I actually wrote was my name. I was too distracted to write and I sat quietly in my parka, holding my ping-pong paddle. I had no reason to be unhappy, no reason to pity myself, not one valid thing to complain of, and yet I was so sorrowful for several minutes that I couldn't have moved or spoken. I hated myself when I got that way. It wasn't manly. I was too healthy. It was ignoble to be so depressed, but I was anyway. I had acquired an independent depression. I was beyond my control, much like the fog. It didn't take orders from strong, healthy, soon-to-be-successful, unself-pitying me. It came from a place of Fogs and Depressions and held me in my chair for hours at a time, making me feel lonely and unwanted and tired of everything in my life.

I was in the kind of mood Jenny Salomea would not have tolerated for five minutes. In my mind I often heard her lecture me. Jenny Salomea had become the voice of reason, but in my life reason was like a ninety-seven-pound weakling in a Charles Atlas ad. My depression was twice its weight and could kick sand in its face with complete impunity. Reason's lot was one of constant humiliation, and there was no likelihood that it was ever going to weigh more than ninety-seven pounds. I didn't care. I had known all along that my brain was not going to win any fights—or impress any girls.

Sally fed me supper and then went downstairs and spent the evening talking to the Beaches. I got in bed, or rather, on the mattress, and read *The White Nile*. I liked it very much and intended, as soon as I had finished it, to read all the river books that were mentioned in it. Almost every evening Sally went to talk to the Beaches, and almost every evening I sat on the mattress and read river books. Almost every day I went out to play ping-pong and see movies, and almost every day Sally stayed in the apartment, enjoying her new life. We inhabited the same place but sort of at different times. It was a very strange life—not a life anyone in his right mind would have wanted to lead. At least mine wasn't. Part of the strangeness of it was that Sally was extremely happy.

She had become happy shortly after our arrival, upon discovering that she was pregnant. "It'll come about April," she said, the evening the doctor told her it was positive. She sat by the window all evening, sipping wine and looking happy, and from then on she went through her days looking happy. She had beautiful color in her cheeks and she looked good with her hair in a knot and she became even quieter than usual. She sat around quietly, looking beautiful and peaceful. It was easy for me to imagine her with a baby. She would be a tall, lovely mother. Right away she bought a back pack so she could take the baby with her on walks through San Francisco. I could easily imagine that too. The one thing wrong with my many mental pictures of Sally and our child was that I wasn't in any of them. All I could picture was Sally and the baby, and the reason was that Sally made it perfectly obvious to me that that was how she pictured it. I don't think she used the pronoun "we" at all, after she knew that she was pregnant. For her our marriage seemed to have ended on that day. From then on she said "I'll," never "we'll."

But pronouns were only the subtler manifestations of what really happened. What really happened was that she dropped me from her life. She dropped me so completely that she didn't bother moving out, or making me move out. I had no tangible existence for her from then on. I couldn't even manage to get in her way. I knew women were supposed to act strange when they got pregnant, and I knew they were supposed to make unusual demands on their husbands at such times, but I hadn't expected to be required not to exist. That was the gist of it, though. It took me months to articulate it to myself, but my one practical function in Sally's life had been to get her pregnant. I had performed it, and that was that. All she had needed of me was my seed. I gave it and that was that. In all other respects she was self-sufficient. She didn't even say thank you for the seed.

From then on she served me meals as if I were a ghost, a hungry vapor that had happened to drift into the room. Her judgment on my existence carried a lot of authority with it, too. I began to feel like a ghost or a vapor, and to act like one as well. At first I didn't accept nonexistence. I continued to try to act like a living human. The evening we got the word about her pregnancy I wanted to make love. I touched Sally and she gave me such an odd look that I took my hand away immediately.

"What's wrong?" I asked.

"I don't want to fuck," she said.

Apparently she thought it was something that would be self-evident, though I don't know why. We had made love almost daily, since we had met, and Sally seemed to enjoy it as much as I did. Then, abruptly, we weren't making love anymore. What she really meant when she said she didn't want to fuck was that she was through with me sexually. At first I couldn't believe it. It was too abrupt. We didn't taper off, we didn't grind slowly to a halt, we just stopped. I made passes and Sally rejected them with a single look, a look that made me feel I had absolutely no right to touch her. For a few days I held back, thinking it was a mood. Surely it was a mood. She liked sex too much for it not to be a mood. We had been having enjoyable times—there was no reason for them just to stop.

But they stopped without a reason. I let a few days pass and tried again. Same look. She looked at me the way she might have looked if a total stranger had walked up and put his hand on her cunt. The look made me a little desperate. I was her husband—I had some rights. I decided to be firm. I tried to ignore the look and keep on with my pass. Sally frowned once, but then her look changed. She looked completely indifferent. She didn't let my making a pass at her discommode her at all. She didn't even look unpleasant. She looked as if she were lying in bed alone, thinking about something remote, like the isles of Greece. I had proceeded to the point of getting between her legs—I was pretty determined—but somehow her look of pleasant indifference wrecked my play. I felt awkward and stupid. Why had I thought I wanted to make love to a woman who wasn't even affected by my presence between her legs? It was absurd. Sally didn't look cold or stiff or frigid. She looked like a warm, lovely woman who happened to be lying in bed alone. The attentions I tried to pay her were so ghostlike they didn't even make her look jostled. It was an eerie moment—I didn't entirely forget it for months, and as months followed months I became very unclear about it. Maybe I didn't really get between her legs or go inside her. I ceased to know. But when I spoke again that night I wasn't between her legs.

"Sally, what's happening?" I asked.

She was completely silent. I was not sure she had heard me. I couldn't make her feel and I couldn't make her hear.

"Tell me what's wrong," I said. "I don't understand why."

"There doesn't have to be a why," she said, turning over.

That was virtually her only comment on the change in our lives. She sat up and picked up her comb and began to pick the hairs out of it, and when she had done that she went to sleep. I stayed awake for hours, maybe for weeks. I can't remember having really slept, in my months on Jones Street. I made no more passes at Sally and I didn't even try to talk to her about what was happening. The fog, San Francisco, and the new Sally were too much for me. She had convinced me of my nonexistence, I guess. She was not a talking person, and I all but lost my powers of speech. She never complained and she was not bitter. She was just finished with me. Her body told me so a hundred times a day. If I put my hand on her shoulder at night her body automatically shrugged it off. The authority with which I was rejected simply numbed me. I sank within a few days into a state of glum will-lessness. In my most optimistic moments I assumed that things would change, sometime, somehow. Sally was very happy. Sooner or later she was bound to notice me again. A light that had been switched off would be switched on again, eventually. Even if she didn't love me she was bound to want to screw, sometime. She liked it too much to give it up overnight.

It was trying, living with someone who had forgotten my existence, but I consoled myself with the thought that it was temporary. She was sort of an odd girl. Perhaps her pregnancy was just odder than most. She might remember me, after a while. I played ping-pong, lived in my parka, wrote bad pages, met writers in bookshops and never saw them again, read Wu's novel, went to the movies and slept sex-lessly beside Sally, who seemed to grow happier every week. I thought a lot about Texas, but couldn't remember it. Finally I tacked a Texaco road map over my typewriter and stared and stared at it. I was hoping it would solidify me in some way, but it didn't. For four whole months I didn't feel solid at all.

8.

MY QUIET LIFE in San Francisco lasted until almost Christmastime. One foggy week went by, then another foggy week went by. One silent evening was followed by another silent evening. Sally and I never raised our voices, to each other or to anyone else. We waked chaste, and I heard myself murmuring good morning; often the next thing I heard was myself again, murmuring good night. Sally was only morning-sick three times. Then one day I was ejected from my quiet life, and just as cleanly as I had ejected myself from my quiet life in Texas, a few months before.

That afternoon I had put on my suit and had gone to a photography studio and had had twenty-five dollars' worth of pictures made. Random House had been bugging me for a picture, to put on the dust jacket of my novel. Their publicity lady had written me three letters about it but I was so habit-ridden that it took me three weeks to get around to doing anything new. I figured twenty-five dollars ought to get them a nice selection. If I had thought about it I would have gotten a haircut, but I was already at the studio before it occurred to me that my hair was awfully long. The photographer didn't seem to think it odd, and I hoped Random House wouldn't. It was the first time I had worn a suit in San Francisco.

Sally wasn't home when I got back, but there was a letter in my mailbox from Emma Horton, and also one from my editor. I hadn't heard from the Hortons since we had moved, and the sight of Emma's name, in her handwriting, unnerved me a little. I wanted to save it for a few minutes, so I read my editor's first. He was coming out for

New Year's, for some reason, and wanted to get together with me. He said there were going to be literary parties. I tried to imagine a literary party and was unable to. It was a very abstract effort, like trying to imagine a triangle or a cube. Wearing a suit made me feel even more abstract. I had a mental picture of me inside my suit, inside a party, inside a building, inside San Francisco. I didn't know what I was doing, inside so many things that were unlike me. Emma's return address, written in a ball-point pen on the outside of her envelope, was the only thing that pertained to me that I had seen in months. It had a power that return addresses on envelopes don't usually have. I felt really shaky, but I was just about to open the letter anyway when there was a knock on the door. I supposed it was Wu, and stuck the letter in my hip pocket, a little glad to have an excuse to save it longer. It wasn't Wu, though. It was Andrea Beach, her skinny face full of anger.

"I'm tired of waiting for you to do something," she said. "I'm going to *see* that you do something. That's why I took off early."

She walked past me, into the apartment, and stood by the window, screwing up her face and biting her thumbnail. She was a redhead and she wore a very proper, pretty suit. She was obviously very exasperated, and I had no idea why.

"Look, what are we going to do to them?" she said. "We have to do something. I can't stand it anymore."

I suddenly had a bad feeling. Andrea Beach was a cool, composed girl. She was not the type to get upset at random.

"Do to who?" I asked.

"Don't play dumb with me," she said. "They're down there fucking and you know it. She fucks him every afternoon. Why don't you stop her? Don't you ever fuck her yourself?"

She must have seen from the look on my face that I was just getting a message. Her look changed a little.

"Well, you're pretty dumb," she said. "You must not notice anything. It's been going on for a least a month."

I was speechless. For a moment I took refuge in the hope that Andrea Beach was incredibly paranoid. But that hope was the tiniest of canopies. In no time I passed out from under it.

"Why do you think I took off early?" she said. "I never take off early. I've been waiting all this time for you to stop her. Do you think she goes down there to listen to Willis practice his goddamn cello?"

"But aren't you her friend?" I asked. "I thought you two were friends."

Andrea suddenly began to cry. "No, no!" she said. "That was just the only thing I could try. I thought if I made her my friend she wouldn't be able to do it. I know Willis has no resistance—he just sits down there helpless. It gets boring, being blind. I don't really think he likes classical music all that much. I don't blame him. But I couldn't make her my friend. She doesn't have feelings. She'll take anything."

She was so upset she couldn't stand still. She kept pacing around our apartment, biting her thumbnail. I just felt sick. I wished I hadn't been wearing my suit. The fact that we were both dressed up made everything all the colder and the more unnatural. I felt as if I were on some kind of stage, only there wasn't an audience, just a skinny girl crying because my wife was fucking her fat, blind husband. I knew I had to do something for her but I didn't feel capable of choosing what to do.

"Do you have friends?" I asked.

"One or two," Andrea said, sniffling. "Why?"

"I don't have any here," I said. "I was thinking that if you had some you might want to go see them for a while. I'll do something about Sally and Willis. Right now I don't know what, but I'll do something. You don't have to stay here if you don't want to."

"It's not that simple," Andrea said. She shook her head dejectedly. "Willis thinks he's in love with her," she said. "When you make her stop seeing him there's no telling what he'll do. I better stay around. He might hurt himself. I guess if I didn't leave him alone so much it wouldn't have happened."

"Don't you have to work?"

"No," she said. "I have money. I just like my job."

We were at a strange impasse. Neither of us wanted to go down to the Beaches' apartment. We both felt indecent, I think. I felt very indecent. Even if what was happening was happening two floors below us we were somewhat involved in it. We didn't want to go down and get more involved in it, but we couldn't help being involved in it to the extent that we were. I was a husband and she was a wife. I didn't know what it meant, but I realized suddenly that, whatever it meant, I hadn't been equal to it. Maybe Andrea felt the same way. She gnawed her thumbnail.

"I'll stop her," I said. "I don't know how, but I will, even if I have to take her back to Texas. Do you want to take a walk?"

"I guess," Andrea said.

We took an unusually silent walk. I think we walked twenty blocks without saying a word. The city was very gray. We didn't see anything interesting. We were both deep in thought. I had never been so deep in thought. Sally had been with Willis every afternoon for a month or more. Andrea had convinced me. It gave me plenty to think about. When we got back to Jones Street it was late in the afternoon.

"She's gone by now," Andrea said blankly.

"Don't worry," I said, at the door of her apartment I don't know why I said it. Her face looked pinched. She had plenty to worry about.

Sally was sitting by the window when I got in. She was wearing her black sweater and eating a peanut butter sandwich. She looked tranquil and lovely. She didn't look at me. She was looking at the bay.

It was a hard moment. I took a deep breath. Then I put myself between her and the window. I blocked her view. This made her look at me. I wasn't so nonexistent that she could see through me. She looked at me to see why I was bothering her.

"Andrea was just here," I said. "I know about things. Why don't you pick on somebody who has a chance?"

She only changed expression very slightly. She looked slightly annoyed with me. "Get out of the way," she said. "Who do you think you are?"

She was sitting on a cushion. I leaned down and put my hands on her shoulders and shoved as hard as I could. She scooted halfway across the bare floor. She wasn't hurt and she didn't change her expression much now either.

"Why don't you go out on the street and look around the next time you're bored," I said. "The Beaches were getting along fine until we came along."

Sally sniffed. She could look complacent and scornful at the same time, somehow. If I could have killed her for anything I could have killed her for that look. Nothing could make her uncomplacent.

"He'd never even fucked anybody but her," she said.

"That's nothing to be scornful of," I said. "Maybe monogamy is the way things should be. Now they'll have awful trouble."

"She could have stayed out of it," Sally said. "It was none of her business."

"Yes it is!" I said. "She's married to him. She tried to be your friend. Don't you even want your friends to have good lives?"

Sally sniffed again. "I quit seeing Willis three weeks ago," she said. "You could have made me miscarry, shoving me like that."

"Why'd you stop seeing him?"

Sally shrugged. She had said all she had to say on the subject. She sat down on the cushion again and began to read a baby book.

"Andrea doesn't know you quit him," I said. "Tell me the truth. She thinks you're still seeing him."

"Willis probably lies to her," Sally said. "He likes to tell her about me. I guess it gives him a feeling of power."

I thought of Andrea. No wonder she had looked so awful. I had no reason not to believe Sally. She didn't care enough about it to lie. She probably had quit seeing him. My head was pounding. I could argue with her for a week and not change the way she felt by even one degree. I looked around the room to see if there was anything I wanted to take with me. There wasn't.

"I'm leaving," I said. "I don't want to live with you anymore. I don't know where I'm going to live. When I figure it out I'll come back and get my stuff."

"Okay," she said, looking up briefly.

"If you want to get another apartment I'll help you move," I said.

"Why should I move?" she asked. "I like the view."

"It won't be very comfortable for the Beaches," I said. "Not with you living here."

"Tough shit," Sally said.

It made me furious. I stepped over and yanked the cushion out from under her, spilling her on her behind. It made her angry, but I was angry enough so that she didn't say anything. She just looked at me.

"You ought to clean up your language," I said. I went and got my manuscripts. When I came back through the living room Sally didn't say a word. I started to threaten her, so that she'd stay away from Willis, but it didn't seem necessary. If she had already quit him she would stay away from him. I couldn't think of a thing I wanted to say to her, so I left.

I walked to California Street, not knowing what to do. One impulse I had was to give up, to go home to Texas. I could quit trying to be married, and quit trying to write. I got on the cable car at Powell Street and as we were going down the long hill I looked across San Francisco and in my mind all the way across the West, to Texas. It was there beneath the clouds two thousand miles away.

But I couldn't go. I couldn't be a student again. I was already too different from other students. Anyway, Sally was pregnant. I couldn't just abandon her completely. As I was walking up Geary Street I saw what looked like a cheap hotel and went in and took a room. It was only four dollars.

The room had green walls and wasn't very cheerful, but I was too low to care. I had a period of jealousy. It was like a high fever and what made it worse was that Sally was too awful to be jealous of. I knew she was awful. I didn't approve of my loving her anymore. But she had been sleeping with Willis and I still had the jealousy. While I was having it I sat in a chair by the window. I watched a pink neon sign across the street, the sign over a sleazy bar-burlesque. It blinked monotonously. I was hungry inside my fever, but I didn't have the spirit to go out even to get a sandwich.

I kept feeling something crinkle in my hip pocket and finally, sometime about dark, I became curious enough to pull out Emma's letter. It was all wrinkled. I turned on an ugly little desk light, in order to read it. Even Emma's handwriting was round:

Dear Danny,

I keep writing you and throwing the letters away. I think it's because you got your book accepted. You being a writer makes me self-conscious about everything I write. I know you probably don't care, but I keep feeling like you wouldn't like it if I wrote you bad sentences.

But I can't stand not knowing about you—Flap can't either—so I have to take the chance. How are you? How is California? Are you living a wild life? How is Sally?

I wish I had more to tell you, but there really isn't much. It seems like years since you left, but nothing has happened. Flap's gotten an obsession with fishing. He and his Dad go almost every weekend, leaving me to languish. His Dad doesn't think women can be fishermen. I don't really care. I never learned to tell one fish from another.

We've had rain all fall and there are billions of mosquitoes. I read *Wuthering Heights* again last week. I don't think I'll ever like any novel better, not even yours. Flap decided to be an English major. He says hi, and to tell you to read *The Medieval Mind*. It's his other new obsession.

There's really just no news. Are you coming home for Christmas? I guess you love it out there so much you'll never come back, but if you do please come and see us. We didn't realize that you were our only friend. Being part of a couple makes it hard to have friends, for some reason. I have one named Patsy you might like, but she'll probably get married anytime now and I'll lose her too. Why does marriage do that to friendships? I don't know if it's worth it.

Please come to see us and please write. We worry about you. That's really all I have to say.

Love,
Emma

I looked out the window, above the pink sign, across the two thousand dark miles of country to where the Hortons were, wishing I could be back where I had been. The sight of Emma's round words made me sniffle. I had always been too impulsive. No one had told me not to marry Sally. It was because I didn't have a family to advise me. Momma was dead and Daddy and my brothers too busy running their Pontiac agency to advise me about my life. In small towns every family needs a black sheep and I was theirs. I think they were glad I had gone wrong, to the extent that I had. If I hadn't, one of them would have had to. I had no one to tell me who not to marry except my friends, and they didn't advise me on such matters. I should have listened to Godwin. For all his problems, he knew more about things than I did.

Rivers and streams of emotion began to rush around in me, and I was too tired to handle them. I watched people walk up and down Geary Street and felt like I was back in the flash flood. I couldn't see properly out of my eyes. I let the rivers and streams run out. When I had to go to the bathroom I discovered there wasn't one on my floor. No wonder the room had only cost four dollars. I remembered something about there being one off the downstairs hall. I went down, still sloshing with emotion. A door was open and a thin old lady stood in the doorway. She was one of the most made-up old ladies I have ever seen. She must have had literally ounces of makeup on, including eye-shadow. In the crook of her arm was a tiny black and white terrier. As I passed she pointed the terrier at me like a gun. The terrier bared his teeth and snarled. I went on to the john and when I came back she was still standing there. Her eye shadow was bright blue. She had a heavy string of amber beads around her neck.

"Hello," I said. I felt embarrassed, passing without speaking.

Once again she pointed the terrier at me. It bared its teeth again and made ugly low snarls. It was a nasty little dog.

"A gentleman wouldn't require the lavatory at this time of night," she said, raising the terrier a little so it would be easier for him to spring at my throat if the need should arise.

"I'm new to the hotel," I said. "I'm sorry if I disturbed you.

"I'm waiting for my husband," she said. "Usually he is in by this time. He must have been detained at his club. I am Russian by birth. There are no standards here. I've asked him to let me return to my country and my people."

Her voice was old and throaty. The floor of the room behind her seemed to be covered with newspapers and movie magazines and there was a huge birdcage with a moldy black bird of some kind in it. The terrier stood up on her arm, leaning toward me, dying to bite.

"I've never used firearms," she said. "You may come for tea sometime, but you must send in your card three days in advance. That is our inflexible rule. No impromptu callers. In our youth we made exceptions on occasions, but we found that was not wise. Send in your card.'

She turned, and as she was shutting her door, I saw the little dog hop off her arm.

I stayed in the hotel almost three months, but her door was never open again.

9.

NOTHING HAPPENED for a while—actually, for a month or two. Sally lived on Jones Street, being pregnant, and I lived on Geary Street, in the Piltdown Hotel. Days and weeks passed. I had moved out on Sally in October and somehow it became Christmastime, with nothing changing. Once I had been amazed at how abruptly things could change, but what was just as amazing was how long they could go without really changing.

When my editor arrived, the week after New Year's, and saw where I lived, he couldn't believe it. He was staying only a few blocks down the street, at the St. Francis, but the ambiance of the two places couldn't have been further apart. The Piltdown was full of old ladies with cats and birds, and the St. Francis, as near as I could judge, was full of people like Bruce.

Bruce was the sort of man who looks comfortable in three-piece suits. He was good-looking and sharp and quick-minded and universally informed, as I assumed all New Yorkers to be. My room at the Piltdown put him off badly. By the time he saw it it was half full of empty Dr. Pepper bottles and Fig Newton boxes. In those days Dr. Peppers and Fig Newtons were among my staples. When I tired of them I ate other trashy things. I loved pork skins and potato chips, Mounds candy bars and Fritos. When I felt really nostalgic I ate jalapeno peppers and bean dip. Nutrition had never interested me and in the weeks after I left Sally it came to interest me even less. I got through my days on Fig Newtons and candy bars and an occasional chili dog. Nibbling took my mind off my troubles, so I nibbled all day. I ate wieners and rat cheese, Butter Rum Life Savers, Peanut Planks and Tootsie Pops. Anything would do. Trashy food was my heritage. I could live for months on cheeseburgers and an occasional plate of eggs.

Bruce was different. He had standards in food. I liked him sufficiently to conceal my more atrocious habits from him, and when he took me out to dinner at a famous French restaurant I ate every bite he ordered me and pretended I liked it. I watched Bruce eat and tried to conceal how ashamed I was of my palate. Fortunately I liked the wine. The big news he had was that my novel had sold to the movies. It was such big news that I had a hard time taking it in. It had sold for forty thousand dollars. When he told me, I couldn't think of much to say. He expected me to go crazy with joy, I think. It was not an unreasonable thing to expect and ordinarily I would have complied. But somehow it was all abstract. I had led a numb, indifferent life for several weeks, writing bad pages and wondering what to do about Sally. I spent a lot of time watching the pink neon sign blink, and even more time on Market Street seeing cheap movies. Having forty thousand dollars was really so unimaginable, I couldn't even become excited. Bruce was a little disappointed in me, I guess, but I couldn't help it. Other than Jenny Salomea I didn't even know anybody else who had forty thousand dollars.

"Well, you can certainly afford a decent place to live, now," Bruce said cheerfully. He had a twinkly expression, combined with what I supposed to be instinctive suavity. I couldn't imagine his not being able to control his destiny. It made me slightly uncomfortable with him. I felt as ashamed of myself as I did of my palate. It had to be obvious to him that I wasn't controlling my destiny. Sally had not even wanted to let me into our apartment to get a necktie, so I could go to the fancy restaurant.

"They want to see you as soon as you can go down," Bruce said, eating profiteroles in chocolate syrup. By "they" he meant Hollywood. I could even write the screenplay of the movie, if I wanted to, Bruce said. I couldn't think of any reason not to. My second novel simply wasn't coming out right. It seemed to me I could probably do a better job of it if I waited until after my first novel was published. Writing a screenplay might be fun.

After dinner Bruce drove me down the peninsula to a literary party at Stanford. I was a little drunk from the wine, and the prospect of a literary party, after so many days of gloom and bad writing, was very exciting. Bruce wanted to know about Texas. He had heard that in Texas people fucked cattle and he wanted to know if that was so. I assured him it was a common practice. Then he wanted to know about millionaires. I was no help to him there. I didn't know any. I only knew people who fucked cattle.

We wove up somewhere into Atherton and were at a party. Numerous real writers were there. Within half an hour Bruce had introduced me to John Cheever, Philip Roth, James Baldwin, Herbert Gold and Wallace Stegner. None of them noticed me and I was just as glad. I could tell it was an occasion at which I didn't really want to be remembered. At the same time, it was interesting to watch. I went off to a corner to get drunk and watch. The writers at the party were obviously different from the writers I met in the bookshops of San Francisco. These people had auras. I could enjoy meeting them and watching them because I knew I would probably never see any of them again.

The party was almost as abstract as my effort to imagine it. It was in a very elaborate house, with new art and old art, and a big garden. Lots of fancy women were there and I stopped watching the writers and watched them. I had never really been exposed to fancy women. They looked a lot more interesting than the writers, who were all drinking and talking intently of literature and things. The women smiled and moved about gracefully. I had felt dead for months but seeing so many women made me wonder if I had to be. I had assumed that things were hopeless, but maybe they weren't. Conceivably a woman could happen to me again.

I watched Bruce move around the room, smiling and talking to people. I felt a little proud of him. He was wearing a handsome dark-red tie and he seemed to me the epitome of what an editor should be. He obviously knew everyone and what to say to everyone, and he had been in New York only that morning. It was amazing that he could cross the country and still know everyone. I didn't even know anyone on the other side of Geary Street.

Watching the party made me realize how much I had to learn.

Writing was obviously an intricate profession. I didn't know if I was ever going to master the writing part of it, much less the knowing-everyone-and-everything part of it. Despite the exciting women, I became depressed. I had only written one slight book. It all began to look beyond me, over my head. I wondered if the Hortons would be very disappointed in me if I gave up writing and went to work full time as an exterminator. For half an hour the idea really appealed to me. Then I was drunk and it stopped appealing to me. My pessimism began to seem cowardly. I decided I didn't like most of the people at the party, perhaps not even the writers. Why were they talking so intently about literature? They knew it wasn't really that important. And even if it were that important it seemed cheap to talk about it so knowingly at fancy parties. I felt high-minded in my drunkenness. Somebody had to live in the Piltdown Hotel. Atherton began to disgust me, it was so rich. I felt that something good was being cheapened. If I were famous I would undoubtedly cheapen it, too, at fancy parties, but I didn't like the picture I had of things. I didn't want anybody there to be a better writer than I was—I didn't like them enough. I wouldn't have wanted them to be better exterminators, either. I would have to keep writing out of pride, until I was good enough at it to be able to quit. Until then I wouldn't have the right to give it up.

I felt complex bad feelings about things. I wasn't even proud of Bruce, anymore. It was probably all too easy to fly from New York to San Francisco and still know everybody. Maybe it wasn't an essential achievement, or even one to be admired.

No one spoke to me, so I had nothing to do but drink. Late in the party, I realized that most of the people were gone and that Bruce was introducing me to a beautiful lady. I had noticed her that evening. She looked rather haughty.

"Renata Morris," Bruce said. "Danny Deck. He's the luckiest thing to happen to Random House since you."

"Hello," I said. The lady nodded. She had long, lustrous black hair, but it was done up on top of her head. She had a very graceful neck. I had heard of Renata Morris and fumbled in my memory unsuccessfully.

"I know Danny knows your books," Bruce said. "I wanted you to meet him." He kissed her on the cheek. "Renata's a love of former days," he said to me. He made it sound like a compliment. My memory finally coughed her up. She had written a famous first novel called *The Diary of a Jaundiced Woman* and two or three other novels that weren't so famous. My memory refused to supply their titles. She looked at me silently. She seemed quite comfortable with her hauteur. Bruce was a little at a loss for conversation.

"The West Coast does have its charms," he said.

Renata looked as if she wanted to give him the finger. "I haven't had a decent meal since I left New York, eight years ago," she said. "Except when I'm in New York, of course."

"I'm just learning to eat decently," I said, I guess inappropriately. Bruce looked embarrassed. No doubt he was thinking of the pile of Fig Newton boxes in my room at the Piltdown.

A man put his hand on Bruce's arm, and Bruce walked away with him, talking intently. I expected Renata Morris to vanish, but she stayed in front of me.

"What a fucking bore he is," she said. "I'm glad I left Random House. I can't believe I ever screwed him. Love of former days, my ass. He caught me on a horny weekend. Long Island used to do that to me."

She kept looking at me. I felt socially awkward. I had no fund of small talk.

"You don't have to talk to me," I said. "I like your writing."

"For a kid you've got sexy hair," she said.

"Do you live nearby?" I asked.

"I live here," she said as she moved away. "This pile of shit was my bridal portion."

I never found out where her husband was, or if he was even still her husband. I became too drunk to be perceptive. Renata Morris didn't return to me for almost an hour, by which time Bruce had gone somewhere with someone and all the writers had vanished. I assumed they had vanished to boudoirs, with various of the fancy women, but I didn't care. In the midst of my drunkenness I began to wish badly not to be drunk. If I could stop being drunk I wouldn't miss anything, but I had the sense that I was going to miss everything I didn't want to miss. I remember walking upstairs holding hands with Renata. It was odd, because she wore a black dress and looked much too elegant and haughty to hold hands with. She had a very sexy, graceful neck. She took me out on a balcony and we looked at the lights on the peninsula hills and at the stars above the hills.

"I wish I weren't so drunk," I said. It seemed to soften Renata a little. She was almost drunk herself.

"Your hair's not drunk," she said. We lay on a vast bed for a while. I napped and we necked and Renata Morris played with my hair. I don't know why she liked it. Hers was far more spectacular, when she finally took it down. I had forgotten how much I liked to watch women take down their hair. She began to tell me about her sexual adventures, in between my naps and our necking. She seemed to have had many. She once even had a cat that was good to her. Sexual adventures seemed to be her interest in life. Her voice changed when she talked about them. I began to swear to myself that I would never drink again. I hated myself for cutting myself off from the most interesting part of the evening. Even when we managed to escape from our dress-up clothes and were in the middle of the huge bed having a sexual adventure, I wasn't quite there. Generally I was making love to Renata, but it was all too general. I couldn't sense Renata. I was making love to her, but I didn't know what she was like. It was disturbing. Locally, where I was supposed to feel the most, I felt the least. My only distinct impression was of the abundance of her hair. Renata kept saying dirty words in a breathy voice. It was very unlike her haughty voice. Maybe saying dirty words worked for her, but hearing them didn't work for me. Liquor had made me numb. I was just as glad to go to sleep. I dozed off, hoping I would get a better chance in the morning, but instead I got no chance. Renata was wearing tennis clothes and had two rackets under her arm when I woke up. It was very early, barely dawn.

"Who do you play tennis with, this early?" I asked.

"My pro," she said. "We play at sunup. For seventy-five dollars an hour he can goddamn well get up when I do."

She was beautiful, but she looked a little sour. It occurred to me that keeping beautiful must be almost as hard as keeping writing. Maybe it was even harder. I was glad not to have to do both. Her hair had a gold comb in it. It was very lustrous hair.

"You better get out of here," she said. "My Jap servants are mean. If they find you in here they'll strangle you."

"Are you okay?" I asked.

"I haven't had a good lay since I left New York," she said. She put her foot on the bed to knot a sneaker. She didn't look at me.

"I wish I hadn't been so drunk," I said.

"It's a good thing you were," she said. "You wouldn't have lasted any time sober."

The phone rang. Renata picked it up, listened a moment, said, "Maybe" and clicked the receiver down. The authority with which she clicked it down was kind of marvelous. While I was looking for my socks she left the room. As I was leaving I saw two of her servants, tiny women in black aprons. I imagined they had garrotes under their aprons.

Atherton was lovely in the morning. The great estates were hidden in mist. I imagined Renata, playing tennis in the mist; only maybe she wasn't. Maybe, being so rich, she had a special place to play tennis where the sun always shone. I would have liked to sit by the court and watch her. I felt melancholy, walking past the great estates. I felt sad because I hadn't been able to feel anything when I made love to Renata. Even if I hadn't lasted very long it would have been nice to be able to feel. It would have made the morning different. I told myself it would have made Renata different too, but I would never know if that was true. If I had been sober I would at least have had a good memory, something I could recapture from time to time, but as it was I only had a memory of disappointment, of something that might have worked and never would. Once in a while, as I walked, the mist broke and I could see the humpy green hills.

Bruce had told me about a young Texas writer who went to Stanford. His name was Teddy Blue. He was from Fort Worth, and Bruce had given me his address. I was in no hurry to get back to the Piltdown or to my novel, so I decided to go to see him. Maybe he was an early riser, and we could have breakfast together. If not, I could wait around until he woke up.

I've always been a lucky hitchhiker. I always get a ride immediately. When I reached the Camino Real the first car along stopped and picked me up. The driver was a dignified old gentleman who was on his way to San Jose. He was using the Camino instead of the freeway because he was too old to drive fast. He was a retired grocer who grew asparagus for a hobby. He wore a blue suit and had a diamond tiepin. I like old men who dress neatly and keep themselves up. He gave me a lecture on the varieties of asparagus and shook hands with me when he let me out.

"Young man, I hope you stay in college," he said. "Get your education. If you don't do it now you'll never do it." Then he drove on.

I found a gas station and asked directions to the street where Teddy Blue lived. It was called Perry Lane. Later I found out it was a very famous street. Thorstein Veblen had lived there, and others after him. A vanished host of writers had lived there and brought the street fame. It was near the Stanford golf course and was extremely hard to find. I walked all over the brown Stanford campus, looking for it. I couldn't even find another gas station, in order to ask where I was. Finally, almost by accident, I stumbled onto Perry Lane. It was only a block or two long and if I hadn't happened to see the street sign I would have stumbled out again, none the wiser. There were a few small wooden houses along the street, and beautiful spreading trees. The sun had just burned through the morning mist, and its rays came slanting down through the trees. Perry Lane was streaked with sunbeams.

The house where Teddy Blue was supposed to live wasn't very large, but it looked pleasant. The part of it that faced the street was painted blue. There was a pretty, grassy yard, with two good trees and lots of bushes. Croquet wickets were scattered erratically among the bushes, and little paths led through the bushes, presumably to other little houses. As I was going through the yard I saw a small girl. She was naked, had curly golden hair, and looked to be about two. She was toddling about happily, pulling up croquet wickets.

"Who you?" she asked, when she saw me.

"Danny," I said. It seemed to satisfy her. She pulled up another wicket, looking at me coquettishly, to see if I would stop her. I liked her. She was obviously a little power, of some independence.

I knocked at a blue door and a feminine voice called, "Come in." I obeyed, and was immediately confronted by a surprising sight. There was a pile of people on the floor—not several people sitting

[90]

near one another, but literally a pile of people, right in the middle of the floor. There must have been a dozen people in the pile. At its highest point it was four people deep. Most places it was only three people deep. Many of its heads were pointed my way and several sets of wide, apprehensive eyes fixed themselves on me when I stepped into the room. It was unnerving, like suddenly coming into a stranger's living room and finding a hydra. It was not an aggressive hydra, but it was still unnerving. When I moved, all the eyes moved too. Certainly it wasn't a well-dressed pile. Most of the bodies in it were wearing blue jeans and old shirts. All the feet I saw were bare. The room it was in was large and pleasant. Over the fireplace there was a red, white and blue sign that read WE ARE THE NEW AMERICANS. In one corner there was a bed with three people on it. A man and a woman were lying in it normally, under the covers, and a short, plumpish, dark-haired girl was lying across its foot. She had her head propped against the wall and was reading a John O'Hara novel.

"I'm Leslie," she said. "Come over here so those kids won't panic. They're still very anxious. This is Pauline and this is Sergei."

Sergei was reading too. He glanced at me from behind a copy of the *Eranos Yearbooks* and then went back to it after saying hi. Pauline just smiled. She was lovely. She had curly golden hair, exactly the color of the little girl's hair. She was from Oklahoma. Sergei was a psychiatrist. I stood awkwardly by the bed, talking to them. Teddy Blue had gone to Fort Worth for Christmas and hadn't returned, so Leslie said. Though plump, she had a tiny face and remarkably big brown eyes.

"Are we having breakfast today?" Sergei asked. Pauline seemed to regard the question as a command. She crawled out of bed and went off silently to the kitchen, looking happy. She wore a white nightgown. Then she stepped back out of the kitchen and addressed the pile. "Are any of you hungry?" she asked. The pile didn't answer.

"That's Sergei's fault," Leslie said, nodding at the pile. "Don't let it put you off. He brought home some mescaline and wanted everybody to take it. Everybody that did got scared, except Pauline. It didn't seem to bother her. The others aren't over it yet. Look at them.

They got so anxious they all just piled together. Sergei says it was bad mescaline. It shouldn't scare people like that."

Sergei put his book down. He had a crew cut and an authoritative manner. "I did not say it was bad mescaline," he said. "Those kids all took too much. Most of them were still high from the mushrooms, too."

"I often wonder if you know what you're talking about," Leslie said, turning a page of O'Hara.

"I often wonder if you'd like to go get fucked," Sergei said.

"Sure," Leslie said. "Tell me where."

Pauline returned, bringing Sergei scrambled eggs and coffee. She went back to the kitchen and reappeared with some for me. The small naked child came into the room suddenly and slammed the door, causing several members of the pile to jerk apprehensively. One boy stood up, looked carefully in his pants pockets and then wandered out the door. The child paid the pile no mind, but in one corner of the room there was another pile, this one of coats. As the little girl passed it she suddenly stopped and pointed at the floor. "Who dat?" she said. "Who dat?" I hadn't noticed, but there was a hand and an arm protruding from under the coats. Leslie hadn't noticed it either. She peered at it.

"I don't know who that would be," she said.

"It's Charlie," Sergei said. "I saw him crawl under there."

The child sat down on the floor to watch the hand. People began to peel off the human pile. Most of them stood up, looked vacantly about and walked out the door. One went to the kitchen and came back with a plate of scrambled eggs. He sat down where the human pile had been and ate his eggs. The child suddenly stood up and stamped on the hand with one bare foot.

"Don't be a brat, Cleo," Sergei said. "Why wake up Charlie?"

The pile of coats began to stir, and a Jewish youth emerged. As I was, he was dressed in a suit, but his was even more rumpled than mine. His eyes were glazed. He looked about eighteen.

"You can sleep at my place if you're still tired, Charlie," Leslie said.

"I have a case to try," Charlie said. He walked slowly out the door.

Leslie informed me that he was twenty-four years old and a precociously brilliant lawyer.

I took my plate to the kitchen. The eggs had been delicious. Pauline was happily scrambling more. The windows of the kitchen were painted yellow. "Are you a friend of Teddy's?" I asked. Cleo came in and Pauline swooped her up and kissed her.

"Oh no," she said. "I'm his wife. This is Cleo Blue. Did you get enough eggs?"

Her curly hair and scrubbed face made her look about eighteen, but misjudging Charlie had made me cautious. I didn't ask her her age.

Leslie came in and had coffee, and Sergei came in and straddled a chair and began a learned lecture on mescaline and Aldous Huxley. Cleo was eating raisin bread. The four of us ignored Sergei's lecture, but each in his own way. When Pauline finally stopped scrambling eggs Leslie took me over to her place, which was just down a little path. It was a tiny house with yellow floors. One room had a loom in it.

"I can't take dope," Leslie said. "I have fits. I can smoke pot though. Want to take a shower?"

I did, actually. I had been in such a hurry to escape Renata's Japanese servants that I hadn't cleaned up. To my surprise Leslie turned a shower on and stripped off her one garment, which was a faded blue dress. Since it was her one garment she was naked in about two seconds. She was shorter and plumper than she had looked reading O'Hara. "Come on," she said. "We better take one together, unless you're a cold-shower type. There isn't much hot water."

It was obviously a practical rather than a sexual suggestion. The one thing that kept Leslie from being ugly was that she had made peace with her body. She looked happy, and was a pleasing person, naked or clothed. If she had been modest or clothes-conscious she wouldn't have been pleasing. She went into the shower and came out a minute later wet and somewhat irritated.

"People are always stealing my soap," she said. "I'm the only one on the Lane who buys soap." By the time she found some more I had shucked my clothes and was hiding in the shower. Leslie politely offered me the soap first, but I declined. Even though Leslie was completely unembarrassed, I was embarrassed. It depressed me not to be able to be comfortable naked, but I just wasn't. Apparently there were bourgeois shackles I still hadn't shaken off.

Leslie put on the same faded blue dress and we went out and sat in her sunny yard. She had been born in California and couldn't imagine any life but the one she was leading. She asked me what my situation was and I gave her a brief rundown.

"You should bring your wife here," she said. "There are a lot of guys around. Somebody would take her away from you and when you got over it you'd be a lot happier."

A croquet ball came rolling down the path from Teddy Blue's house. It explained the sounds we had been hearing. Sergei, wearing a pair of old shorts, came strolling after the ball carrying a mallet. Another ball came down the path and a long-haired boy followed it. Sergei ignored us and studied the position of his ball. The long-haired boy studied the position of *his* ball. Neither of them spoke. Finally Sergei hit his ball down a little trail that led away from Leslie's house.

"There are ninety-nine wickets you have to go through," Leslie said. "They're all over the Lane. The one thing you have to remember, if you start coming here, is never to move a croquet ball. There're a couple of balls down the street that have been where they are for two years. Everybody's afraid to move them. The guys who started it may come back some time to finish their game."

Pauline and Cleo came walking down the path, Pauline still in her nightgown. They sat on the grass, and Cleo played in her mother's lap. I lay back on the grass and considered taking a nap. The sun was very pleasant to lie in.

"He has a bad wife," Leslie said. "She won't sleep with him."

"She must be unhappy," Pauline said.

It was a generous comment, but it wasn't true. I couldn't have made Sally unhappy if I'd tried. Cleo crawled under her mother's nightgown and after much giggling wormed her way between Pauline's breasts and out the neck of the gown. It was a loose gown. They were a lovely sight, so healthy-looking that their mere presence made me feel that my own existence was inexcusably grubby and unhealthy. I should have been spending my days lying in the sun in Palo Alto instead of eating trash all day in the Piltdown Hotel. A thin kid came up dribbling a basketball and asked if anyone wanted to play. The girls didn't, but I did, sort of. I was torn between a desire for basketball and a desire to nap in the sun. There was a little court at the end of Perry Lane and I went with the friendly kid and played a couple of games of horse, both of which he easily won. He had a beautiful jump shot from the corner—he missed it only twice in two games.

Leslie came riding up to the court in an old MG and asked me if I needed a ride to the city. She was going to Berkeley. I did, of course. It was a convertible and she drove so fast that talking was impossible.

"If you need a place to hide out, come down," she said when she let me out on Geary Street. "I can always make room for you."

I had no one to hide from, but I thanked her anyway. She was a hospitable girl. I felt almost cheerful. I felt as if I had found some possible friends. In the interests of healthiness I went in and cleaned out all the Fig Newton boxes and Dr. Pepper bottles. My room took on a more healthful aspect. I even tidied up my manuscripts. As I was going down the stairs with the last load of trash I met Wu. He had his ping-pong paddle in his coat pocket. Since I didn't particularly want to go near Sally, he came to the Piltdown when he felt like a game.

"You are looking friendly," he said. "If you will excuse, you have not been looking friendly lately. Are you having a mistress?"

"Nope," I said. "I feel like some ping-pong though."

"Sure," Wu said. "Very good exercise. You will be having a mistress at a later date."

We broke even, four games to four. I took a long walk through the Mission District, before I went home, and when I did go home I sat down and wrote Emma and Flap a nine-page letter, telling them all about the wild life I was leading. The next morning I reread the letter and decided it was better than my novel. Half of it was fiction, but it was inspired fiction. My novel was uninspired fiction, at least so far. While I was rereading the letter Bruce called. He had been in Sausalito, with another love of former days. He wanted me to go to L.A. with him, immediately. "They" wanted to see me right away.

An hour and a half later, at the airport, I mailed the Hortons their letter. Bruce was very well dressed. I had never been on an airplane before, but I was ashamed to admit it. When we took off, Bruce tried to point out Atherton to me, but I couldn't see it. I imagined Renata down there keeping beautiful. Bruce didn't mention her. I imagined the New Americans, only I couldn't imagine what they might be doing. Probably I had caught them on a quiet day. I liked the world of the sky. When we went above the clouds I really liked it. The world there was new and beautiful. I admitted to Bruce that it was my first plane ride and he couldn't believe it. "How can that be?" he said, several times.

"I just never went anywhere before that I couldn't drive," I said.

He bought me several drinks and I watched the world above the clouds as I drank. Bruce was okay. He had got me laid and he was also giving me my first plane ride. By the time we got to L.A. I was so drunk that I missed my first hour in the city. When I came to myself Bruce was shaking my hand and wishing me good luck with "them." I was standing on a red carpet in front of the Beverly Hills Hotel. Bruce was going to the Beverly Wilshire. His cab began to pull away. Several bellboys looked at me curiously. I sobered up just in time to get intimidated. The last time I really noticed myself I had been swigging an early-morning Dr. Pepper at the Piltdown and it was hard to believe I was standing here, high from gin and tonics, in front of the Beverly Hills.

It was not like having a fantasy come true before you're quite ready for it; it was more like having a fantasy come true before you've even had the fantasy. I had never given ten minutes' thought to being a screenwriter. I had never even seen a screenplay. I felt as if I had suddenly become the puppet of remote but very powerful powers. The elegant bellboys kept looking at me, so I went inside. Everyone was extremely courteous to me. The remote powers had made me a reservation, and no one seemed to doubt that I was who I said I was. My room had a view of the city. I had some Dr. Peppers sent up, hoping they would steady my nerves, but they didn't, really. The city I looked out on was smoggy. The palm trees had a gray cast. I had a huge television set and watched movies on it. I didn't dare go out, for fear the remote powers would call me.

As I was finishing my third Dr. Pepper a bellboy arrived with a wrapped package. He assured me it was for me. I opened it and it was a large bottle of scotch. The card with it said Leon O'Reilly. While I was pondering the card the phone rang and it was Leon's secretary. Leon O'Reilly was the power that wanted me to write the screenplay. I remembered that Bruce had mentioned him, but his was only one of scores of names Bruce had mentioned in the last few days.

Mr. O'Reilly hoped I was enjoying Los Angeles, his secretary said. His driver would pick me up at eight and Mr. O'Reilly would have dinner with me. I said that was fine. The secretary hung up, leaving me alone and at a loss in my huge posh room. It was nicely carpeted and had lamps and tables and closets and a huge bathtub in the bathroom. The bed was as large as the bed Renata Morris had. Nothing in the room bore scars. The carpet was white and looked like no one had ever walked on it. There was no sign that anyone had ever slept in the bed, or turned on the television set, or taken a bath in the bathtub. There were no hairs in the lavatory, no ring around the toilet. The room had led a spotless life and I felt that any move I made might blemish it. It was so different from my room at the Piltdown that I felt like someone I didn't know. I had the creepy feeling that I was living my first hours with someone I was about to become. The changing of the years always disorients me. I never feel quite right in January, not because I worry about getting old, but just because I hate for particular years to go. I hadn't really adjusted to the fact that it was 1962 instead of 1961, and the quiet, luxurious room only made my January melancholy the more pronounced. The room was so unlike any of the other rooms of my life that I felt like I must have skipped several years. It was the sort of room I shouldn't have been living in until the 1970s, or maybe the 1980s, after I had become famous and begun a rich decline. The room made me uncomfortable but I knew right away I could get to like it. I was beginning to be able to imagine having forty thousand dollars—or even more. Renata Morris would probably come to see me, if I lived in such rooms.

The whole tone of my fantasies would begin to change. Soon it would be the Piltdown that was unimaginable. It wasn't that I liked the Piltdown. I didn't like it, and I didn't like poverty either. It was just that I had expected it to take longer than three hours to leave them behind. I was zooming again and there was no telling where I'd stop.

To slow myself down a little I went outside. After I walked a block or two I noticed that I was on Sunset Boulevard, which gave me a real thrill. I like to walk on famous streets. The farther I walked, the more normal I felt. The Beverly Hills Hotel receded behind me and I felt happy to have escaped from it, if only temporarily. I walked along, staring at things, and when I got down into Hollywood I felt normal enough to be hungry and stopped and ate two chili dogs. I felt slightly rebellious. Bruce would have been disgusted. They were great chili dogs—far superior to any I'd eaten in San Francisco. These were huge baroque L.A. chili dogs, with melted cheese and onions and even tabasco if I wanted it. I had mine with tabasco and drank a malt to cool me off. I felt like it might be my last real meal. Once Leon O'Reilly's driver came for me there was no telling where I might have to go, or what I might be required to eat.

The tall, soft-spoken kid who made my chili dogs told me he was only working at the chili-dog stand in order to get enough money to go to the Islands, where he planned to spend his time surfing. He had a friendly grin and his face was so innocent that it was impossible to imagine him ever being forty years old. I often try to imagine teenagers as they will be when they're forty years old, but it wouldn't work with this kid. "Waves are my life," he said shyly, as he was making himself a malt. I had no reply. For the time being, zooming seemed to be mine.

10.

SHORTLY after meeting me, Leon O'Reilly grew despondent. I don't really think it was my fault. We were in the back seat of his yellow Bentley, and his fat secretary, whose name was Juney, sat between us. Leon was a small, neat man, with neatly combed hair and a neat black tie. His tie was very thin. Juney held one of his hands in both of hers and looked at me as if she expected to become despondent too. She was obviously standing ready to hold my hand, if the occasion required it.

"Danny, I want you to know I think your novel's great," Leon said, when we were shaking hands. He avoided my eye when he said it, and I avoided his. We almost looked at each other accidentally, while we were avoiding each other's eyes. I felt very embarrassed. I hadn't gotten used to the fact that strangers out in the world had read my novel.

"I'm out here wasting my education," Leon said a little later. We were purring out the Hollywood Freeway, in the Bentley.

"I was brought up to believe that a gentleman does as little as possible with his education," he said. "I think I've achieved pretty near the minimum. No one could expect me to do less than I've done."

Juney looked at him tenderly and patted his hand. She was a motherly blonde. "Tough it out, baby," she said. Leon did not respond.

"Leon went to Harvard," she said, turning to me. "He operates from a very high level of ____. He really hates ostentation and affectation, but ____ ____ ____ ____ his industry you can't escape it. You have to be ostentatious, you have to have affectations. Leon actually has to *affect* affectations. It's a sad thing. This Bentley is one of the affectations he's affecting. He doesn't really want to drive a Bentley."

I couldn't see why not. I was already in love with the Bentley and planned to buy one the minute I reached that level of affluence. I loved the way the leather seats smelled and the quiet way the car purred along. It obviously worked no wonders for Leon O'Reilly though.

"I have the only private jai alai court in the United States," he said. "It's lit, too. I could play jai alai at night if I wanted to. I also have a twenty-two-pound rat. We bought it for a science fiction movie I produced a few years ago. I kept it. It only weighed seventeen pounds at the time."

"Those are some of his other affectations," Juney explained. "You have to make the people in the industry feel like you're one of them." She patted Leon's hand in sympathy. There was no doubt but that her heart bled for him.

"Nobody wants a movie producer to have a Harvard education," Leon said. "I've had to adapt. I hope you won't be offended by this restaurant we're taking you to. It's a relic of another era. We always take writers there because writers seem to prefer that era. I've never understood why."

"You don't have to worry about me," I said.

"He can't help it," Juney said. "Leon's a born worrier. He worries about every detail. All his pictures bear his individual stamp. I think you'll find he's the most meticulous person in Hollywood."

The restaurant was Scandinavian in decor. It had a tiny little sign on the front gate. The sign said THOR'S and was far and away the tiniest thing about the restaurant. After we parked we got in a boat. It was a Viking warship, poled by a muscular young man in Viking costume. He poled us up an imaginary fjord. The bluff they had cut the fjord through was only about ten feet high, but I was impressed anyway.

After the boat trip we had drinks in a huge mead hall, full of a lot of other muscular young guys in Viking costumes. One banged rhythmically on a huge skin drum. The drink Leon ordered for me tasted like honey, but it affected me like straight whiskey. Leon and

Juney sat holding hands. Leon was looking a little less despondent. Just as I was beginning to get drunk he stood up, snapped his fingers and said, "Coats, coats!" He became authoritative suddenly. Three young Vikings came running up and helped us into three huge fur coats with big fur hoods. Leon's coat weighed more than he did, but it didn't daunt him. We were shown into the room where we were to eat dinner. It was an ice cave, or perhaps the inside of an iceberg. The walls were literally of ice. Literal ice. The room was freezing cold, which seemed to invigorate Leon O'Reilly. He looked happier and happier.

"In the old days this was the place," he said. "All the great stars came here in order to be able to wear their furs. It's the most vulgar restaurant in Hollywood. There won't be anything like it in another ten years. I absolutely hate it but I thought you'd appreciate the experience. It's like a set by De Mille, don't you see? It's life copying art. We're going to have raw fish. When you go to Thor's you have to go all the way. All the great stars ate raw fish here. What the hell, Juney. Anybody could have taken him to Chasen's and fed him chili mac. We'll show him a little of the Hollywood that was."

It was an eerie place and we were the only customers in it. Little seal-oil lamps flickered on the tables. Three shivering Viking youths brought us three huge raw fish and three huge knives. I touched my fish and it was cold as an ice cube.

"Maybe he should have had the seal," Juney said, noting my hesitation. She looked at me from deep in her coat. I was even deeper in my coat and I was freezing anyway. Leon didn't seem to mind the cold. He was hacking at his fish with the huge knife, and his eyes shone.

"Nonsense," he said. "No seal. This is Viking food, not Eskimo food. I've always objected to them having seal on the menu."

Leon seemed to love raw fish. He lectured us learnedly on its nutritional values while he ate. I felt as if I were freezing. Fortunately the shivering Viking youths returned with mugs of hot buttered rum. Juney and I seized them gratefully. Juney even choked down some of her fish, out of dedication to Leon, but I wasn't that dedicated. I swallowed a bite or two without chewing it, but I spent most of the meal cutting the fish in bite-sized pieces and throwing the pieces under the table. Leon didn't notice. I drank two mugs of rum, to keep warm, and almost fell in the fjord as we were getting back into the Viking warship. Leon had a few squid for dessert and he took more squid home with him in a doggy bag.

"I want the rat to try them," he said.

Later, at Leon's house, I was shown the rat. It lived in a very clean cage in one corner of Leon O'Reilly's greenhouse, and it went at the squid like it had been eating squid all its life. Juney said she couldn't stand to watch it, so she went outside and watched Leon's teenage son ride his Honda around and around the jai alai court.

"I used to hate the rat," Leon said quietly. We were drinking brandy and watching the rat eat squid. "I made it a symbol of my fall," he said. "But after all, it's just an animal. It's not the rat's fault I became a producer. It isn't even the largest rat in the world, for that matter. There's one in Baltimore that weighs twenty-five pounds. We've been negotiating for it. I thought it might be fun to mate them, since the one in Baltimore is female. Maybe I could develop a strain of giant fur-bearing rats and breed them on rat farms, like the mink farms I used to see on Prince Edward Island. This rat is bigger than most minks. You'll notice it likes seafood. It's particularly fond of abalone. Whenever we have abalone we give it the scraps."

The huge rat looked at us complacently. It could clearly afford to be complacent. The greenhouse was full of jungle-like foliage. After a while we strolled out with our brandy and rejoined Juney. I guess I was drunk. I had nothing to say. Neither did Leon. Neither did Juney. My head felt like it was a long way from my feet, or even from my hands. I felt more or less absent. Then I was in the Bentley, being driven back to my hotel. I couldn't remember any words being said, at the end of the evening. Juney was in the Bentley with me, but she was asleep and snoring, slumped in her corner. I stayed awake, in order to enjoy the ride in the Bentley.

When I got out onto the red carpet at the Beverly Hills Hotel, Juney was still snoring. I went and sat in my room awhile, wondering where I would have to look to find someone with whom I had something in common. All the people I had things in common with were thousands of miles away, in Texas. Finally I turned on the television set and watched a movie with Rhonda Fleming in it. It was called

The Golden Hawk. I hadn't seen her in a long time and I enjoyed the movie thoroughly. By the end of it I had ceased being drunk. It also had Sterling Hayden in it. The movie was all about pirates, but I felt right at home with it. I didn't feel at all at home with Leon O'Reilly.

The bed I lay in to watch the movie was almost as big as my whole room at the Piltdown. For a few minutes I thought I was going to cry. I had never felt less snug. Only the thought that the Beverly Hills Hotel was a silly place in which to cry kept me from it. What I really wanted was to be a student again. It occurred to me that I hadn't been reading much, and I suddenly had a great longing to sit in the library and read. In my mind I kept seeing the thirty-nine-volume set of John Ruskin, the one I had never taken time to dip into. If I could have just been back in Houston I would probably have stayed up all night reading *Fors Clavigera*. For some reason it was the one Ruskin book I felt like I wanted to read. Also there were innumerable books about rivers I hadn't read. I decided to start reading again and the decision cheered me up. While I was trying to decide in my mind what to read first, I went to sleep.

The next day, just as I was about to leave Columbia Studios, I met a person with whom I had something in common. It was five o'clock in the afternoon and I had spent the whole day in an office with Leon O'Reilly. He was extremely neat and brisk and talked about my novel until it made my head swim. We went completely through the manuscript, a page at a time, trying to work out how to turn the novel into a movie. It was just a simple novel about a good old man whose one son had gone bad, and when I went in the morning I didn't envision many problems about it at all. To my surprise, Leon O'Reilly immediately suggested that we give the old man another son.

"Certainly," he said. "Two sons, one good, one bad. As the story stands, our picture is too simple. What it needs is some ambiguity, some timbre it doesn't have. Let's give him a brother and let the brother be good. Maybe he's even a preacher. Or maybe he's just something dull. A grocer. He devotes his spare time to working with the Boy Scouts. I'm not sure, I'm just thinking out loud. And maybe deep inside himself the old man really likes the bad son better than he likes the good son. Only they fight anyway, and maybe it's the good son that really gets broken. I don't know. But you can see how that makes for a richer brew."

I could see, but at the same time I didn't have any good son in my imagination. I didn't let Leon know that though. While we were talking a Negro came in and gave us each a shoeshine. He never said a word, and all the time he worked Leon kept adding ambiguities to the script I was going to write.

We decided to have the bad son get killed while illegally roping antelope from the hood of a speeding Cadillac. We also decided that the good son would have a sexy wife and that the bad son would either rape her or make her fall in love with him or both. Leon's phone kept ringing and he would pick it up and I would faintly hear Juney's voice coming through it and then Leon would say things like, "Not today," or "Send him a little cognac," or "MGM can go fuck itself," and briskly hang up. We spent two hours debating whether the good son and the bad son could have an idiot half brother. Leon speculated at length about my old man and decided it was not unreasonable to suppose that he had had a mongoloid son by a prior marriage. "I know an actor who's perfect," he kept saying. "I've always wanted to cast him as an idiot."

Then he decided it might be even more dramatic if the bad son had a wife who was secretly in love with the good son but was too good a woman to break her marriage vows. "There's conflict for you," Leon said. "You're wonderful to work with, you know." When five o'clock came I was exhausted, not from talking or even from thinking, but just from listening. Leon had not so much as loosened his tie all day, and his eyes were as bright as they had been when he was hacking at the raw fish.

"I think we're solid," he said, when he shook my hand. "I'll have Juney type this up in outline form and send it right off to you. It's not to be considered restrictive, of course. Feel free to invent and embroider. I want Brando and Burton for the two sons, maybe Spencer Tracy for the old man. Think what a picture that would make."

I went on out. Just being in the hall made me feel better. It seemed to me I had been listening to Leon O'Reilly talk about my novel for several weeks. I didn't mind all the things he wanted me to do to it.

Most of his ideas were better than my ideas. I couldn't imagine why I hadn't had sense enough to give the bad son a good brother, and a wife who would be in love with the good brother. It would have made the book twice as interesting. But it was too late for me to do it and talking about it for eight hours was a big bore. My brain felt fuzzy from trying to keep myself listening to what Leon was saying.

I hadn't gone more than ten steps down the hall when I heard a woman yelling. She was yelling from an office, behind a closed door, and I didn't really pick up what she was yelling. It was incoherent yelling, about someone destroying her. Then, just as I was passing the door behind which she was yelling, there was the sound of a very loud slap.

"I'll tell you why," a man's voice yelled. "Because you're a fucking no-talent establishment creep, that's why! You won't fuck and you can't draw!"

The door opened just then and a heavy-set redheaded man hurried out, trying to get into his coat. He glared at me, as if he suspected me of intentionally eavesdropping on the fight, but he didn't stop to challenge me. He hurried on down the hall. Just as he was about to turn the corner a thin girl in a green dress stepped out of the office. Tears were streaming down her face. "I can *draw!*" she yelled after the man. "Don't you ever tell me I can't *draw!*"

The man went around the corner without ever pausing or looking back and the girl walked over and leaned her forehead against the wall. She rubbed her cheek with one hand and sobbed. I felt very awkward, but I didn't feel that I could just go on and leave her sobbing, her forehead pressed against the wall. The slap might really have hurt her. Before I could think of what to say she turned and looked at me, her eyes overflowing. She had mousy blonde hair.

"Oh, why does everyone want to fuck me?" she asked. "Why does everyone want sex, anyway? I can't even know anyone without sex messing things up. I can't even have a simple job! Somebody always has to try and fuck me. I hate it! I hate it! I don't even get to have friends."

She wiped away her tears and gave me a very direct look, as if she suspected me of being someone else who wanted to fuck her. I wasn't, though. She seemed very thin and lonely, and not sexy at all. What she touched were my sympathies.

"Can I be of some help?" I asked. "My name's Danny. Does your jaw hurt?"

"Not enough to complain about," she said. "Will you help me carry some stuff downstairs? I can't work here now. He'll just try it again. I'll have to take my sketches home. My name's Jill Peel."

She went back in the office and threw what seemed like about a hundred pounds of sketches into some big portfolios. It turned out that she did drawings for animated cartoons. Not ordinary Tom and Jerry stuff, but serious animated cartoons. One she had worked on three years before had won an Oscar.

"That's why he called me establishment," she said. "He really feels very inferior."

She had a red Volkswagen bus parked in the parking lot across Gower Street. I put her drawings in the back for her and she got in the driver's seat and shut the door. But she didn't drive off. Once she was under the wheel she turned and looked at me. She had a thin, sweet face, and very blue eyes. Her look was very direct. We hadn't talked much, but I felt that I was going to be lonelier once she drove off, and I tried to think of something to say that would delay her a few minutes. To my surprise she thought of something to say.

"What do you do?" she asked.

I told her I was a novelist, writing a screen play for Leon O'Reilly.

"He's the straightest man in the industry," she said. "What's your novel called?"

"It's called *The Restless Grass*."

"You're not from L.A., are you?"

I told her I was from Texas, and we began to talk. She put her arm on the car window and her chin on her arm and I stood in the parking lot and we talked. She didn't really want to drive off and be lonely, either. She just wanted a car door between us, so there would be no chance of my deciding to try anything sexual.

She gave me very straight, clear looks, to determine if I had any intention of trying anything. I didn't have any intention at all of trying anything and I did my best to let her know I could be trusted to be friendly. After we had spent an hour and a half talking about

Texas and Hollywood and novels and drawings we were both a little bit less nervous. I really wanted to ask her to have dinner with me, but I was afraid it might spook her. While I was debating with myself it occurred to Jill that I had been standing up for an hour and a half.

"You can get in if you want to," she said.

"Okay," I said.

I got in the front seat with her and we both felt awkward. Fortunately we really liked to talk to each other. I don't think either of us had talked to anyone in a long time, not anyone of much sensibility, anyway. We liked to talk to each other so much that we managed to beat the awkwardness. The sky to the west had turned purple, and from a distance we could hear the low roar of evening traffic out the Hollywood Freeway.

"Would it scare you if I asked you to supper?" I said. "I don't know anyone in L.A."

Jill had a way of straightening her head suddenly so that I was forced to look her full in the face. She did it when I asked her to supper. I had never in my life met such a direct look, in such an uncompromisingly honest face. Her eyes weren't blank, like Sally's. They were clear and gray and intelligent.

"I'm glad you said supper," she said. "No one's ever asked me to supper before. Guys here ask you to dinner, which means they buy you a cheap steak and then try to fuck you before you even get it digested. Let's go to supper."

I was very pleased and did my best not to make her nervous. We ate at a diner near her place, which was in Westwood. After we ate we walked around UCLA for a while. To my surprise she invited me to her place. "*Viva Zapata*'s on TV," she said. "I love it. Come watch it with me".

She looked at me once more, very straight. I guess she had decided I wasn't dangerous. We went to her apartment, which was extremely neat. It had white walls, hung with her drawings. Most of the drawings were of strange, curvy cartoon-creatures who reminded me of Reddy Kilowatt. Jill had black modern chairs, but we sat on the floor to watch *Viva Zapata*. I loved it too. "It was filmed in Roma, Texas," I said. Henry, the old screenwriter in the Rice library, had told me that. He had gone down to watch them film it, hoping that Darryl F.

Zanuck might be there. Jill cried twice during the movie. The sight of Texas made me sentimental, but I didn't cry, mostly because it was such a great relief just to be with somebody again. As soon as the movie was over Jill and I began to talk. We talked for several hours. I told her about my life and career and she told me about hers.

At two in the morning, when it was very foggy, we got in her Volkswagen bus and drove to the Beverly Hills Hotel. We ordered a big pot of tea and sat on my huge bed, drinking tea and talking. We were also holding hands. I never expected it to happen and didn't make any moves. Jill just took my hand.

I had hardly had my eyes off her face for six or eight hours and despite myself I was beginning to love her. She had an honest, unpretending face, and it had already become dear to me. It seemed to me I knew it much better than I knew Sally's. I stopped being able to imagine myself living with Sally. Even before she took my hand I had begun to imagine myself living with Jill.

All the time we were holding hands Jill was telling me a wild story involving a baby bed. She was actually twenty-four years old and had a six-year-old son who lived with her parents in Santa Maria. The story was about a baby bed she had had when her son was an infant. It had been given her by the wife of one of her own former boyfriends. That was only the mere outline though. The baby bed, in only ten years, had passed from one young couple to the next all around the country, and the couples themselves were a great interlocking swirl of lovers and boyfriends and mistresses, ex-mistresses, wives, ex-wives. In its travels it had gone from UCLA to San Miguel de Allende, Mexico, then to Utica, New York, then to Edmonton, Canada, and had come almost back to where it had started. It was presently in Redondo Beach. All the people it had belonged to had been friends or lovers of Jill's at UCLA. She had a soft, rapid voice, and she filled out the story of the baby bed with wonderful, intricately detailed vignettes of the lives and personalities of the various girls and boys whose off-spring had been infants in the same baby bed.

Almost before she completed the story I knew I wanted to steal it. I told her so right away and she didn't seem to care. It could be my second novel. I didn't know any of the people, so I could invent everything but the baby bed itself. It seemed to me the perfect subject—a picaresque novel with a baby bed as hero.

Jill thought it was very interesting of me to think of such a thing. Her clear eyes lit up and we began to try and think of a title for my novel.

"I wish I could illustrate it," she said. "I've never done drawings for a book."

She got some Beverly Hills Hotel stationery out of a drawer and did a quick sketch of a baby bed with twelve funny babies in it. She drew very fast.

I thought the sketch was charming. She had personified the baby bed, somehow. It looked like a mother. In a way it reminded me of Emma Horton. "That's wonderful," I said. Jill blushed. All the funny babies looked different. While I was watching, Jill drew some more. She was very bold and funny in her drawings. She drew a sketch of the baby bed hitchhiking through Mexico. Then she drew one of the baby bed on the banks of Lake Louise. Her face changed when she was drawing. She became very sexy. I leaned forward gently and tried to kiss her. She let me for about one second and then drew her face back. She was very tentative and hesitant. She wouldn't let my face near hers again. She stopped drawing, though, and we lay on the bed looking at each other.

"I'm older than you," Jill said.

I didn't say anything. I was very tired, and I was thinking how accidental things were. If I had left Leon O'Reilly's office one minute earlier I would have been in the elevator when Jill was having the fight. I wouldn't even have met her. I noticed she had gone to sleep. I guess she trusted me. I went to sleep too. When we woke up the room was full of sun and Jill was sitting up, drawing sketches of the baby bed. She had used up all the stationery and was drawing sketches on the back of other sketches. She looked much perkier than she had the day before.

"I shouldn't have given you that story," she said. "It would make a great cartoon."

"Go to San Francisco with me," I said. "We'll compete for it. If your cartoon is better than the novel I write I'll burn the novel."

"No, you should never burn things," Jill said, looking at me seriously for a second. "What you should do is give it to the sea."

She was drawing again. When she drew her face became beautiful. I tried to kiss her but she ducked. While I watched she did a little sketch of my novel being given to the sea. I had just dropped it off the Golden Gate Bridge and a scholarly-looking sea gull was trying to read it as it fluttered down into the bay. Then she did a sketch of me. My hair was very uncombed and I was standing on the Golden Gate Bridge looking forlorn. In my hand I held an empty box on which was written THE GREAT AMERICAN NOVEL. Finally she did a tiny sketch of herself being presented an Oscar. Jayne Mansfield, mostly bust, was making the presentation. When she finished Jill let me kiss her for one second.

"I mean it," I said. "Go with me."

"I know you mean it," she said. "You couldn't be insincere if you tried."

"You'd like it," I said, though I realized it was a silly thing to say. What I meant was that I liked her.

"I'll go," she said quietly, looking me straight in the eye. "But you'll be sorry. I've got nothing to lose. I may come back here in two days. I probably won't even sleep with you."

"Why not?" I said.

"For one thing, I'm in love," she said. "He's a cinematographer and he's been in Europe for two years and he never loved me anyway but it's still there. Carl's one major hang-up. Sex is another. I've had problems and I'm scared of it now. Also my son's a big hang-up. I have bad guilt feelings about him. I've got more hang-ups than I've got good points. Besides, you've got a pregnant wife and you're obviously very dutiful. If she wants you back you'll go. I'm a very weak person or I wouldn't even think of going with you. I just want someone to make my decisions for me."

"I don't mind that," I said. "I make decisions easily."

"Of course you do, dummy," she said. "Ninety-nine percent of them are wrong, but you make them."

"Can we go in your bus?" I asked. "I don't know how to get to the airport."

"A cabdriver could probably direct you," Jill said dryly.

Cabs had just occurred to me as she said it. I still wanted to take the Volkswagen, though. Driving to San Francisco would be fun. Jill didn't care. "You're making the decisions now," she said. She did a funny little sketch of two people fucking under the baby bed. Three babies hung over the rail, trying to get a glimpse of what was going on.

We went to her apartment and she showered and put on a blue and white striped sweater that made her look ten times as sexy as she had looked standing in the hall at Columbia Studios. When we left for San Francisco, late that afternoon, she left a light burning in her apartment.

"I don't know when I might be coming back," she said. "I hate stepping into dark apartments." At Santa Barbara we stopped and ate seafood. While we were eating the sun went down into the Pacific Ocean. Jill sat in the same side of the booth with me. We held hands. From time to time I tried to think of Sally, and of what might happen, but I couldn't. Jill was too present. She continued to tell me about the adventures of the people who had had the baby bed. "We were a wild lot," she said. "I had an abortion when I was sixteen."

I was thinking about sleeping with her. She was awfully shy and nervous and I knew it was probably going to take a few days. I didn't care. We ate and drove on and Jill talked until midnight and then flaked out in the seat, her head on my thigh.

At three o'clock in the morning I parked the bus in the tiny little parking lot across from the Piltdown and led Jill up and left her on my creaky bed. I went back down to make sure the bus was locked. At the other end of the parking lot a couple of drunks were throwing rocks at a garbage can. I couldn't imagine where they'd got the rocks. There was no one watching the counter at the Piltdown so I went back myself and got my mail. There were two air mail special delivery letters, practically the only two special deliveries I'd ever received in my life.

I took them to my room to open them—Jill was sleeping peacefully so I settled down in a chair. The first letter was from Leon O'Reilly and contained an outline of the movie I was to write. Sure enough, he had given the bad son a wife who was in love with the good son. In order not to lose the rape scene, he had had the bad son get drunk and rape his own wife. He had even given the good son a bad wife. Maybe I would make her rape her own husband. I felt very lackadaisical about the whole project.

Then I opened the other letter. It was from Bruce and contained a check for thirty-six thousand dollars. A note from Bruce said, "Leon pays promptly." I held the check in my lap for several hours, and sat and watched Jill Peel, who stayed asleep.

11.

WHEN I woke up, still clutching my check, Jill was trying to put a pillow behind my head. She looked great. She had only to wash her face to look fresh and intelligent and lovely, and she had washed her face. She had even cleaned up my room, somehow. It was the cleanest it had been since I moved into it. Jill had on another striped sweater, and pants and sneakers. She was somewhat put out with me.

"You've probably got a crick in your neck," she said. "You're already letting me trample you. You could have slept on the bed. I'm not that hung up."

"I didn't mean to go to sleep," I said.

"I'm really compulsively neat," she said, noticing me looking the room over. "It's one of the reasons nobody can live with me. I guess it's all connected with my sexual problem. Everything seems to be."

Her face had already become dear to me. I liked the little blue shadows under her eyes. She gave me one of her looks, to see if I was going to hate her for having a sexual problem. Meeting Jill's looks made me wonder why I had ever been fool enough to think Sally was vulnerable. She might be vulnerable to cannonballs, but she wasn't vulnerable to people. Loving her didn't make her face change— neither did hitting her. She was not affectable.

Jill's face changed constantly. She was always affectable, always vulnerable. The penalty she paid for being honest was that she lived most of her life poised on brinks. They were real brinks too. At first the sight of Jill poised on a brink scared me badly. I had no confidence in my ability to pull her back, and if I said something false or wrong and she went over she would really go over, into some kind of different life. She never poised on phony brinks.

"I don't mind your being compulsively neat," I said. "I'm compulsively sloppy. We'll complement each other."

She looked so darling that I got up and tried to hug her. She wanted to be hugged, but the hug didn't really work. We were awkward and unfamiliar with each other, and just nervous. We weren't used to being in small rooms with each other.

Fortunately we were both hungry. The minute we got on the street we both relaxed. Jill had a blue windbreaker, to go with her blue sneakers. She hooked her arm in mine and we walked several blocks and went in a diner and ate sweet rolls and drank several cups of tea. We talked about things we read in the paper.

"Gee, I'm glad we still like to talk to each other," Jill said. I put my thirty-six-thousand-dollar check on the table. Now that I was back in the neighborhood of the Piltdown, that much money was an unreal thing. "What should I spend it on?" I asked.

Jill frowned, considering. "You could save it for when you grow old," she said. "I've always thought I'd go to India, if I got a sudden windfall. I've always wanted to go to Benares."

I couldn't think of any place I wanted to go, which surprised her.

"You ought to be more interested in the world," she said.

I agreed, but I just wasn't. I was interested in her. My interest made her slightly fidgety. It was a lot more serious than the thirty-six thousand. After breakfast we walked over to California Street and put the check in my bank. Jill said she would talk to her broker and find out what I ought to do with it. In the meantime, I just put it in my checking account. The teller was absolutely flabbergasted.

The sun was out and we decided to take advantage of it and find a place to live. Jill had kept the want ads from the morning paper and had circled several places that might be possible. She turned out to be extremely picky about apartments. I wasn't, so I let her do the picking. I enjoyed just following her through apartments, watching her response to each room. She had extremely keen responses. We finally took a beautiful four-room apartment on Vallejo Street. It had two bay windows, and very white walls. Jill loved it immediately. It was always full of light, and we could see the bay from every window.

It was pretty expensive, but with thirty-six thousand dollars in my checking account I couldn't have cared less.

Jill wouldn't let me give up my room at the Piltdown, though.

"Not yet," she said. "Not until we see if I stay. If I stay for a while we have to think of your work, you know. You need a place completely away from me. You have to get back to writing. If we try to work in the same place we'll use each other as an excuse to sluff off."

I didn't care. The thought of living with her entranced me, and I really sort of liked the idea of going down to the Piltdown to write. Jill was very firm about my writing. She insisted that I start the novel that afternoon, while she went off in her bus to look for furniture. She had extremely high standards in secondhand furniture. She refused to spend my money on anything that cost over twenty-five dollars, so she ended up buying most of the furniture herself. We started off with two mattresses and one chair. Two days later she found a table. Eventually we had two beds, a table, four chairs, two bureaus, and a couch made from a door. We also had lots of bright cushions. All our kitchenware was blue except for a yellow teapot and an orange frying pan. We had a bookcase made from dark bamboo. It took Jill ten days to find the things she wanted. Only one room had a rug, a beautiful green rug from India.

Jill was choosiest of all about colors and wouldn't let anything in the apartment if it wasn't a good color. White was her favorite color, but she also liked yellows, blues and oranges. She couldn't exist without flowers, either. They were a necessity of her life. Fortunately there was an old man with a flower shop only two blocks away. Jill soon became his darling, and he sold her irises and pansies and tiny roses. I could always make her blush and look pleased by buying her a bouquet. She was very shy when she was pleased and wouldn't come near me at such times, but she was often very pleased, anyway.

In no time Jill had me enthusiastic again. Mostly I was enthusiastic about her, but some of my enthusiasm spread to other parts of life. She made me get up in the mornings and take an early morning walk with her, no matter how cold and foggy it was. I soon got so I loved to walk in the early morning. Then she made me all the breakfast she felt it was proper for me to have. She had very strict ideas about food and was very opposed to people overeating.

"Not only is it wasteful, it's bad for you," she said, giving me a sliced orange on a blue saucer. She also let me have wheat germ and honey and milk and lots of oranges. Sometimes I got a sausage, because Jill knew I loved them.

"I'm indulging you today," she said. She didn't indulge me often. One of the things that really griped her about me was that I was by nature self-indulgent. I was very casual about it, which according to Jill was the worst possible way to be.

"Sprees and feasts are one thing," she said. "I don't mind them. But just casually buying things or gobbling things is awful. How can you ever really appreciate anything if you slop around indulging yourself?"

"I appreciate things," I said. "I appreciate many things."

Jill admitted that I did. "I guess it's one of the things I like about you," she said. "You let yourself do anything you want to do. I repress myself too much. I could have lived in Sparta. If I were left alone I'd probably repress myself right out of existence."

After breakfast every morning I went to the Piltdown and wrote. I invented a hero named Jerry and dashed right into my baby-bed novel. I felt very reckless about it and wrote very rapidly, probably to keep my mind off the fact that I didn't know where I was going in the novel. Jerry was incorrigibly foolish, especially with women, so I decided to call the novel "The Man Who Never Learned." I took the novel home to Jill, a chapter at a time, and she read it sitting on my bed. One of the wonderful things about her was that she was not jealous of anything I did. She loved for me to write, and she loved for me to read. Her only complaint about my novel was that Jerry was too foolish, but she giggled while she read about him, even so. I figured that if it was good enough to make Jill giggle it couldn't be too bad, so every day I went to the Piltdown and dashed off ten pages more.

Once I finished my daily writing I went to the San Francisco public library and carried home books for the night. Almost all of them were travel books, or narratives of exploration. I developed a fascination with South America and read myself right down the continent, night after night, all the way from Mexico to the Strait of Magellan. I enjoyed books about the famous explorers, but I got an even greater kick out of obscure travel books by obscure and forgotten travelers, ordinary little people who for some reason or another decided to journey up the Amazon or explore the Andes. I even read nine books on Patagonia.

Almost every night I read a travel book or two, with Jill sitting beside me on my bed. She had a great capacity for quiet, but it was not an ominous quiet, like Sally's was. Often, in the late afternoon, we saw a movie and ate dinner out at some place cheap and came home slightly tipsy and just sat around all evening. I read, and Jill drew, or hummed, or listened to FM music on a radio she had brought with her from L.A.

She drew hundreds of sketches of the two of us going about our lives — most of them very comical sketches. Sometimes she drew Wu. Jill liked Wu, and we had him over often. He liked Jill and would stay for hours, sipping tea and talking about Andrew Marvell or Richard Crashaw. Another nice thing about Jill was her likableness. I couldn't imagine anyone who would like me not liking her. During the day, when I was gone, she worked on her current project, which was an animated version of a weird Russian story called "The Nose." It was by Gogol. Jill let me read the story, but she wouldn't let me see her drawings for it. That was what she had been working on at Columbia when she had the fight and quit. Technically she was still under contract to do it, and it was something she took very seriously. She worked at least as hard on her animation as I did on "The Man Who Never Learned." One of the many things I didn't understand when I brought her away with me was that within the world of the animated cartoon she was very famous. She really had won an Oscar; she really was establishment. Walt Disney had offered her fabulous money to work for him. As soon as her agent found out where she was she got daily calls and letters, imploring her to come back. No one in Hollywood could understand what she was doing in San Francisco, living with an unknown writer.

What she was doing was making me happy. She did it but it was a complicated kind of happiness, not simple at all. She hadn't lie<

about being in trouble herself, and making me happy cost her a lot. "I've been ruined," she said, after I had made love to her the first time. She said it flatly, as if it were just a fact she did not permit herself to feel sorry about. I didn't believe it. I held her and kissed her face and looked in her eyes and tried to get her to tell me what had ruined her, so I could change it, but she wouldn't tell me. "I don't want to talk about it," she said, and we never did. Jill was always true to her own statements. She would never talk about it. I didn't believe it anyway. I kept trying to make her happy without knowing what had hurt her in the first place and it was very complicated. She could be happy—often I did make her very happy, very pleased. But not by making love to her. She let me make love to her, after a while, but only for my sake. Her ethics wouldn't allow her to live with me and frustrate me. "I have to be fair or I can't live," she said one time. I didn't know what to do. Once I began to love her she became very sexy to me. I wanted her all the time. We had such fun everywhere else, I couldn't understand it. Sex was virtually the only thing we did together that we didn't enjoy. Jill just couldn't. It was not an act she wanted to do. She only did it because I needed it. I didn't know what to do. The reluctant way she took her blue gown off made me very sad. "We have to stop," I said one day, when I couldn't stand it any longer. Jill looked at me solemnly, her gown half off. "Why?" she said. "I can't stand it if you don't like it," I said. "I'm destroying something." "That's right," she said. "You're destroying my modesty. And I was letting you." And she put her gown back on and went and put a pink robe over the gown. After that I seldom saw her without her robe on. We didn't make love anymore. We sat on my bed and held hands and drank a lot of tea. Jill went back to being very modest again, which was her way. I could delight her and make her feel touched again, in little ways. When she was delighted, desire made me giddy. Jill's instincts were delicate, beautiful things—it was painful but wonderful to observe the way they handled me. I was convinced all would change, though. I was convinced I could really win her, sometime. She didn't think so.

"My son is my first problem," she said. She always cried when she ~ied to talk about it. "I have too many traumas to raise him happily. lso I work too much. But if I don't work I get in bad involvements and have worse traumas. It never really works out when I go to Santa Maria to see him. He's really happier with my folks than he could ever be with me, and it makes us both feel awful. That was the nice thing about Carl. He took us on a couple of picnics and Johnny enjoyed them. A time or two I almost felt like a normal mother. But Carl was never very interested in me, really. He could always get sexier people than me. He just had a kind heart."

It made me terribly sad, to hear Jill talk about her son. I wanted her to love me more than ever, not just for me but so she could feel normal. I never really said much about love, though. Jill was very intelligent, and I have no knack for hiding my feelings. But we didn't talk much about it. If I had poured out statements of love it would have just made her feel worse. I let it be tacit. One thing we agreed on was that love was something there was no point in asking for. It was either simple or impossible. If you had to ask for it, it just meant it was impossible.

A month after Jill came something really ugly happened with Sally. She had achieved her ambition and gotten a motorcycle, it turned out. She also had a boyfriend. His name was Chip Newton and he sold motorcycles in south San Francisco. Apparently he had given Sally one.

At Jill's insistence I had fixed my money so Sally couldn't check on it. I sent her three hundred and fifty dollars a month. It seemed to be enough for Sally but it wasn't enough for Chip. He wanted to buy things. One day while I was at the Piltdown writing, they came to our apartment. Jill had never seen Sally and was curious about her. She let them in. Chip was a young hood, according to Jill. He did all the talking. Sally merely looked contemptuous. Chip walked right into the room where Jill drew and started picking up her drawings and looking at them. He didn't ask permission or show any trace of politeness. The extent of his conversation was to say that they needed bread, and if I could afford to rent such a fancy place I could spare lots of bread.

Jill said he should take that up with me, and to please leave he drawings alone. Sally had wandered into my bedroom, without asl ing permission. Jill lost her temper and tried to grab the drawin away from Chip. He pushed her in the face with one hand. She went to the telephone to call the police and he strolled in and took the phone away from her and held it over his head. He made a remark or two about how skinny she was and how screwing her would involve too many bones and got a Coke without asking permission and left. Jill wasn't hurt but their total arrogance left her quivering for hours. She came to the Piltdown and cried.

"I shouldn't," she said, crying. "I ought to be above it. They're both too cheap to bother about. It just made me feel so futile."

I hugged her until she quit quivering. The insult to Jill made me furious. I hadn't even got to see her drawings. As soon as I got her calmed down I walked her back to our apartment and headed for Jones Street. Foolishly Sally had never bothered to make me give back my key. The more I thought about somebody pushing Jill in the face the madder I got. I was hoping Chip would be there, so I could hit him with a chair. I knew just which chair I was going to hit him with. He wasn't there, though. Sally was there, running a bath. She stood in the bathroom door, in jeans and her black sweater, looking at me haughtily.

"Who asked you in?" she said. "If my boyfriend was here you'd have to leave."

The bath was running behind her. I didn't say a word, or break stride. I had an inspiration, a gift from Godwin. Sally barely had time to change the expression on her face before I had shoved her backward and into the bathtub. I took her completely by surprise. When I shoved her in, water sloshed everywhere and I got almost as wet as she did, but I didn't care. Sally thrashed wildly and for once looked more scared than mad, but she was in no danger. I just wanted to get her good and wet, and I succeeded. Her black sweater looked awfully soggy. "I'm going to call Daddy," she said, sitting in the tub.

I left without saying a word and went to our apartment. I expected Chip to come and fight me. I waited that day and the next but he never came. Later I learned he had been arrested for selling stolen motorcycles. The third day a deputy sheriff found me at the Piltdown and I was taken to court and served with a peace bond. Jill was more upset about it than I was. So far as I was concerned it was a small price to pay for wiping the smug look off Sally's face for once.

*

Despite all the good times we had Jill and I developed a mutual, internal sadness. Sex caused it. It wouldn't let us alone. It wouldn't work for us, so it worked against us. I tried to approach it gently, I tried to approach it roughly, I tried to approach it drunkenly, I tried to talk about it, I tried being silent about it, and everything failed. She was right: she had been ruined. I didn't know how, I didn't know for how long, and I didn't know what to do about it. A month passed, while we tried to live around it. Despite that much of the month was good, it was really no good. One night Jill came to my bed and woke me up. She sat on my bed in her robe and gown, twisting her hands.

"I worry about you," she said. "What have you let me do to you?"

"I was dreaming," I said.

She went to the window and stood looking out at San Francisco. "I wish I was loose like I used to be," she said. "I can't do it out of charity anymore. You should just rape me.

"Maybe so," I said.

"No you shouldn't," she said. "You wouldn't be you if you could do things like that. Somebody has to be like you."

"What does that mean?" I asked.

She shook her head and went and made a pot of tea. We sat on the bed and drank it. I knew things were serious. Jill kept her robe wrapped tightly around her. We held hands. She was extremely modest.

"You're the most modest person I've ever met," I said.

She blushed and smiled. "At least you've made me positively modest," she said. "Before you I only had negative modesty. Let's drive to Berkeley. I have to go back to L.A. I can't take advantage of you any longer."

At four in the morning we drove to Berkeley in her bus. I was numb and unable to think of good arguments. She had an old mentor in Berkeley, an aged Danish theologian who had once been at UCLA. Once we had had a picnic with him, in the Berkeley hills, and he had brought along his equally aged love, an old woman who had lived in Berkeley forty-eight years, studying the Homeric poems. The theologian was named Stigand and his lady friend was known Lady Northford. She was English. They were both renowned scholars both had snow white hair, and both were remarkably healthy.

quick of mind. We sat in a backyard high in the hills and watched the sky behind the Golden Gate. The sun disappeared early, behind Mount Tamalpais, and soon great rollers of fog came in and hid Mount Tamalpais and the Bridge and San Francisco and then the Bay. As we watched the white fog come toward us Jill drew sketches and the old man and old woman talked of the Greek Islands, which they had both often visited, and of D. H. Lawrence, whom they had both known well. They were a very argumentative old couple and gave each other no rest, but they were extremely polite to Jill and I. They invited us to join them for their daily swim, which they took in an ice-cold lake somewhere in the hills. Jill said they had been lovers thirty-five years before, and had separated, and married, and had their respective spouses die, and then had come together again, widow and widower. The old woman spoke of Homer with extraordinary respect, as if he were an honored relative whom many misunderstood. Their features were not the tired features of the old people I was used to, but lean and chiseled, perhaps from years of swimming in cold lakes.

When Jill and I got to Berkeley there was nothing to do but drive around Cal in the fog. We were numb with the imminence of parting, and didn't talk. After twenty minutes or so we went back across the long bridge to San Francisco. On Vallejo Street the light was dim. We stood in front of the bus in the cold fog, holding hands.

"I'd ask you to come with me down there, but it wouldn't work there either," Jill said. "I don't want to love anybody. I don't want to repress you out of existence, either. I'm not a woman anymore, I'm just an artist. All I can do is draw. It'll happen to you if you don't get a girl who'll sleep with you. You'll wake up someday and you'll just be a writer. I'm not worth it. Nobody's worth it. You'd be better off staying a man."

I was too depressed to talk. "Drive careful," I said. It was all I could think of to say. I knew I couldn't stop her from going. She was right to go. We couldn't be any different. We had tried to change things, and we hadn't.

"Don't stand there thinking it's your fault," Jill said. "This is my fault, damnit! You're so lovable some girl will glom on to you five minutes after I leave. No normal woman could ask for more than you and a nice apartment."

"Oh, horseshit," I said.

"Some girl will come along in five minutes," she insisted. It was a silly point of controversy. Jill went around to the rear and opened a big portfolio and gave me the two sketches that she liked the best. I kissed her, sort of. She kicked me lightly with her sneaker and got in the bus and left.

Three days later I got a note from her, in a big package. The big package contained a sketch, protected between two heavy pieces of cardboard. The sketch was of Jill, just of her face.

The note said:

Dear Danny,

My light was still burning. It burned for two months and two weeks. Light bulbs get better and better. This is how I looked when I got home. I looked at myself in the bathroom mirror and drew it for you. It shows how mean and critical I look.

Put it where you work, so you won't be tempted to write sloppily. I put what little trust I have in your doing your work right. I don't want you to be cursed like me, but I'm afraid you may be already. I hope not, but if you are, at least you must do your work right.

You mustn't leave San Francisco until you finish the novel. When you finish it you can come and see me and I'll read it. Please don't go back to eating trash.

Love,
Jill

12.

JILL didn't call for ten days. When she did call the first thing she asked was, "How much have you written?"

"It doesn't matter," I said. "I don't want to be a writer all that much, anymore. You didn't have to go away."

She was silent a minute. "Don't be that way," she said. "You don't have to sound so bitter. I miss you too."

"I *am* bitter," I said. I was. The more I thought about it all the bitterer and more hurt I got. She hadn't had to go away. She could even have slept with me. In retrospect it didn't seem like either of us had tried very hard.

Jill sighed. "You mustn't be bitter, even if you are," she said.

"Why not? It wasn't just a flirtation. I love you."

"You're being very stubborn," she said. "It's a little late for you to be so stubborn. Why didn't you think of some way to keep me?"

She sounded hostile suddenly, and I felt hostile. We hadn't been when we parted, not at all. I was surprised to feel so hostile. I had been brooding for days. I guess I blamed her for not making us work. I guess she blamed me for the same thing. When she told me she was leaving I had felt paralyzed. I felt really helpless. I watched her leave in a kind of blank daze, as if I were drugged.

"I just couldn't think of any way," I said. "You didn't want to be kept."

"How much have you written?" she asked again. We talked for an hour, keeping our hostilities and resentments under control. Afterwards I missed her terribly. I went outside and sat in a park. Jill and I had sat there often, in the late afternoons, watching people come home from work and go in houses and come out with their dogs and walk them. It was a pleasant park. Jill had a long green scarf she always wore. When I went to the park after talking to her on the phone I was utterly convinced I would never be happy again. An old fat lady with a golden cocker walked up to me and said, "Where's the nice girl with the green scarf? We miss her."

"I do too," I said.

It was horribly true. My life was scarcely a life at all, since she had left. She had educated me to certain qualities and properties that I hadn't known before: the properties of food, of nice rooms and nice light and good colors, the pleasures of walking and looking at things with someone intelligent, new qualities of affection, the pleasures of talking. I had never done those sorts of things with a woman before. For a time I almost hated the concept of love and the fact of sex, because they were the missing ingredients that kept me from having all the other good things I wanted. With Jill gone, the nice things she had taught me to enjoy seemed flat and meaningless. They weren't all that enjoyable, intrinsically: she had made them enjoyable. She started calling often and we argued about it over the phone. She hated my attitude.

"There's no reason for you to slop around like you used to, just because I'm not there," she said. "That's ridiculous. You see? That's what I hate about love. You get so dependent on a person that you can't lead an intelligent life without them. It's sick."

"Maybe it is if you're interested in living an intelligent life," I said. "I don't particularly want to live an intelligent life."

"Well, you certainly aren't," she said. "Damnit. Are you going to movies again?"

"Sure," I said. It was true. Every day when I finished my work on the novel I scuttled down to Market Street and killed five or six hours going to movies.

"Why do you do that?"

"The apartment's lonesome," I said.

"Don't give me that. That's pure self-pity. You lived alone all your life up until a few months ago. How come you can't live alone now?"

"Because I lived with you two months," I said. "I don't want to live like I used to live."

"What do you have for breakfast?" she asked ominously.

"A Milky Way, usually," I said. "Sometimes a Coke."

"Danny, you're being deliberately cruel," she said. "I'm going to hang up and cry. You're hurting me."

She hung up. I called back and apologized. I *had* been being cruel. I was hoping I could convince her I was deteriorating, so she would come back and stop me. It didn't work. It just made her doubt me.

"I want you to have standards," she said. "I want you to keep them."

"But standards are so empty," I said.

"So what!" she yelled. "Life isn't exactly gushing with fullness down here, either. That's no excuse for not living intelligently and having standards and eating well and working and keeping some order in your life. Emptiness is easier to bear if you have a little order in your life."

"I don't doubt it," I said. "I just don't care."

Jill sighed. "I don't either," she said. "You oughtn't to eat trash, though."

Actually my lapses into old habits were not very major. I worked twice as hard on the novel as I had before Jill left. I wanted to finish it, so I could go to L.A. and see her. Besides movies, I went back to ping-pong and saw a lot of Wu. It was from Wu that I learned that Sally had left.

"You can be coming to my house again," he said one day. "Sally is not living there anymore. An Englishman came, very jolly fellow. He was taking her to Texas."

That was interesting news. At first I was relieved. With Sally in the city I always felt slightly conscious of her, as a responsibility. She was still my wife, and she was going to have a baby. The time was drawing nigh. It was March and the baby was due in April. I tried to forget about it but I couldn't. It would be my child. I would have to do *some-thing* about it. I couldn't let a succession of Chip Newtons raise my child. I tried to talk to Wu about it but he was no help. He had children in China, but he was very vague about them.

"Children are always problems," he said. "Good thing there are women."

When I tried to talk to Jill about it we had fights.

"You'll go back to her," she said. "Or she'll come back to you. It's another reason I left. You're already worrying about her. If I'd have fallen in love with you I'd have been stuck in about two months, you see. You'll be back in Texas changing diapers."

Her attitude infuriated me. She seemed to think that because I had some normal concern about my child that I still loved Sally, or preferred Sally to her. I told her a hundred times that it wasn't true, but her convictions were unalterable. She believed what she wanted to believe.

"I know you," she said. "You're a sucker. I would have been a sucker to love you."

"I wish you had been," I said. "It would have helped a lot."

"I didn't dare," she said. "I can't even raise my own child. I'd have to be crazy to try and help you raise yours, even assuming we could get it away from that bitch."

"You ought to take more chances," I said.

"I took too many earlier," she said. "I'm sorry."

In late March, for two weeks, I did nothing but work. I was into the last hundred pages of *The Man Who Never Learned*. I gave up movies and ping-pong and worked ten and twelve hours a day. When I got within two days of the end I called Jill.

"I'll be through in two days," I said. "Can I come down?"

"You better not have written it sloppy just so you can see me," she said. Talking to her on the phone was not like looking her in the eye.

"I didn't," I said.

There was a pause. "I'm sorry," she said. "I shouldn't have said that. I know you wouldn't. You're going to be mad at me.

"Why?"

"I have to go to New York tomorrow," she said. "I've got a project that has to be done there. I didn't know about it until yesterday. I may be gone three weeks."

I was very let down. "Are you going because you don't want to see me?" I asked.

Jill sighed. "At least we're still blunt," she said. "No, it's really a job. I wouldn't avoid you that way. On the other hand, I'm not sure I want to see you."

"You said you would," I said.

"I know, Danny," she said. "Please don't sound so hurt. I *will* see you, of course. What I said was I'm not sure I want to."

"Why not?"

"Because it will hurt," she said. "We already didn't make it. It's not going to be any different. It's not your fault, it's probably totally mine, but it's still true. What's the point of our hurting each other?"

In my mind I had become convinced that it would be different, when I went to L.A. But Jill sounded very convinced when she said it wouldn't. I stopped being sure. There was no real telling what would happen.

"I still want to come," I said. "I want to see you."

"You wanted to write," Jill said. Suddenly she sounded terribly hostile.

"What?"

"If you'd really wanted me you'd have come the day I left, or never let me leave," she said. "You'd really rather write than cope with me. I don't blame you a bit. I'd really rather draw than cope with you. I just don't think you ought to be so goddamn righteous about wanting me. You did what you really wanted to do."

"Oh, fuck you!" I said. "You're crazy. I hate simple-minded people who think other people only do what they want to do."

"Then you hate me," she said. "That's what I think."

"You're the one who's scared to get involved," I said.

"I admit it," she said.

"I'm *not* scared to get involved," I said. "I'd marry you tomorrow."

Jill was silent awhile. "Maybe you would," she said quietly. "I guess you would. Only you *are* married. Too bad. I might have gambled on you."

"Oh, stop it," I said. "I can get divorced."

"I've got cramps," she said. "I don't want to fight anymore. I'm sorry about New York. I really didn't plan it, Danny."

"I believe you," I said. "I don't know who I'll celebrate with, now."

"Wu, probably," she said. "He's handiest. There *are* planes that go from San Francisco to New York, you know. Anybody with money enough can get on one."

"I never thought of that," I said.

"That's why I mentioned it. It's on the order of your wanting to drive to San Francisco because you forgot about cabs."

"I never claimed to be bright," I said.

"You're bright. You're just not used to thinking. Write me a good ending."

I did. I finished the novel in the middle of an afternoon. Wu came by just as I was finishing it, and I took him to Berkeley and we ate Mexican food at a fairly good place on Telegraph Avenue. Wu was very congratulatory. "You will be getting fame and money," he assured me several times. "Also mistresses. I think I am not very commercial."

It was true. I felt sorry for Wu. He was a middle-aged exile with nothing going for him but gentleness. He would never get fame, money, or mistresses, neither from writing nor from anything else.

By odd coincidence, the first copy of *The Restless Grass* had come to me in the mail that morning. It didn't move me much. I didn't really like the dust jacket or the binding, and I felt only a dry interest in the book. I flipped through it, but I couldn't read it. My heart was with the people in *The Man Who Never Learned.* They were alive, to me. I didn't want to stop writing about them, or knowing them. The people in *The Restless Grass* I had stopped caring about. I was so dead to them that I didn't like seeing their names on the page. I didn't really want to keep the copy of my book. Handling it made me feel sick, in some way.

That night, on Jones Street, on impulse, I wrote an inscription in the copy and gave it to Wu. He was extremely pleased.

"You will be going to Texas to see your son?" he asked.

"I don't know. How do you know it will be a son?"

"Always hope for sons," he said.

It shocked him a little that I would give him my only copy of my first book, but I really felt like it. Of all the people I knew in San Francisco, he had been kindest to me.

The way he mentioned Texas made me think of it, for the first time in weeks. My thoughts had mostly been of Los Angeles and Jill.

I could go anywhere. New York, Texas. I could start roaming the world. We stood on the steep doorstep of the house we had shared, and looked at the dark bay. I didn't have the novel to work on, anymore. I couldn't stay in San Francisco. With nothing to work on and no one to be with I would just see ten thousand movies.

"I may go to Texas," I said. "My editors want me to be at an autograph party."

Bruce had mentioned the autograph party several times. I could go home. Texas was still over there, waiting.

"Sure, you will be going," Wu said. "It is your land, is that not so? There are no borders in the U.S., very nice. Can always go home. Not so with me. Only heart can go home, for me. Too many borders."

I saw that he was moved. He clutched the book tightly, and looked at me sadly.

"You are touching me with this gift," he said. "Also you are young. You can go. I am sorry we will not be having games. We are not having world enough and time, now—this is so? Texas you are wanting. A mistress, wife—many things for you to seek."

"Oh, I don't know," I said.

"Oh yes, yes, very important," Wu said. "Go on away, we have been friends, this gift very fine. I keep writing, maybe get published someday. Is not major. You will be sending letters, is this so Danny?"

"Sure," I said.

"Welcome to literature," he said, holding up my book. Then he went in.

I went back to the Piltdown and promptly checked out. I never wanted to sit there and write again. I put my typewriter and the manuscript of my new novel in the back seat of my car and drove to Vallejo Street, very uncertain what to do. Usually abrupt action in my life is initiated by someone else, but no one else was around, or likely to come. I would have to do something myself.

Staying in San Francisco without Jill or without my novel to work on was clearly out of the question. I had to go somewhere. There was nothing to hold me but a little furniture and I didn't want that. Jill wouldn't want it either. I wrote the landlord a note telling him the furniture was his to dispose of as he wished, and I put some blankets and cushions and a couple of Jill's drawings and the green Indian rug in the Chevy. That was enough. I was going. I could hardly bother to pack. I really suddenly wanted to be gone. Objects weren't going to stop me. I had a few travel books that belonged to the San Francisco Public Library, and I took them right to the library and dropped them in the night-deposit box.

Then I left. As I was curving out the freeway I glanced behind me a second at the city I was leaving. It was sort of misty-foggy and the lights of the city were lovely. In the second I had to glance at it as I was leaving, it seemed a beautiful, romantic city. It occurred to me that I hadn't got to know it at all well. For a brief moment I felt regret. In a way it felt like San Francisco was leaving me. I had just glanced back and seen it go. We had barely known each other—like two people who notice each other at a party but never get to talk.

Then I was over the first hills and San Francisco was gone. A few minutes later I passed the airport. I heard the roar of a plane overhead and remembered Jill, all the way across the country, in New York. I had no concept of New York, I had no idea what kinds of things might happen there. I pulled off the freeway for a few minutes and watched the airplanes come and go. I had taken a thousand dollars out of the bank that afternoon. I could go. I was very uncertain, though. Going to New York felt wrong. I had a feeling I would get there and not be able to handle the city or myself or anything. Finally I drove on down the freeway, but I kept thinking of Jill, and I was uncertain. Maybe the surprise of seeing me would make her love me. I had no way of judging, but I kept driving. What I really wanted to do was drive all night. There were other airports along the road. I could fly from Phoenix or El Paso and get to New York in the daytime, instead of in the middle of the night. In the daytime I might stand a better chance.

Still, passing the airport didn't feel right. None of my possibilities felt right. As I was passing Palo Alto I suddenly turned off. I had never gone back to see the New Americans and meet Teddy Blue. I thought I might as well. There was no knowing if I would ever return to California. Perry Lane was almost as hard to find in a car as it had been on foot. My thoughts kept going back to the airport and to Jill.

I found Teddy Blue's house, finally. When I got there things were very quiet. I knocked and went in and found Pauline and Leslie and Sergei sitting on the floor playing Monopoly. They greeted me as if they had known me for years.

"How's your awful wife?" Leslie asked. "Has she had a baby yet?"

"Don't be so personal," Sergei said. He was wearing a maroon sweater. Leslie had on the same green dress she had worn the first time I saw her, and Pauline was in her nightgown and a blue terry cloth bathrobe.

"Are you hungry?" Pauline asked.

"She can't stand not to feed people," Sergei said. "Play Monopoly with us. Everyone's gone to Tijuana."

"It was Teddy's idea," Leslie said. "He can't stay out of Mexico."

"I'm on my way to Texas," I said.

"Oh, we have mushrooms tonight," Sergei said. "Bring him some of the mushroom shortcake, Pauline. The mushrooms are from Mexico. They're great. Monopoly's a lot more fun when you're high."

"He ought to eat first," Pauline said. She got up and went and made me a baloney sandwich and brought it to me on a plate. She also brought me a boiled egg and some milk. While I was eating Sergei and Leslie argued about how they would divide the properties already acquired with me, so I wouldn't be unfairly handicapped by starting so late. Sergei already had two hotels on Park Place. I thought we ought to divide with Pauline too, since she had practically nothing. What she did have was lovely calves. Nice ankles too. Sergei explained to me that the mushrooms in the shortcake were vision-inducing mushrooms. Mexican Indians had been eating them and having visions for centuries.

"I'm not having any mushrooms," Leslie said. "Visions always make me cry. I'm too unstable. I have visions of myself unraveling."

I ate the shortcake, which was good. I had no reason to refrain from having visions, that I could think of. Perhaps I would see Jill in a vision and know what to do about her. But instead of having visions I got into a very competitive Monopoly game. Leslie and Sergei competed fiercely and I competed fiercely too. Pauline smiled and looked lovely and palpable and quiet. Occasionally she bought a cheap property. Long before we finished she dropped out of the game and went over and took off her robe and went to bed. "Night," she said. "Stay for breakfast if you want to. You might have a wreck, driving at night."

Sergei was bold with his capital, but he was also lucky. He was keen and zestful and awfully intelligent. Leslie groaned often and wrinkled her brow, trying to decide what to do. She was essentially cautious. I was reckless and did about as well as Sergei.

Pauline had gone to sleep. She was so lovely that I kept wondering why Teddy Blue kept running off and leaving her. I ate some more shortcake and began to feel effects. I was not having visions but I felt the distances of things begin to alter. Both inside me and outside me the distances altered. It was a little like being drunk except much dryer and lighter and all in the head. My hands and feet felt distant from one another, and the pieces on the Monopoly board seemed larger, the size of dollhouses. At moments we seemed to be right by the bed, watching Pauline sleep. At other moments the bed seemed miles away. At two in the morning we stopped playing Monopoly. We went out in the yard so Sergei could identify constellations. While we were out in the yard the desert shrunk. It seemed to me that Texas was only a few miles away. I would ease down the road and be there soon. It was absurd to go to the airport, with Texas so close.

"He ought to take some mushrooms with him," Leslie said. "I can tell they make him feel good."

I did feel very good. I was delighted I had stopped by to see them. It was wonderful to feel Texas so close. I thought of Emma. I could have breakfast in her kitchen. She'd be very pleased to see me. Sergei gave me a brown paper bag with some mushrooms in it. I stuffed it in my parka.

"Save them for sometime when you're playing a game," he said. "They improve all games."

I thanked them and got in the car. Leslie said she would read my book as soon as she could get a copy. I drove away. When I got to the freeway I slowed down very slow, so I could read the exit signs clearly. I was looking for familiar names. I expected the first exit to be El Paso. Then there would be Van Horn. Then San Antonio. But that wasn't the way the exits read. It didn't bother me, though. I felt wonderful. I expected to be arriving in front of the Hortons' house in a few minutes. I had keen dry light visions of everybody. If I missed the Hortons' I could just go on and see Jill. I imagined her sitting on a big bed in a hotel, in her bathrobe, solemnly watching TV. There were many homes where I could spend the night. Jenny Salomea would let me in. All the exit signs kept saying San Jose, which was a little odd. Then they began to mention Salinas. I saw Mr. Fitzherbert drive right through my room. He drove right through it with a lovely splintering sound, and the apartment flew everywhere. Pieces of it settled lightly and quietly to earth, as I was passing San Jose. Emma kept hugging me while she was fixing breakfast. There wasn't much traffic. Then a bad vision came: Sally. She loomed out of a bathtub with her belly like a whale's back, a little spout of water coming from her navel. She looked contemptuously at me, for being so distanced from myself. She made me feel guilty for being spaced out. While I was looking for hotels I noticed that two of my wheels were not on the pavement. Jill said I was a dummy, speaking kindly. I let the Chevy drift off the road and stop. I had many cushions and pillows in the car and I piled several of them in the front seat and got the green Indian rug and huddled under it. Sergei had not noticed any constellations. It was very dark. I didn't want to drive anymore. That would be stupid. I felt very wise, much too wise to do stupid things. I covered myself with the green rug and shut my eyes. I had never felt so wise, or so nicely sleepy.

When I woke up I felt great. The world had become absolutely white, not only the earth but the air as well. I was in a thick, milk-white fog, the whitest, milkiest fog I had ever seen. It was like the Chevy was at the bottom of a lake of milk. Actually it sat somewhere in the Salinas Valley, as I realized when I got my wits about me. The old man and old woman of the Berkeley hills had had a long argument about Odysseus' visit to the underworld, the day we had had the picnic. They had argued about the spirits that came out of the fog, and I had gone right home and read the chapter they had argued about. The spirits came out of the fog and approached the pool of blood at Odysseus' feet and he kept them back with his sword. It seemed to me I was in such a fog. The spirits of the dead ought to be moving in it. If I went and found a heifer and slaughtered it and got a club to fight the spirits back with perhaps the spirits would come. I could talk with Granny and Old Man Goodnight and ask them if I had their stories right. I got out and walked across the ditch to piss. No real spirits came but to my surprise I had a faint intimation of Godwin Lloyd-Jons. It was unlikely he was abroad in such a fog, and anyhow he was in Austin, but I thought anyway that I heard him say my name.

I got back in the car and eased along in the fog, scared to death that someone would run into me from behind. When I finally ran out of the fog the green country was beautiful and I was starved.

I drove on to Bakersfield in the bright morning sunlight, feeling extremely fresh and extremely happy. Being on the road was wonderful. By the time I had been driving an hour I could understand what had been wrong with me for so many months. I should have taken Jill on the road. I loved watching the land as I passed through it. I stopped at a filling station and had a Coke and some peanuts. The filling station was far out in the Valley, and flat green fields stretched all around. While I was stopped I called Bruce and told him I was going home and would be at an autograph party if he wanted me to.

Bruce was all business. He had already arranged a party, and had been about to call and tell me. I felt generally aimless and happy. Bruce read me a review from *Publishers' Weekly*, which said I was very sentimental. That struck me as fair enough. I got in the car and drove on and before I had driven fifty miles I had forgotten that I was having a book published, or even that I was a writer. All that day I was just a happy driver.

That night I slept in my car, just east of Las Cruces, New Mexico. The swish of the trucks and cars that passed me put me to sleep, and when I woke up there was no milk-white fog, as there had been outside Salinas, but only a cold, absolutely cloudless desert sky overhead, with stars still bright in the west. I huddled under my rug and covers for a while, watching the sky change. It was very cold in the car. I remembered driving toward Las Cruces on my way to California, with Sally waking up in the back seat, smelling like a warm sleepy girl. I didn't really want any more of Sally, but despite myself I missed the way she smelled when she woke up.

Finally I shook myself out of the covers and drove on toward El

Paso. Ahead of me, forty miles away, the sun was about to come up, over Texas. The rims of the desert had all been dark when I woke up. Then, to the northeast, a line of pink edged along the rim. Slowly the pink became red and widened into a band. Soon the band stretched itself in both directions, north toward the Staked plains, south over Mexico. The curve of the sun appeared and the red became orange. As I approached El Paso the whole great spread of sky in front of me shaded from orange to yellow.

Texas was there, beyond the sunrise, looming as it had loomed the day I left San Francisco. "It is your land," Wu had said, but Wu had never seen the great sky that opened above me. It was the sky that was Texas, the sky that welcomed me back. The land I didn't care for all that much—it was bleak and monotonous and full of ugly little towns. The sky was what I had been missing, and seeing it again in its morning brightness made me realize suddenly why I hadn't been myself for many months. It had such depth and such spaciousness and such incredible compass, it took so much in and circled one with such a tremendous generous space that it was impossible not to feel more intensely with it above you. I wanted to stop at the first filling station and call Jill and get her to come to Texas. No wonder I hadn't been able to make her love me in San Francisco. I couldn't feel anything in a place where I hadn't even noticed the sky. Maybe I hadn't been very loving—I couldn't be sure.

Below me, to the south, I could see Juarez and El Paso, nestled in their crook of the Rio Grande. I was almost home—at least I was almost to some part of home. It was an odd feeling, because I had no real idea what I had come home to do. Perhaps I had come home to be a father, but that notion was very confusing. I had no sense of what being a father might be like, and of course if I even went near Sally I might be put in jail. All my prospects were nonspecific, indeterminate.

That being the case, it was nice to be just on the rim of home. At the very least I had another whole day to drive. If I stopped to see Uncle Laredo, as I had promised myself I would if I ever came back, I could put off getting to Austin for two or three days. I wanted to see Uncle Laredo anyway. He was ninety-two years old and there was no telling how many more chances I would get to visit him. Once he was dead I would never get a chance to visit anyone remotely like him—that was certain. There was no one remotely like him.

In Van Horn I stopped at a dusty filling station and asked the attendant if Uncle L was still alive. He was only an in-law, and my family wouldn't have bothered to tell me if he had died. The filling station man was fat and wore a dirty green baseball cap. He looked at me as if I were a freak, and when he found out whose nephew I was he almost stopped putting gas in my car. He was about forty and he chewed tobacco.

"If that old bastard ain't alive he's the stinkinest ghost I ever met," he said. "We got a barbershop downtown, if you'd like to get a haircut. Must not be no barbers where you come from."

"I come from Texas," I said. "I just like hair."

"Aw yeah?" he said. "If a feller was to drop a match on your head it'd go up like a haystack." He gave me a mean wink. He didn't want me to ignore the fact that he was insulting me. I ignored it anyway.

"I could squirt a little gasoline on it," he added. "Might help it burn."

"You could mind your own fucking business, too," I said, stung. No one had commented on the length of my hair in so long that I had forgotten about it. I was home again, and I didn't feel like being trifled with, especially not by fat rednecks in green baseball caps. He hadn't bothered to check my water, so I got out and checked it. Then I went around to the trunk and checked the air in my spare. I had forty-seven miles of dirt road to cross. The man pitched my gas cap about ten feet in the air, and caught it when it came down.

"You oughtn't to sass around and use your goddamn profanity with me," he said. Suddenly he hunched over, made a fierce face, and gave the air a hard karate chop.

"See that?" he said. "I just finished a karate class, up in Midland. These hands is lethal weapons. I'd about as soon give a curlyheaded little fart like you a chop or two, for practice. Hai! Karate!"

He concentrated on what must have been an imaginary brick and gave it a terrific chop. Then he looked at me to see if I was properly intimidated. I wasn't. I was back home. Nobody had the right to push me around. Also my trunk was open. All I had to do was reach down and pick up my tire tool. The minute I did the look on the man's face changed. He looked forty, and foolish. I shook my hair at him and smote the air once or twice, for effect.

"Hai!" I said. "Tire tool!"

"Let me get them windshields for you," the man said. I put the tire tool in the front seat with me and it had a wonderful effect. Not only did the man clean my windshields, but he chased me halfway down the driveway as I was pulling out.

"Say, young feller, you must not be awake good," he said. "You's about to drive off without your green stamps."

13.

UNCLE L was my most colorful relative, but there was no denying that he had his drawbacks. Ninety-two years had not mellowed him at all. The minute I stepped out of my car and heard his rasping old voice I began to remember his drawbacks, and to wonder why I'd come. The voice came from somewhere in what he called his kitchen pasture—a little twenty-acre pen north of the house, where he kept an assortment of animals he planned to eat.

When I walked up he was down on his knees, stabbing at a hole in the ground with a big crowbar. It was a hot morning and he was sweating like a Turk. Three bedraggled Mexican cowboys sat on the ground nearby, looking unhappy. Uncle L still had freckles, at ninety-two. His little blue eyes were as clear and mean as ever. The ground was so hot it was burning my feet through my sneakers.

"I still got ever goddamn one of my teeth," he said, opening his mouth to show me. His teeth looked perfect. While he was showing them to me his mean little eyes scrutinized me inch by inch. He was not a man to pass lightly over one's faults.

"What the hell, you got the mange?" he asked.

"I don't think so."

"Your hair's a foot long," he said. "Thought you must be hiding the mange. How old are you?"

"Twenty-three."

"That's old enough to remember to go to the barbershop," he said.

He spat in his gloves and went back to stabbing at the earth with the crowbar. Holes were one of his obsessions. Over the years he had scattered some three hundred corner postholes about the ranch, to the peril of every creature that walked, including him. The theory behind them was that if he ever got around to building the fences he meant to build it would be nice to have the corner postholes already dug. But he had lived on the ranch fifty years and it only had two fences, both falling down. My own theory was that he dug the holes because he hated the earth and wanted to get in as many licks at it as he could, before he died. The earth might get him in the end, but it would have three hundred scars to show for it. Uncle L was not the kind of man who liked to be bested in a fight.

"Hey, Pierre," he yelled to the cowboys generally. "Get off your asses and strangle one of them goats. We got company for dinner."

The kitchen pasture held a motley collection of edible animals, all of which were standing around in a half-circle behind the Mexicans. Perhaps they hoped to be fed, rather than eaten. They managed to look disheartened and desperately belligerent at the same time. There were six or eight goats, a yearling camel, a scruffy young buffalo cow, a flock of malign-looking guinea hens, five spotted pigs, and a dozen molting turkeys. All of them looked as desperate as the cowboys—on Uncle L's ranch it was an open question as to who would eat whom.

The three cowboys all scrambled up and made a run for the animals, shaking out their ropes as they ran. The animals immediately scattered to the four winds, all except the pigs, who formed a tight little phalanx and stood their ground. Uncle L hired only Mexicans and called them all Pierre—by accident the first man he had ever hired had been French. Pierre was a generic name for hired hand; only old Lorenzo, the cook, was exempt from it.

The three Pierres were not charismatic ropers. They never got a loop within ten yards of anything. The goats, most of whom had looked half-dead, fled around and around the pen with the fleetness of gazelles. The buffalo cow lowered her head and bellowed and pawed the ground. Pierre, Pierre, and Pierre left her alone. They ran wildly after the goats and caught nothing. One accidentally ran behind the young camel, who kicked him flat. The minute he fell the five pigs started for him, squealing horribly. His companions rushed over and got him to his feet. They beat the pigs back with their lariat ropes. Everything on the ranch seemed to be starving. The three men picked up rocks and began to throw them at the guinea hens and the turkeys. They were clearly desperate to kill something quick, before Uncle L's temper rose. It seemed to me it was rising. His face was turning red.

"Look at them shitasses," he said. "Can't rope a goddamn goat in a goddamn pen. Pierre! You shitass! Bring me that goddamn rope," he yelled. All three Mexicans came hustling back, their eyes downcast. Uncle L took the first rope that was offered him and strode off. He was only five feet four—in his fiercer moods he reminded me of Yosemite Sam.

At his approach all the animals stopped dead. They knew who was boss. The fight went out of them and they stood meekly, awaiting their doom. Uncle L slipped the rope over the head of the first goat he came to and led him toward the gate.

The tallest and most desperate-looking of the Mexicans wore yellow chaps. To my surprise, and everyone's, he suddenly yanked his chaps loose and began to take down his pants. He looked crazed, and apparently was. His companions started toward him, but he shook his fist at them. They backed off and glared.

"You filthy toad, what is it you do?" one of them said. He was a humble little fellow with symmetrically broken front teeth.

"Go away, people!" the crazed Mexican said. "Do not stand in my way."

Something, perhaps his madness, had given him an erection. Suddenly he flung himself on the mound of earth beside the posthole and began to fuck it passionately. I was amazed and his two companions were profoundly annoyed.

"Antonio, stop this you are doing," the little one said. "You lizard, where is your religion? What do you think you are doing, fucking this dirt? Do you want me to kick you?"

The man in the yellow chaps paid him absolutely no mind. Finally the others turned their backs on him. They both spat loudly, to show their contempt for his moral standards. I went over to the gate, glancing behind me from time to time to see if the man was still at it. He was. The little goat Uncle L led looked like it might drop dead at any moment, from pure resignation.

Ahead of us, beyond my car, loomed Uncle L's house. It rose from the floor of the valley like some kind of great tabernacle, not Mormon, not English, not American. Russian, maybe. What it really looked like was a great black Russian church. It had four stories, three turrets, seven porches. On the top was a huge cupola, with a spire rising from it. The wood had long ago been scraped by the sand until it was almost black. When I had driven along the rim of the valley that morning and saw the house, ten miles away, rising out of the desert like a great grotesque mirage, I had thought immediately of Leon O'Reilly. He would buy it on sight, if he ever saw it.

The house had been built before the turn of the century, by an English architect named Lord Montstuart. Lord Montstuart had come to America and gone broke in the cattle business, and had spent the dregs of his fortune and the last ten years of his life building the house. I think it must have been his vengeance on England, or America, or both, but unfortunately it was situated right in the center of an isolated, forty-thousand-acre valley, fifty miles south of Van Horn, Texas, and neither America nor England ever knew what Lord Montstuart had done to them.

On the east side of the house, attached to it by a little catwalk, was a praying tower made of adobe brick. Lord Montstuart had had a fling with Mohammedanism and had sometimes gone out at dawn and bowed toward Mecca. He had had earthly flings, too. One day in an excess of bitterness he had flung both himself and his last mistress, a Mexican woman, to their deaths from the fourth-story porch. The two of them were buried on a small knoll in the horse pasture, as Lord Montstuart had wished it.

The house had twenty-eight rooms, most of which had never been used. It was a kind of bitter, demented parody of everything Victorian, with marble bathtubs, all half full of sand, and quarters below ground for three cooks, two valets, and a laundress. Lord Montstuart's last mistress had been the laundress. The living room was sixty feet long and contained a grand piano and an orchestra pit, with instruments laid out for a nine-piece orchestra. There was even a bassoon. The instrument cases were half full of sand.

In the center of the living room, snarling eternally at the non-existent orchestra, was a stuffed lobo wolf. It was Uncle L's one addition to the house. It was the last wolf killed in the Pecos country, he claimed, and he himself had killed it, after an intermittent hunt that had lasted sixteen years. Uncle L was as obsessed with last things as he was with holes. He never did anything that wasn't a last thing.

I followed him and the sad little goat around the towering black house to the backyard, where Uncle L had made his permanent camp. He never slept in the house and seldom went in it at all. All his life he had slept around a camp-fire. His ranch was called The Hacienda of the Bitter Waters. Lord Montstuart had named it, and it was a very apt name. The waters were so alkaline that no normal person could drink them without disastrous effect.

As soon as we turned the corner of the house old Lorenzo, the cook, got up and came over. He had always seemed to like me.

"Señor Danny, your hair is beautiful," he said.

"It ain't no such a goddamn thing," Uncle L said, handing Lorenzo the rope that held the goat. Lorenzo was even tinier than Uncle L. He was fifty times as wizened, and claimed to be even older, though their respective ages had been a bone of contention between them for many years.

Lorenzo looked contemptuously at the hopeless little goat.

"This is a terrible goat you have brought me, Jefe," he said. "I think it has got the worms. Am I supposed to cook a sick goat for Señor Danny? Why didn't you rope me a nice pig?"

"This goat'll do," Uncle L said, sitting down and leaning back against his saddle. Two camels were tied to the windmill—they placidly chewed their cuds. For years Uncle L had ridden nothing but camels. He had had a great studhorse named El Caballo, and when El Caballo died he had sworn off horses.

Lorenzo took the rope off the little goat's head and gave the goat a kick. "Go away, goat," he said.

"Cook that goat," Uncle L said.

The goat itself did not believe it was alive. It only took one step when Lorenzo kicked it.

"No, it is not possible," Lorenzo said. "Who knows what this goat may have? It may have the cholera."

"Goddamnit, it don't have no cholera," Uncle L said. "The goddamn pigs have probably got cholera. Just cook the sonofabitch. I never asked you to diagnose it."

Suddenly the goat saw its chance and darted away. It was quick but Uncle L was quicker. His Winchester was right by his saddle and he snatched it up and shot the goat just before it went around the corner of the house. The crack of the gun echoed strangely off the distant ridges. The goat had been right the first time, when it concluded it was dead. Now it was undoubtedly dead. Probably I had inherited my shooting eye from Uncle L. Lorenzo went over and cut the goat's throat, but he took his defeat with bad grace.

"All right," he said, dragging the goat to the cook fire. "I will cook this filthy goat. You had to go and shoot it, Jefe, instead of going to rope one that was fat and healthy. I myself am much too old to rope now, or I would have done it gladly. You are young and can still rope well. There was no excuse for what you have done."

"You never could rope worth a shit," Uncle L said. "You couldn't rope a goddamn stump when you was twenty years old."

"I would not rope a sick goat, that is for sure," Lorenzo said. "I would have roped a pig, if I had been there."

He was very grumpy. I could smell some bread, baking in two big Dutch ovens. A pot of frijoles and peppers was already bubbling over the fire. A clothesline strung with jerky stretched from the windmill to the house.

"This goat will probably kill us all! Wipe us out!" Lorenzo yelled. Uncle L ignored him. Lorenzo spitted the goat and soon had it cooking. The three Mexicans slunk around the corner of the house and went to their camp, which was in Uncle L's extensive junkyard. The junkyard consisted of every machine that Uncle L had ever owned. There were twenty or thirty cars, two broken-down bulldozers, several tractors, a hay baler, a combine, and an old cattle truck. The vaqueros lived in the cattle truck.

When the goat was cooked we ate. I had brought a case of Dr. Peppers with me, as protection against the water on the ranch. I drank three of them with lunch. Lorenzo's frijoles were incredibly peppery. I gave Uncle L a Dr. Pepper and he took one sip and poured the rest on an anthill. In the distance, toward Mexico, we could see

Uncle L's camel herd grazing. He had about forty. He hated cattle and wouldn't have them on his ranch. Besides camels, he kept goats, buffalo, and antelope. He had tried at various times to raise llamas, guanacos, javelinas, and ostriches, but none of those animals had cared for The Hacienda of the Bitter Waters. They had all promptly disappeared. Uncle L was particularly bitter about the ostriches, and referred to them again as we were eating.

"Always wanted an ostrich ranch," he said, gnawing on the shank of the goat. Might get me in a few cassowaries. They ain't as fast as ostriches. Been trying to get a couple of giraffe, too. Always wanted a few giraffe."

"They will just run away, if you get them," Lorenzo said. "All the good animals run away, when they come here. Only stupid animals and crazy people live on this ranch."

While we were eating a fight broke out in the camp of the vaqueros. The junkyard began just beyond the windmill, so we got to see it all. The vaquero in the yellow chaps wrenched the hood off an old blue Plymouth and threw it at his companions. It hit the man who had been kicked down by the camel—he had not been having much of a day. He scrambled up and he and his ally took possession of the hood. They refused to leave the field, and actually there was no need for them to. The vaquero in the yellow chaps had lost interest in them. His passion was up, again. His companions screeched at him in Spanish, but he paid them no mind. He unscrewed the gas cap from an old black pickup, dropped his pants again, and began to fuck the gas hole. Old Lorenzo thought it was a hilarious business. He doubled up with laughter. Doubled up, he was only about two feet tall. The other vaqueros were outraged, at seeing a pickup fucked. To them it was unpardonable license. They dropped the blue hood and began to throw handfuls of sand at the vaquero. He continued to hump away.

"Those men must be starving," Lorenzo said. "They have been cooking the seats out of those old cars. Who wants to eat such things? You should give them a pig, Jefe."

Uncle Laredo ignored him. The two stumpy Mexicans came over, looking huffy.

"Señor Jefe, we are going to quit now," the one with the broken teeth said. "We cannot live with this Antonio no more. He has got no morality! These days he is fucking everything. We had better go to town."

"You should have let him have at that goat I give you last week," Uncle L said. "You ate it too quickly. It might have taken some of the ginger out of him."

"Go on to town," Lorenzo said. "We do not need complainers on his ranch. Go on now. It is only forty-seven miles. Take a piece of my jerky if you haven't had your breakfast."

It occurred to me I could take them to town, if they weren't in too big a hurry. When I told them so they both looked so grateful I was afraid they might cry. They were pulling jerky off the clothesline and stuffing it in their pockets.

"You are a kind man, Señor," one said. "Can we wait in your car? This is not a safe ranch."

"Sure," I said. "Have some Dr. Peppers if you're thirsty."

Uncle L clearly didn't care whether they stayed or went, or lived or died. He was over saddling his camel.

"This here's a Bactrian," he said, when I went over to watch. "I can't stand them goddamn dromedaries. They belch all over a man."

Behind him, piled up in a heap, was what looked like two or three hundred manhole covers. I had never seen so many manhole covers, if that was what they were. The camel Uncle L was saddling was big and yellow and absolutely expressionless. It was still chewing its cud, and its thoughts were elsewhere.

"Are those manhole covers?" I asked. Uncle L looked at me as if I were simply too much. He was one of the many people who made me feel that everything I said was stupid, that everything I asked was obvious, and that everything I did was ineffectual.

"You better get your ass back to that school you're supposed to be going to," he said. "Can't you even recognize a manhole cover when you see one?"

"I thought that's what they were," I said apologetically. I would have bitten my tongue off rather than ask why he happened to have three hundred manhole covers piled behind his windmill. Uncle L didn't explain. The camel kneeled, Uncle L got on him, and the camel rose again. "I'll be back about dark," Uncle L said. The big yellow camel seemed to float away, into the distance.

Old Lorenzo hobbled over and began to milk the other camel.

"The Jefe is getting old, Señor Danny," he said. "He will not last many more years. His constitution is not so good, you know. Now myself, I am as good as ever, even though I am older than him. I seem to be made of iron. Often I do not even sleep at night."

When he had finished milking he drank from the foaming bucket and then offered the bucket to me. I took it, thinking of Jill Peel. She had sometimes drunk camel's milk. I remembered how nice she looked in her windbreaker and pants and blue sneakers. The milk was warm and full of foam and smelled of camel's hair. I took a swallow and almost gagged. Uncle L and the camel had floated almost out of sight.

To get out of the blazing sun for a minute I went in and reexplored the house. On the third floor there was an exercise room, equipped with a chinning bar, wall weights, and a rowing machine. The rowing machine was in a kind of solarium, from which one could look out across endless miles of desert. I tried a little rowing, but the machine was badly rusted and squeaked horribly.

In one corner of the solarium was the largest medicine ball I had ever seen. I decided at once to steal it. I took a nap in the library, on a lavender Victorian chaise, and when I woke up I kicked the medicine ball down three flights of stairs and lugged it out to the car. The sight of it seemed to delight the two vaqueros. They were stretched out, one in the back seat, one in the front, drinking Dr. Peppers. Relief seemed to have made them giddy.

"You had better steal the wolf, Señor," one said. "If you don't steal it Antonio is going to fuck it one of these days. Goddamn he is fucking everything that's got a hole."

"I don't think the wolf has a hole, anymore," I said.

"If he has got a hole Antonio will fuck him, pretty soon," the man said.

I went back to the fourth-story porch and sat there with an old spyglass I found, until the sun fell. The great black shadow of the great black house gradually stretched itself across the kitchen pasture. The five spotted pigs were trying to root out a fence post. To the west, the lower sky became purple. It was eerie to imagine how Lord Montstuart must have felt, sitting there evening after evening for ten years, watching the empty land and the great sky. Perhaps his mistress had talked when he hadn't wanted her to. Perhaps she had had the upper hand, and had given Lord Montstuart a bad time. Perhaps he drank too much brandy, watching the sunsets all alone. In the stillness I heard the clomp of hooves and Uncle L came riding in. From where I sat it was a long drop to the ground. Perhaps Lord Montstuart had fallen in love with the air, or with the distance, or with the thought of the plunge, and had decided to share his new love with his old. The sky was purple, orange, golden, yellow, blue.

Below me, Uncle L was trying to start his jeep. It was an old green army jeep, without a seat. He had piled some of the manhole covers in it, to sit on. Lorenzo was sitting in the back of the jeep, on some firewood, holding a Winchester. Uncle L held a Winchester across his lap. I ran downstairs and grabbed my parka out of the car. The blazing sun was gone. Before I could get to the jeep Uncle L had begun to honk.

"Martha's particular about when she eats," he said. Martha was his wife. He had married her only three years before, after eighty-nine years of bachelorhood. I had never met her. She lived on her own ranch, some miles away.

We bounced off into the desert just as the sun was setting. In the three years that he had been married Uncle L had established a traditional route from his ranch to Martha's, but it was only a route, not a road. He roared down into gullies and across washouts as if he were on El Caballo instead of in an antiquated jeep. We bounced and rattled. The ridges in the far distance were black and the first stars were very bright gold. Neither Uncle L nor Lorenzo had a word to say. We passed Uncle L's buffalo herd, dull brown shapes in the dusk. There was the smell of dust and sage in the clear air.

Seeing the buffalo reminded me of a story I had always loved. It had to do with Old Man Goodnight. Some Indians had broken off their reservation and come to Goodnight and asked him for a buffalo, and when he reluctantly gave them one they ran it down and killed it with their lances, on the plains in front of his house.

To me it was the true end of the West. A few sad old Indians, on sad skinny ponies, wearing rags and scraps of white man's clothes and carrying old lances with a few pathetic feathers dangling from them, begging the Old Man of the West for a buffalo, one buffalo of the millions it had once been theirs to hunt. He got tired of being pestered and gave them one, and they flailed their skinny old horses into a run and chased the buffalo and killed it, in the old way. Then all they did was sit on their horses and look at it awhile, the winds of the plains fluttering their rags and their few feathers. It was all over. From then on all they would have was their longing. I wondered what Mr. Goodnight had felt, watching it all from his front porch. I didn't know. I just knew it was a great story, full of tragedy. I didn't know exactly whose story it was, but I knew it was great.

We roared up on a high ridge and came out on a kind of plateau. Suddenly Uncle L veered over right to the rim of the plateau and stopped the jeep. Far to the west we could see a light blinking.

"That's Martha's house," he said. He took his Winchester and walked over to the rim of the hill and looked south. There was a pile of stones near where he had stopped the jeep. It was where El Caballo was buried—El Caballo, the horse. It was also where Uncle L and Lorenzo kept their nightly watch for Zapata. Long before Uncle L had married Martha he and Lorenzo had come to the plateau nightly, to watch for Zapata. They had both fought with him. They had also fought with Villa. Before that Uncle L had fought with the Texas Rangers, and before that—literally—had fought with the Seventh Cavalry, in Wyoming in the 1890s. After the battle of Wounded Knee he came south, first to the Rangers, then to Zapata. That was where he had met Lorenzo.

Lorenzo got out of the jeep and began to unload the firewood. He would stay near the cairn of El Caballo and wait for Zapata, while Uncle L and I went on to have supper with Martha. Any night, Zapata might come. He might need them again. The man who had been shot, whose picture had been shown to the world—that was not Zapata at all. It was only his cousin, a stupid fellow. Zapata was in the hills, biding his time. Some night he would cross the river and come to the campfire of his old companions. They would sit on the rim-rock and make plans and clink their gold. Uncle L actually kept a sack of gold in the jeep, in case Zapata needed money when he came.

Lorenzo built his little fire and Uncle L waited until it was flaming. Then he fired three shots into the dark sky. It was a signal— actually, two signals. Ten miles away, in the house with the winking light, Martha would hear the shots and set the supper table, and, somewhere in the hills of Mexico, if he needed to, if he was ready to come, Emiliano Zapata would hear them and know that things were ready. Pancho Villa had been stupid—Pancho Villa was mortal flesh. It had been good sport to ride with him, but in the end he was only another bandit. Zapata was immortal. El Caballo was the Horse. The shots cracked across the darkening land, and Uncle L got back in the jeep without saying a word. We left Lorenzo crouching by the fire.

The stars were very bright when we left the ridge. I felt apprehensive. I didn't know what I was doing, in a jeep in the desert with Uncle L. He wasn't my kind of man at all. He wasn't crazy and nice, he was crazy and mean. I had nothing to say to him and he had nothing to say to me. He drove grimly, swerving now and then to avoid running over goats.

Unlike Uncle L, Martha raised goats seriously. They seemed to be everywhere. Uncle L seemed to resent having to swerve. He honked furiously. The yard of Martha's house was full of bleating shapes. Uncle L parked right in the center of a sea of goats. There must have been hundreds. The ranch house was a one-story adobe building, a dark bulk beyond the goats. Through the open door we could see a table with a kerosene lamp on it. A woman stood by the table, holding a rifle by the barrel.

"She sees that hair she's apt to think you're a goddamn Comanche," Uncle L said. A number of goats poked their noses into the jeep. Uncle L kicked a space clear and got out. I did the same. At the door of the house Uncle L stopped and took off his hat.

"You don't need no firearms," he said. "It's just me and my idiot nephew."

Martha was silent. Her silence had something of the uncomfortable quality of Sally's silences, only it was a great deal more formidable. She was a statuesque old woman, and had not put down the rifle. Her face was in shadow, but the hand and forearm that held the gun looked as brown and strong as wood.

Uncle L tried to open the screen door and it wouldn't open. It was latched from the inside.

"What in the goddamn hell's the matter with you?" he said, rattling the screen. "Ain't you gonna let us in the house? We come to get fed, not to stare through a goddamn door screen."

The old woman shifted the rifle to the crook of her arm and came slowly to the door. Her face was still in shadow.

"I don't know that I want you in my house," she said.

Uncle L was a little taken aback. It was obvious that he had expected a different reception.

"Since when, by God?" he asked.

"Since yesterday," Martha said. She wasted no words—I don't think she wasted anything.

"Lemme in," Uncle L said, rattling the door screen. "I got a goddamn right to come in, ain't I?"

"I don't know that you do," Martha said.

Her voice was as level as the desert, and about as unappeasing. I had the feeling that I had blundered into a show-down of some kind. Uncle L was literally hopping mad. I expected him to hop at any moment.

"What kinda goddamn airs are you putting on now?" he said. "I'm your husband, ain't I?"

"We might be getting a divorce," Martha said.

Uncle L was taken aback.

"Why?" he asked.

"Because you're an old sonofabitch," Martha said.

Uncle L was enraged past reply. He dug in his pocket and came out with a yellow-handled pocketknife. He opened the longest blade and jabbed it through the door screen, near the latch.

"All right, I'll cut my way in," he said. "I ain't gonna stand out here and listen to you call me names."

Martha shifted her weight and put the barrel of her rifle against the screen, exactly covering the point of Uncle L's knife. An instant later she fired. Fortunately Uncle L had jerked his knife back. A hole appeared in the screen and behind us there was the sudden crack

[151]

of glass. The goats, some of whom had followed us onto the porch, immediately stampeded. Hundreds of small hooves drummed the earth—white forms vanished. The three of us stood and listened to them run. There was nothing left in the yard but a jeep with a shattered windshield.

Uncle L was too shocked to speak, but Martha was not shocked at all. She levered another shell into the chamber and put the rifle back in the crook of her arm.

"Just because I stood up with you don't mean you can ruin my screens," she said. "If I want 'em ruined I'll ruin 'em myself. You ran over six goats last night, going home. I'd like my money in cash. Then we'll see about supper."

She flicked the door latch off and turned and went back to the table. It was just a plain wooden table, with a kerosene lamp sitting on it. All the chairs were plain and wooden. Martha laid the Winchester across the table and turned and planted herself, facing Uncle L. She was an angular woman, and she really did stand in the room as if she were planted there. Uncle L kicked the door back and stomped into the room, but it was obvious to all of us that he was facing his match. He was like a wildcat who had been insulted by a tree. He could gnash his teeth and bare his claws but he was not going to be able to hurt the tree, much less break it down. He hung his hat on a peg.

"I never run over six of them *going home*," he said. "I ran over two of them coming. The little shitasses are as hard to see as rocks. You don't need to be so goddamn ornery about it."

"If you can't see where you're going you oughtn't to *drive*," Martha said. "Why don't you hire that boy there to drive for you? He looks like he needs a job."

"All he needs is a haircut," Uncle L said. "Let's eat. I smell the cooking."

"I'll see the money," Martha said. "I ain't no rich woman. I can't afford a husband if he's going to run over my goats."

Uncle L took out his billfold disgustedly. "I don't know why in the goddamn hell I married you," he said. "I got by eighty-nine years without no wife. All you've been to me is expense, expense, expense. I can't recollect now why I was fool enough to do it."

"Because you got tired of eating that old Mexican's cooking," Martha said. "A hundred dollars'll be fair."

Martha's face was neither thin nor full—her features looked firmer than leather. They had the quality of bone. Her mouth was neither contemptuous nor welcoming.

"I ain't passing out no food to a man who ain't honest enough to admit his mistakes," she said.

"A hundred dollars?" Uncle L said. "You can go shit in the sea. Two of them goats was cripples anyway. A goddamn accident ain't no goddamn mistake."

"Six accidents in one night is a mistake," Martha said. "I've had enough of this talk. If you ain't going to pay me, you can leave."

Uncle L paid. His billfold was bulging with money, doubtless made gambling. It was his real profession. He was famous all over the West as a poker player. He gave Martha a hundred-dollar bill and sank into injured silence. That suited Martha fine. Evidently conversation was not what they had married for. Probably she was determined to outlast him and get his ranch. Probably he was determined to outlast her and get hers. The determination to outlast was the bond that joined them, just as it joined Uncle L and Lorenzo. All of them were bound and determined not to be the first to die.

Martha brought us in buffalo steaks, cooked rare. They were served on old pewter platters. The only other dish was a stew made of beans and goat sweetbreads. Uncle L got a tumbler of whiskey and I got a glass of goat milk. The table looked like it had been used for a hundred years. Everything in the house was simple. Martha sat a flat slab of cornbread in the center of the table, and a dish of goat butter beside it.

Not one word was said during the meal, and there was no sense of sociability between the three of us at all. We were three separate people joined in the performance of what was essentially a common duty. Uncle L had told me he was Martha's third husband, and I ate the bloody steak and peppery beans and tried to imagine what life had been like for the other two. Presumably they had actually lived with her. Her hair was iron gray, parted in the middle. The strings of muscle in her forearms were like the markings of driftwood. Her face had a certain beauty, but beauty of such a severe nature, so spare and unswerving and unself-glorifying that it hardly seemed feminine at all. After we had eaten we got scalding hot coffee, served black. When we finished that Uncle L abruptly got up and put his hat on. I mumbled a word about the meal and followed him out. Martha came out too and stood on her low porch.

"Is this boy still going to school?" she asked. "He looks peaked. Probably don't get no exercise. I'll hire him if you ain't got a place for him."

"He wouldn't be worth a shit," Uncle L said. "All he's ever done is read."

Martha stood on the porch, watching us silently. The thought of working for her was a vision of hell. I could tell she knew no variables. Life was lived in one way and one way only. It was hard to imagine anything unnecessary happening within a certain distance of her person. I was unnecessary, and all variables. It was an immense relief not to have to justify myself in her eyes.

"Yell if you see any goats," Uncle L said, as we drove off.

Soon we passed a small flock and he braked the jeep. "Get out and help me catch some," he said. "She ain't getting away with that goddamn robbery. I got some string in the back, here. You catch 'em and I'll tie 'em up."

There was no need to chase the goats at all. They practically leapt in the jeep. Uncle L took ten and tied their feet with string. The ten of them made quite a pile, and also quite a bit of noise.

"Sit on 'em," Uncle L commanded. "I don't want none falling out. I ought to steal fifty. Two dollars is enough to pay for a shitass goat."

When we drove up on the ridge old Lorenzo was still squatting by the fire. His rifle was propped against his knee, and he was nodding. Uncle L got out and kicked him awake and the two old men took their Winchesters and went over to the edge of the rimrock again. They squatted and peered into the night, across the long barrenness to Mexico. Faint starlight lit the desert, and a wind had come up, a late norther. It was an eerie scene. The fire threw shadows on the rocks that covered the bones of El Caballo. I zipped up my parka and scrunched down, using the warm smelly goats as a windbreak. If I had been drunk the scene would have been even more eerie. Also it wouldn't have been so cold. The wind sped and the fire threw shadows, the emptiness around me was vast and supernal and the skeins of high-flung stars were coldly beautiful. Finally Uncle L and Lorenzo gave it up. Zapata wasn't coming for another night or two. They came back to the campfire and opened their breeches and peed on it. They didn't even pee like old men. Between them they put the fire out. Lorenzo kicked a little sand on it, for good measure, and in a minute we were plunging off the ridge.

As soon as we got back to the house, Uncle L and Lorenzo butchered the ten goats. I guess they were afraid Martha might come and find them. They sat around the campfire most of the night, cutting the goat meat into jerky-size slices and hanging it on the clothesline. I was not in the mood for so much butchering. I didn't like the blood, or the washtub full of goat guts that soon accumulated. Now and then, in the darkness of the windmills, the two camels belched. Uncle L and Lorenzo were very cheerful—they had gotten away with ten goats, and they made short shrift of them.

There was nothing to do that I knew how to do, so I went up and sat on the fourth-floor balcony. The two old men were far below, cussing each other and telling stories about the Zapatistas. Neither of them seemed tired, which was very confusing. I was mortally tired. I was also mortally mortal. I always thought of Uncle L as near death, because he was ninety-two, but it was obvious to me that that was a wrong way to think. I was probably nearer death. It was as if Uncle L and Martha and Lorenzo had already contested Time and won. The contest was over. They had made life theirs. So far as life was concerned they could go on living until they got bored with living, with butchering goats and digging postholes and cooking buffalo steaks.

I felt really insubstantial. I didn't know if I would ever make life mine. Martha was right about Uncle L, though. He was an old sonofabitch. The Hacienda of the Bitter Waters wasn't the Old West I liked to believe in—it was the bitter end of something. I knew I would never want to visit it again.

I sat on the balcony, huddled in my parka, until Uncle L and Lorenzo finally wrapped themselves in their bedrolls and went to sleep. When I went down to leave I found the two vaqueros wide awake.

"You sure Antonio doesn't want to go?" I asked.

"He is too crazy to go," the humble one said. "He is a wanted man. He is always fucking people, stealing cars, drinking whiskey. Someday the Texas Rangers will get him and beat his head. Awhile ago, while the Señor Jefe was gone, he was fucking those camels. We saw him but we didn't stop him. Many times he has threatened to kill us if we don't leave him alone while he is fucking things."

All the forty-seven bouncy miles the two vaqueros praised my generosity and told stories of Antonio's filthiness. At four in the morning, with the norther still blowing, I let them out in front of a dry-goods store in Van Horn.

"Señor, you have help us," the humble one said, tearful suddenly, either from gratitude or the cold. "You are good man."

It made me tearful too. They were the only ones who thought so. They thanked me seven times more. The beginnings of dawn were in the east. I felt tired and ragged, but I didn't want to sleep. I didn't know when, if ever, I would want to sleep again.

Being very tired made certain parts of me numb, and in a way I was stronger numb. Austin was still several hundred miles away. In several hundred miles I could get tired enough to be dangerous for a little while. There was undoubtedly a fray ahead. I gunned my Chevy through the grimy, empty streets of Van Horn, thinking of Martha's poor goats. I didn't want to be a helpless goat. Maybe I should get drunk, as well as tired. If I didn't I'd arrive like a goat and my guts would be in a washtub six minutes later.

Not me. I would drive myself ragged and arrive like Zapata—after so many years in the hills the sight of me would strike terror into my foe. I gunned the Chevy up to eighty, five miles faster than it would usually go. It had risen to the occasion. I would call it El Chevy and bury it someday beneath a cairn of rocks, preferably on the banks of the Rio Grande. El Chevy and I both quivered as we streaked out of Van Horn. We were both tired, but there was nothing for it but to rush on toward the battle.

14.

IT WAS EVENING when I reached Austin. The norther petered out at daybreak, and El Chevy and I grew hot. It seemed almost an endless road. In almost no time I lost my spiritual momentum. Being tired was no fun, and I didn't know if I could stay awake long enough to get tired enough to be high. It was cooler moving than it was stopped, so I kept moving and about five o'clock the buildings of Austin were there ahead of me, beyond their little lake.

I went right on to Godwin's house, not giving myself any time to think. It was a soft, spring evening. A great many young couples walked along the sidewalks, holding hands. It was hard to understand why I wasn't among them. Even in my flat state I was conscious enough to envy the couples.

On just such an evening, a little less than a year before, I had come driving into Austin, partly to eat Mexican food but probably mainly in hopes of meeting someone to walk along a sidewalk holding hands with. I found Sally and maybe we took two walks, holding hands. I had been a feckless student—probably as feckless as any student anywhere. Now I was a feckless nothing, author of a book I already didn't care about and soon to be the father of a child I couldn't imagine.

Godwin Lloyd-Jons met me on the front porch of his house, with two cans of beer. I don't know how he could have known I was coming. Maybe he just happened to have two cans of beer in his hands. Godwin looked thinner and older, but he was still the perfect host.

"Welcome back, my boy," he said. "Is that beer cold enough?"

"It's fine. Is Sally here?"

"No," he said quietly. We sat down on the steps and sipped our beer. He had pretty spring flowers in his yard. We looked at each other and said nothing. We weren't engaging. It was a feeling I had had for weeks, ever since Jill left San Francisco. I hadn't engaged with anyone. I was very separate. My words got across to people, but it was all verbal. At a deeper level, some level of needs and responses to needs, I was separate from everybody.

"Has she had the baby?"

"I don't know," he said. "She's not called." He grimaced, as if his gums were aching.

"Is she with her folks?"

"They took her," he said. "I believe they have rented her an apartment. At least I have an address. I doubt she's entirely alone, though. She expressed some interest in a Mr. Leonard. A genius at the calculus, I believe."

"Mathematicians have no more scruples than writers," I said.

"Oh, fuck it," Godwin said. "Fuck it all." His legs seemed thinner and his socks were slipping down his skinny ankles.

"I haven't had any Mexican food in a long time," I said. "Do you want to go and eat?"

Godwin belched. After he belched, he sighed. "I don't suppose we ought to be breaking bread together," he said. "Not technically. You *did* take her from me."

"I don't live very technically," I said. "Anyway, she never gave a damn about either of us."

I felt very discouraged. Godwin had suddenly become a romantic purist. I would love to be a romantic purist but I knew there would never be any way for me to fake it. I stood up to go to Houston.

"Oh, let's do eat," Godwin said. "I was just remembering how much I hated you once."

I remembered my autograph party was the next evening. It was something I knew I mustn't forget. Godwin and I ate at a cafe by the river. It was full dusk, and the moon had risen. I could see the moon out a window and it grew whiter as it rose. The cafe was full of Mexicans and students. The Mexican food was very hot. I scalded my mouth with hot sauce and cooled it with beer. They brought us beer in large half-gallon pitchers. The beer was cold and the pitchers sweated and dripped. My tiredness turned right away into light-headed drunkenness. The drunkenness gradually seeped down from my head to the rest of my body. The only part of me that resisted was my stomach. In my stomach somewhere, amid the beer and enchiladas and chili con queso, was a hair ball of anxiety. No amount of beer was going to dissolve the hair ball, but I drank anyway. It would dissolve the rest of me. I drank beer like a horse drinks water, dipping my nose in it. Godwin was getting drunk too. I went to the jukebox and punched Elvis Presley records. Out the window the white moon hung over the river. When I got drunk enough not to be flat anymore I noticed that Godwin's face was ravaged. His teeth were awful. I could see their stems.

"You don't look happy," I said mildly.

"You notice everything, don't you?" he said, suddenly belligerent. "Bloody little writer. No doubt you pride yourself on your powers of observation. The ever observant eye, the note-taking mind. Godwin looks unhappy. Why is Godwin unhappy? Find out cause. Put in book. Make great name for oneself. And up the fucking ladder you go, from my unhappiness to the bloody Nobel Prize."

"You got me wrong," I said.

He grumbled for an hour about my Nobel Prize, but I don't think he really cared. We went back and sat on his porch and drank brandy. The Austin night swirled around us, warm and familiar. Crickets made noises. Godwin sunk himself in a deep wicker chair and passed his brandy under his nose.

"A fine brandy," he said. "A rare distillation, like my unhappiness. Only a connoisseur could appreciate an unhappiness such as mine. It would take a mind trained to the finer subtleties. That's what they should be giving Nobel Prizes for, unhappiness."

I was silent, determined not to say anything that would make him purple.

"To Godwin Lloyd-Jons," he said, "for high and singular achievement in unhappiness. Years of dedication. Years of sacrifice. Dedication to folly. The sacrifice of all good sense."

"Come on," I said. "Sally's not that tragic."

I should have kept quiet. He flashed at me.

"Shut your fucking mouth," he said. "What do you think Sally has to do with it? That little cunt couldn't make me unhappy. My unhappiness is compounded of a hundred unworthier loves than her."

I shut up again, and sniffed my brandy.

"Tragic is not a word that is called for in this discussion," Godwin said. "Nothing tragic has ever happened to me, or ever will. I was speaking of unhappiness, not tragedy." He was still bristly.

"I don't know anything about anything, Godwin," I said.

"That's quite true," he said, smiling. "You've a touching humility, really. Never confuse unhappiness with tragedy."

"How do I tell them apart?" I asked.

Godwin stared at his brandy. He was really very sad. "I envy the victims of tragedy," he said, in a very flat voice. "They haven't to feel guilty, or to blame themselves for their own waste and the waste of others. War. Starvation. Loved ones dead before their time. The concentration camps. What have I in common with people who have suffered such things? Nothing."

He sniffed a couple of times—tears, not brandy.

"Tragedy is no achievement," he said. "It happens to you or it doesn't. The foolish can be as tragic as the wise. Look at this house," he said suddenly. "Forty thousand dollars. Completely insured. Look at my job. Twenty thousand a year for walking three blocks and shooting off my bloody mouth six hours a week. That too is completely insured. Tenure, retirement. They'll probably even buy my fucking coffin. I eat the best food that's buyable and drink to excess of very excellent liquor. I have students to fuck—absolute scores of them. A good car, clothes, books, cinema, parties—home to England in the summer, if I want to go. I could waste two thirds of what I have and still have more than any man needs. I *do* waste two thirds of what I have—I'm so fucking bored with having it."

We were silent. The crickets cricked. Students walked by, hand in hand.

"No tragedy here," he said. "My circumstances are hopelessly incommensurate with my capacity for suffering. I can't be tragic when I'm made so fucking comfortable twenty-four hours a day. Who can? One summons all ones resources for the fight for unhappiness. I've no war to fight, no prison to endure. My body's known no duress, no tyrant is out to trample my spirit. It's all in personal life, for such as us. Famine, drought, war, injustice—anything you want. We pump it all into our personal life."

I was well into my brandy, and very tired. I lost track of what Godwin was saying even as I tried to fix my mind on it. Sally was in Houston and I had to get up and go on. Just as I was about to raise myself, a motorcycle turned into Godwin's driveway. A young guy in a leather jacket was riding it. A minute later two more motorcycles turned into the street and stopped at the curb. The first rider killed his cycle and got off. The second two killed their cycles and didn't get off.

Godwin stood up. There was a sudden new tension on the porch. The kid who had driven up first came to the steps. He had a distinct swagger. I decided to hate him. In my state such decisions came easy.

"Well, Geoffrey," Godwin said. "I thought you were coming to dinner last night."

"I got busy," Geoffrey said. The fabled Geoffrey, finally. He wasn't apologizing one bit.

"Quite all right," Godwin said. "I wasn't chiding you. I've been a little worried, I guess. This is Danny Deck, Sally's husband."

"Let's go in the house," Geoffrey said. He squinted at me. His hair was very short, but it didn't look like it had been cut that way. It looked like that was as long as it would grow.

Godwin looked pained. He flashed me an apologetic look and followed Geoffrey in. I got up and followed Godwin in. I wanted to look at Geoffrey in the light. When I got in he had sprawled on Godwin's couch, his arms crossed on his chest. He had a bad complexion and a thin stingy mouth, I had expected him to be a kind of young Adonis, but he was only a young runt. He was just a little Central Texas thug, in greasy Levi's. I had seen a million of him. He put one of his dirty boots on Godwin's mahogany coffee table.

"You got any money?" he asked Godwin.

"Certainly. How much do you need?"

Godwin's hand was trembling when he pulled his billfold out. He was getting the screws put on him by a teenage hood, in full view of me. I should have left the room, but I didn't want Geoffrey to think his dirty clothes impressed everybody.

"Three hunnerd," he said, in reply to Godwin.

Godwin was badly startled. "That's quite a lot," he said. He counted his money. "I'm afraid I've only got sixty. You're welcome to that, of course."

"I gotta have three hunnerd," Geoffrey said flatly.

"I could get it in the morning," Godwin said. "Won't that be soon enough?"

"Naw. Wrote a hot check for a hunnert and fifty. Can't afford no hot checks. Besides, we's going to have a party."

"That still doesn't come to three hundred," Godwin said, pained and plaintive. "Why do you need three hundred?"

He asked for it and he got it. A mean little smile cut across Geoffrey's thin mouth. "We's gonna get laid," he said. "Going down to La Grance to 'at whorehouse. Ain't got no money for the whores."

I decided I didn't want to watch, and I went to the kitchen and got myself a beer to chase the brandy with. When I got back to the living room the argument was ending.

"I'll run and try the Seven-Eleven," Godwin said. "Perhaps they'll cash my check. I'm well known there. I buy there often. Do you want to ask your friends in, while you wait?"

He was very pale.

"Naw," Geoffrey said.

"Do excuse me for a few minutes," Godwin said, not meeting my eye. He left.

"Where you from?" I asked, conversationally.

"Odessa," Geoffrey said. He got up and went upstairs. I assumed he was looking for something to steal. That didn't bother me, but he did. I went upstairs too. There was a nice balcony-patio on the second floor. I went out on it and looked at the stars. Nothing was swirling, but I was tired enough to feel strange. It was a nice little drop from the patio to the graveled backyard—maybe ten feet. The stars over Austin were beautiful. It was kind of terrible, Godwin's life. I could imagine what Geoffrey must do to him when they were alone. I usually like people but I didn't like Geoffrey. I didn't like him getting away with the things he got away with. I drained my beer and waited on the patio. I felt strange and a little dangerous. Zapata was about to come out of the mountains. Zapata's people were needing corn. I leaned against the balcony rail and when Geoffrey came out of Godwin's room and swaggered down the hall I hailed him. For better or worse, old Godwin was one of my own. Boy did he need corn.

"Hey, Geoffrey," I said. "Can I talk to you for a minute?"

Geoffrey stopped and stared at me. I didn't ask again. I waited. He stood. Finally he opened the door and came out. I walked toward him, very unsteady. He saw I was deeply drunk. He didn't know what else I was, though—what else I was deeply. He didn't know what I cared about, or what I didn't care about.

"Watcha want?" he asked, frankly wary.

"Oh, nothing," I said. "I just wanted to say hi to you from Sally. She asked me to. She talks about you a lot."

"Yeah?" Geoffrey said. I wandered back to the rail, and he followed.

"She says you're a great fuck," I said.

Even Geoffrey could be pleasantly surprised. His stingy mouth grinned. He leaned both elbows on the railing and looked down at the gravel.

"'At Sally," he said tightly. For him it must have been expansiveness. I was behind him. His tight smugness was just like hers. For a hot second I could have killed him. I grabbed both his legs and heaved. He was looking down, caught for half a moment by some memory of Sally. It must have been a horrible surprise to him, to find his legs suddenly rising above his head. He tried to wiggle and grab but it was too late. I had caught him completely off guard. I took his legs completely over his head and shoved him out with my body. He had an odd expression on his tight little face. He twisted in the air and hit on his side. I watched—I wanted to know if I was a murderer or what. I was glad the yard wasn't grass. Gravel was his desert and gravel was what he got. It didn't kill him. He writhed on the gravel, not even knocked out. I looked at him. I was silent. He couldn't believe it. He made some groans, looking up at me. I suddenly felt sick. I could never be good at violence. Geoffrey looked up at me in pained innocence. He had no idea what he had done to me, or to anyone. I looked at him silently and went downstairs. Godwin was just coming in the living room door, lots of money in his hand.

"Where's Geoffrey?" he asked.

"I just threw him off the patio," I said.

"My God," he said. "Are you serious? His friends are criminals. They'll kill you."

"Not me," I said. "I'm going to Houston. You can ride along, if you like."

"It would do no good," he said. "You're most inconsiderate. Of course he's a horrible little fucker, but that's not the point. They won't blame me, I've got the money. I must calm down. But you have to run. They'll be on you like wolves."

It obviously did behoove me to get moving, but I felt quite calm. I shook Godwin's hand.

"That kid's too tough for you," I said.

Godwin smiled crookedly. "Best of luck," he said. "I shall buy your book."

The two hoods were sitting on their cycles, right behind my car. They were both about twice as big as Geoffrey.

"You guys better scram," I said. "Geoffrey just committed suicide."

"Done what?" one said, opening his fat mouth incredulously.

"Yeah," I said, getting into El Chevy. "He cut his throat with a paring knife. The cops are on the way. Nice to meet you."

I left. In my mirror I saw them looking uneasily at the house, kicking their engines. I turned right and then right again and idled at a stop sign for a minute or two. When I got back to where I could see up Godwin's street I saw my ruse had worked. Both motorcycles were gone.

15.

EL CHEVY and I slipped smoothly out of Austin, I had become a Driver, apparently. The wheel felt good in my hands. I liked the way the road slipped under me, liked to see signs, to pass cars, to ease into little towns. Once I got moving my feelings seemed to come back. When I stopped, feeling seemed to leave me. I wasn't sure I wanted to go to Houston, where I would undoubtedly have to stop and cope with things.

Three hundred miles to the north was Idiot Ridge, where Granny Deck had lived and died. It was just a little bluff, with lots of mesquite trees and rattlesnakes, but in a way it was the place most truly mine. The ridge was the northern boundary of a valley called the Sorrows, which my mean old grandfather had homesteaded with his first wife. The Comanches came one day, while Grandpa was gone, and shot six arrows into the first wife. After that Grandpa lived alone in the Sorrows, drinking whiskey and trapping skunks. One day an ex-soldier came drifting through, with a sixteen-year-old girl he had tricked into coming west with him. Grandpa was womanless and took a fancy to the girl. He and the soldier got drunk and he offered the soldier half his winter's skunk hides for her. The soldier took the skunk hides and left the next day.

The girl was Granny Deck. Somehow she hung on and survived. She never married Grandpa, but she bore him eight kids. She lived out her life on the ridge. The story of her bartering was one of the best things I had ever written.

I had meant to use it as a prologue to my second novel. Oddly enough, Old Man Goodnight had helped chase down the Indians that killed Grandpa's first wife. Then he had gone on to blaze his cattle trails.

I didn't turn north. I would have liked to *be* on the ridge for a little while, but I didn't want to drive there. Neither did I want to write about it. I didn't want to tell the world about the sadness of Granny, as she sat in a flapping tent in the 1880s, listening to Grandpa count out skunk hides. I didn't want to tell it about the sadness of the Indians, as they sat watching the buffalo grunt out its last grunts. I would have liked to sit on Idiot Ridge for a while and watch the April moon float over the Sorrows, but I was too tired to turn. I kept driving, and El Chevy found his way home to Houston.

She had not reformed. She smelled as spunky as ever. I drifted over to Rice. Nobody was walking, and I didn't have a library key. Didn't matter. I was awfully tired. El Chevy and I needed rest. I drove to my apartment and parked at the familiar curb. I got all my blankets and pillows and Jill's green rug. The grass would be very wet in such a mist. I slunk through the darkness, carrying stuff. Jenny's tree was still there. I put several blankets on the ground. I put me on the blankets. I put more blankets on me, which was stupid. It was hot. I made a sort of nest and rested in it. I put the pillows against the tree.

Parts of my body must have slept, but most of my mind didn't. I was too tired. Too many things pressed at me. I dreamed of Sally. I struggled to know what might happen, but I couldn't. I struggled to sleep. I struggled in sleep.

Jenny found me in my nest. I noticed her standing on her back porch. The sun was well up. She was wearing her same bathrobe. Red. She seemed to take the sight of me in stride. She didn't panic. She didn't scream. She looked in her milk box, to see what the milkman had left her. He hadn't left her anything, apparently. Maybe *he* had seen me and panicked and screamed. I imagined myself as looking horrible. I hadn't shaved for a few days. I felt boneless. I didn't want to move. After a while Jenny came walking across the wet grass toward me. She was smiling. I tried to smile back.

"You're full of surprises, aren't you?" she said. "Why didn't you tell me goodbye?"

"When I left it was the middle of the night," I said.

"Sure it was," Jenny said, sitting down in the grass. Her bathrobe was going to get wet again. For some reason she seemed glad to see me. She had a very pleased expression on her face.

"God, you're even sloppier than you used to be," she said. "How's that slut you married?"

"I don't know," I said. "She's here somewhere, about to have a baby."

"Who got her pregnant?"

"Me."

"What a sucker you are," she said. "You must have changed your mind about me, huh? Otherwise you wouldn't be under my tree."

"That's right," I said. "I've given up on monogamy."

"You hungry?" she said. "I could make you some breakfast. You don't look healthy."

My stomach felt like it didn't want food in it. "You don't play hard to get," I said. "How come?"

"I'm so good at being hard to get that nobody gets me," she said simply. "Let's go get in bed before we lose our nerve. I don't want to talk about it."

She had the right idea. If we had talked any longer we would have lost our nerve. We went right up to her bed, leaving my nest under her tree. She had a huge bed with a purple bedspread. We undressed as quickly as we could and got under the covers, scarcely giving each other a glance. Jenny was shivering. I felt embarrassed. Neither of us could think of a thing to say. We were much too shy to play with each other. After about two kisses we tried to make love. It very nearly didn't work. It was like neither of us had ever done it before. We were terribly awkward. The covers felt like they weighed tons. I was almost too weak to cope with such covers and Jenny's body too. Jenny kept her eyes shut. Fortunately I didn't give up, or become impotent. Technically the basics worked. Things got smoother. It wasn't the summit of anything, but after a while we had actually made love. Jenny opened her eyes. Doing it hadn't been any fun, really, but having done it made us both feel immensely better. Somehow we had triumphed over shyness and separateness. We could never be quite as separate again—at least that was how I felt. I couldn't understand why Jenny was so inexperienced. It was like she had never been touched. But she was Jenny Salomea, the maneater. I asked her about it.

"You're supposed to be very tough," I said.

"I am tough," she said. "That's why I never sleep with anybody. I'm so tough men are afraid to try me. It just makes me worse. If I can scare them I don't want to do it with them anyway. You were my only hope. I cried myself blind when you left. You're too foolish to be scared of me. You were the only one around foolish enough to try and care about me."

Since we had done it I thought we might be comfortable enough to look at each other. I kicked the covers back, but Jenny wasn't that comfortable. She shut her eyes. I covered us up again. She didn't look tough at all.

"I've been shy all my life," she said.

I had almost forgotten how much I liked to be in bed with women. I wasn't shy. I felt happy and kind of horny. We kissed for a long time. Jenny hadn't been kissed much and was sort of delicate about it. We twisted around and got more and more comfortable. The bedroom window was open and we could smell the nice hot Houston morning. I could see the squirrels in the tree. Finding out how inexperienced Jenny was made me admire her terribly. It must have taken great nerve, that time she came to see me. She didn't even know how to kiss. I was determined she should get some happiness. I was feeling very refreshed. I wanted to make love for several hours. I couldn't think of anything nicer than whiling away the morning getting Jenny more comfortable with sex. The fact that I wanted to make love again really took her by surprise.

"Are you sure?" she said. "Sammy usually waits eight or nine months."

I had gotten completely unembarrassed and was a lot smoother about things. Jenny enjoyed herself a little. She was a long way from knowing how to really enjoy herself, but she wasn't hopeless. She just hadn't had any practice. I was slow and easy. Once in a while I looked out at the squirrels, while I was being slow and easy.

Suddenly an incredible thing happened. Something made me look around just in time to see it. Jenny had her eyes shut and sensed nothing, but I sensed that another person was there. I looked over my shoulder and there was Sammy Salomea. Unfortunately I was just in the process of letting myself come. I couldn't stop. Sammy was a short man. He wore a neat blue suit and his red tie had a large knot. I only saw him with part of me. Most of me was with Jenny. Sammy had a large bucket in his hands. I think it was a laundry bucket. It was so large he had to struggle along with it. He wasn't a big man. I supposed he must be carrying a vat of acid or something, to destroy the bodies with. Before I really had time to get scared I got doused. It was too bad Jenny wasn't coming too. It would have been an unbeatable sexual experience. The contents of the bucket were warm soapy water. Half water, half soap suds. Sammy made a perfect heave. In an instant we were both absolutely drenched. I wouldn't have thought he could get so much warm soapy water in a bathtub, much less a bucket. I was nonplussed. It was considerate of him to warm the water, I must say. Cold soapy water would have been awful. As it was I was able to enjoy the last second or two of my orgasm. There was no reason not to. No man who would think to warm the water could be going to kill us. Besides, I couldn't help enjoying it. A flood of warm soapy water is kind of nice. Only the circumstances were bizarre.

It was a great shock to Jenny, of course. Propriety required that I pull out but I didn't. I had just come and I couldn't see what good pulling out would do, anyway. We were certainly caught. I think for an instant Jenny thought I had burst. I hadn't. I was snugly buried in her, and I stayed that way. She looked at me through the water and the soapsuds, deeply puzzled. Then she noticed Sammy. Immediately they began a domestic scene.

"Oh, Sammy, you horse's ass," she said. "Why did you do that? Look at my bedspread. Do you know what that bedspread costs to clean?"

"Listen, Jenny," Sammy said, "what you two are doing is not very hygienic. I saw you the first time you did it. If you had showered, that would have been that. But you didn't even remember to shower!" He was very indignant.

"Oh, shut up!" Jenny said, wiping soapsuds out of her eyes.

"Honestly," Sammy said. "He has several days' growth of beard. Why didn't you insist that he shave? Where are your principles?"

"I was getting fucked, Sammy," Jenny said. "Why are you standing there talking about principles? This is private."

"I've done what I can for you," Sammy said. "I have to rush. I see you forgot to buy dental floss again."

He picked up the empty bucket and left. Jenny and I, soaked and soapy, lay exactly as we were, recovering from whatever it was we had been through.

"Poor guy," Jenny said. "He's flipped out several times, and I can't find him a nut house he likes. It's put a lot of new pressure on me."

Being soapy was kind of sexy, but it didn't do us any good. My penis went into retreat. We got towels and went out on Jenny's sundeck to dry off. I was in a new life again. Jenny had really lovely legs. I remembered them from our badminton games.

"Where are you going to live?" she asked.

"I don't know."

"Live here if you want to," she said. "We have lots of rooms. Sammy won't mind, as long as you keep clean. You'll have to shave, is all."

Her face seemed young—her body too. She was just unused. She had nicely rounded shoulders.

"You have to help me get to be normal," she said, smiling at me.

"Okay," I said. "Maybe I'll just get a room somewhere close. It would be bad for your reputation if I lived here."

"Okay," she said. She fed me a good breakfast. We sat on her woodblock and necked and ate and necked. Then we went out in her yard and I gathered up my nest.

"Seeing you under that tree this morning was the happiest moment of my life," she said.

I almost wished she hadn't said it. It was probably true. My responsibilities were getting constantly more complex. I told Jenny again that I had to go. She let me go, but her eyes were shining and her face was very alive. She skipped back to her house.

I got in El Chevy, feeling odd. I didn't know what life was coming to. Suddenly I felt I had to call Emma. I called her from the nearest drugstore.

"I knew you were back," she said, when she heard my voice. "When you coming by?"

"I don't know," I said. "How are you?"

"Why don't you know?" Emma said. "What's wrong with you? I'm dying to see you."

"I may not be the same," I said. "I may have changed forever."

"That's just bullshit," Emma said. "You quit saying that. How could you ever change?"

"I've had a lot of problems," I said.

"You shouldn't have married her," she said. "It could have ruined your whole life. Why don't you come by? Flap's gone fishing with his dad. They won't be back until Sunday."

"I might come by before my party. I have to find out where Sally is, first."

"Why don't you want to come and see me?" Emma said. Her tone was odd.

"I do," I said.

"No you don't. If you wanted to you would have come already. I've been expecting you for days."

I sighed. There was no use trying to fool her. All I knew about it myself was that I was saving her for emergencies.

"I don't know why I don't want to," I said. "It isn't because I don't want to."

It seemed to reassure her. "I know you want to," she said. "Why don't you then?"

"I have to be in order first," I said. "I can't even explain. Do you want to come to my party with me?"

"No," she said.

"Why not?" I was surprised.

"Flap would get jealous."

It had never occurred to me that Flap could get jealous of me.

"Come on," I said. "You don't know what you're talking about."

"Yes I do," she said, in a small voice. "I can't come with you. That's all."

It made me feel even odder. I suddenly wanted to see Emma. Maybe she was in trouble. She didn't sound so bouncy.

"Can I come tonight then? After my party."

"Yes," she said. "You don't have to, if you don't want to."

"I want to."

"Good luck with Sally," she said. "I hated you for marrying her."

"The universe in general disapproves of me," I said. "For that, and many other things." I was a little bitter. Why hadn't anyone spoken up sooner?

"I don't disapprove of you," Emma said. "I didn't say that. I'll cook you something when you come. You haven't really changed," she added, in a more satisfied voice. "If I'm asleep when you come, bang on the door."

I hung up and went out into the hot April afternoon. I was sort of up against it. I could fiddle around looking for a room to live in, or I could go confront Sally. I didn't want to do either one, but I was getting tired again and I didn't know how much longer I'd have my wits about me. I got back to El Chevy and went to the address Godwin had given me.

Sally was there. As usual, she had been napping. As usual, she hated being awakened. She was wearing a loose, sleeveless dress. I had never seen anything like her stomach. I thought it was large when I had shoved her in the bathtub, but it was nothing then to what it had become. Her stomach amazed me. Sally leaned against the doorjamb, trying to stop yawning long enough to frown. Her hair was tangled and her face a little puffy from sleep. Her stomach almost split her loose dress, it was so big.

"You can't talk to me," she said. "You must be out of your head. You could be put in jail for being here."

"I'm not going to hurt you," I said. "I came home because you were having the baby."

"I'm having it, all right," she said. "I had pains this morning. It's none of your business, though."

"It's my child too," I said. "I came to see if I could help."

"It's not yours," she said. "It's mine."

For some reason, seeing her stomach changed things. I wouldn't accept the words she was saying. The stomach was not Sally. It had a roundness that wasn't Sally. It lived of its own, attached to her. It shook a little, when she moved.

"You better fuck off," Sally said. "Daddy's coming. I'm going to the hospital. You'll never see my baby."

"It's just as much mine," I said.

"No," she said. "It's in me."

"Who put it there?"

Sally shrugged. "I fucked a lot of guys," she said. "You're not important."

"Sally," I said. "I was in Austin yesterday. I think I broke Geoffrey's neck. I threw him off a roof."

"Good," she said. "Then maybe they'll put you in jail, where you belong. I think you're a sex maniac anyway."

"You're utterly illogical," I said.

"I don't care," she said. "I'll tell them you're a sex maniac. I'll really make them put you in jail. You're not going to see my baby. You couldn't be a good father."

"I came home to try," I said.

I wanted to try, too. The baby would soon be alive, like Jenny was alive, like Emma, like Jill. I hadn't realized that. I had only thought of it as a picture of an embryo, like I had seen in books. Seeing Sally's stomach changed things.

"You married me before I knew what I was doing," Sally said. "You ought to have to go to jail."

"Shut up," I said. "I found you living with one queer and sleeping with another. You did screw Geoffrey, didn't you?"

"Why not?" she said. "He's a lot cooler than Godwin."

"I hope I broke his neck," I said. I meant it.

"You tried to murder me, too," Sally said. "You ought to go to prison for life. I don't want this baby to know he has a criminal for a father. He's going to have a respectable life."

I was dealing with a mad person, and I was just making the future more impossible than it already was. I decided to back off.

"Okay," I said. "I'm not going to bother you. I didn't come to fight. You have the baby, but I'll keep in touch. You might need money."

"I can marry Rick Leonard," she said. "He's got ten times as much money as you'll ever have. He's not sloppy and he wears good clothes. If my father saw how long it's been since you had a haircut he'd really beat you up. You're a disgrace to our whole family. None of us ever want to see you again."

"None of us ever did, except you," I said.

"They've heard about you, though," Sally said. "They know how awful you are. Your book's even supposed to be dirty."

"Why'd you pick me to get you pregnant?" I asked.

"I didn't," she said. "That was an accident. I'm not even sure it was you."

"It was me," I said. "Nobody else you know could have made anything live in you. I happened to be able to love you, even if you were a bitch."

"Listen, are you calling me a bitch?" she said. "I'm gonna call the cops and have them get you right now."

We were locked in combat. I was tired of being threatened with cops. I was tired of being threatened, period. I felt strange. For all I knew I was coming apart. Sally's look wasn't blank. It was hot and insolent. I hated her so I thought my temples would burst. She hated me too. Her armpits were hairy. We stood a foot apart, only her belly between us. Suddenly she kicked at me and tried to slap me. I caught her wrist and held it.

"Get your hands off me, you fucking maniac," she said. "Can't you see I'm pregnant?" She wrenched free and stepped back inside. "You maniac," she said again, and slammed the door.

I drove away. She probably would call the cops. I didn't want to go to jail. I went to Hermann Park and parked under some trees and calmed down. It was hot and sultry and I dozed. When I woke, strings of traffic were passing. I felt tireder when I woke up than I had ever felt. I could no longer believe in sleep. It didn't work for me anymore. It was like struggling with my eyes shut. If I had to struggle I would rather struggle with my eyes open.

My party was in two hours and I looked terrible. I was totally scruffy and had no place to clean up. It would be my first evening as an author. Up to then I had only been a writer, and I didn't know if I could make the change.

Rice was nearby so I drove over and cleaned up in the second-floor bathroom of the library. I tried to wash my hair, but I couldn't get my head in the lavatory. All I did was get my hair thoroughly wet and soapy. Getting the soap off was very difficult. I put on my suit and to my dismay the zipper fell off. It simply came off in my hand. My crotch was unclosable. It upset me badly. How could I go to an autograph party with an unclosable crotch? My suit was in bad shape anyway. It had fallen down on the floorboard of the car at some point and had gotten terribly wrinkled. I didn't have the poise to be an author, I didn't think.

As I was going out of the library, my old clothes held in front of my crotch, I met Dame Juliana. Her bosom quivered with indignation at the mere sight of me. It had been in almost constant motion for years.

"Aren't you ever going to mature?" she said. "You look worse than ever. We ordered your book."

"Thank you," I said. I always felt humble in her presence.

"Are you going back to school?" she asked.

"I don't think so."

She snorted and bustled off. It occurred to me then that I should have lied to her. Maybe she would have given me my key back. I could have lived a secret existence in the library. I could live on the fifth floor, amid the religion stacks. No one ever came there. I could sneak out at night and slink over to South Main and buy cheeseburgers. I had thirty-four thousand dollars in the bank in San Francisco. If I lived in the library it would probably last me my entire life. Probably now and then I could waylay a coed. It wouldn't be a bad life. I could read the church fathers, or anything else I wanted to read.

But I hadn't lied, and my crotch was unclosable. I went to a drugstore and got some safety pins. They weren't very long, but they were the best I could do. I pinned myself up. I didn't do a very smooth job, but I was too tired to be patient and effective.

In some respects, life hardly seemed worth living. My hair was unruly, the tie I had meant to wear had fallen out of the car at some point, and my crotch was like a pincushion. Outside, it was coming a thunderstorm. If Bruce had been there to see the spectacle I was about to make he would have resigned his editorship in disgust. I was probably a disgrace to Random House.

I drove through the rain to the bookstore where the party was to be. Perhaps the police were looking for me. They might raid my party, in which case Random House would never forgive me. Lightning was flashing and the rain fell in sheets. It was almost as bad as the flash flood. Perhaps there would be a drowning family for me to rescue. My ability to imagine absurd catastrophes was getting sharper.

Unfortunately the parking lot in front of the bookshop was low. It was raining furies. It was hot, too. Being in El Chevy was like being in a steam bath. My windows were fogged. I was sweating heavily. Most Houston parking lots are altogether too low. An engineer with sense enough to build higher parking lots could make a fortune in Houston. This one had no drains. I had a choice of staying in the car and steaming or else stepping out into a foot of water.

My sense of obligation to Bruce helped me decide. If I had a public, it was waiting. There didn't seem to be many cars in the parking lot, but that wasn't decisive. Perhaps my public had come on chartered buses. I stepped out into a foot of water. If I looked really soppy and awful it might make them love me more. They would think me an inspired madman, like Dylan Thomas.

The bookshop was in the River Oaks shopping center. Hordes of gorgeously attired rich women might be there. I knew the owner of the shop well. Once I had clerked for him. He kept a statue of Petrarch's Laura in the window. That's how I had gotten the job. When I walked in and asked for a job the owner, Mr. Stay, took me over to the window and pointed to the statue.

"Tell me who that is and the job's yours," he said. Mr. Stay was a vigorous elderly drunk, much like Mr. Fitzherbert only more literate.

"But you can't tell me, can you?" he added sternly.

"Sure I can," I said. "It's Petrarch's Laura." It was really just a shrewd guess. Mr. Stay wrote sonnets on the side. He had had a volume of sonnets privately published in El Paso, not long after World War II.

When I slopped in the door Mr. Stay was waiting. He had on a black suit. "Danny, Danny," he said, grasping my hand warmly. "By God, you've come back. Why didn't you get a haircut?"

"No time," I said, panting.

I saw a table with a big pile of my books on it. There was another table with a big champagne bucket on it. There were four bottles of champagne in the bucket. A blue-eyed teenager in a sports coat stood by, ready to uncork the champagne and serve it to the crowd. But there wasn't any crowd. The three of us were the only people in the shop.

"I presume the crowd has been deterred by the present storm," Mr. Stay said gravely.

The present storm passed, almost as he said it. The rain ceased. As usual, it had rained just long enough to get me wet.

"Well, son, I'm proud this day has come," Mr. Stay said. He stood poised by the cash register.

"Me too," I said, insincerely.

For the next forty-five minutes not one soul entered the shop. None of us knew what to do. Mr. Stay was not a master of small talk. Neither was I. The blue-eyed teenager never showed his tongue, if he had one. We all stood silently, waiting for someone to come in and buy a book for me to autograph. The teenager twitched at the sleeves of his sports coat. Occasionally people walked by the front window, and hope sprang up in our breasts, but none of the people came in.

"Some days things go a little slow," Mr. Stay said, finally.

We stood. I was embarrassed for Mr. Stay, and, somewhat more remotely, for Random House, but inwardly I didn't feel too bad. Being an author was only a little boring, a little silly, and mildly awkward.

At the end of forty-five minutes we were all startled to see a little fat woman enter the store. I think we had resigned ourselves to standing eternally as we were, positioned near my pile of books. It was a shock to see that the arrangement wasn't eternal. The little fat woman wore a raincoat and gloves and bustled right over to me. Even so she wasn't as quick as Mr. Stay.

"Break out the champagne, Chester," he said.

Chester sprang at the champagne.

"Oh, I'm so glad to meet you, Danny," the little woman said. "I'm Mrs. Ebbins. Dorsey's mother. Dorsey's talked about you for years. We're all just real proud of your success."

Luckily I remembered Dorsey Ebbins. For a moment I was afraid the little woman had strayed into the wrong autograph party. Dorsey had been a classmate of mine when I was a freshman. I sat next to him in English class. Dorsey was very sensitive, and the rough and tumble of college life was too much for him. He dropped out of school after six months. It was lucky he hadn't dropped out of my mind. I asked about him.

"Oh, Dorsey's just doing real well," Mrs. Ebbins said. "We're all just real hopeful now. He lets us take him on walks every day or two. He'll even go around the block if somebody goes with him. You know for years Dorsey just stayed real shut in. But he always remembered you. He said you were kind to him. I'd just be so happy if you'd autograph one of your books for Dorsey. I know it'd just give him a real thrill."

The only book I had ever autographed was the copy I had given Wu. When I sat down in front of the three neat clean piles of new books to autograph one for Dorsey I almost broke up. His little fat mother stood there in front of me looking so thrilled I couldn't bear it. I almost broke out crying. My eyes were hot. I didn't know what to do. I *had* been kind to Dorsey. I liked him. We used to play tennis, sometimes. He hadn't been much crazier than me—he just happened to have a mother to retreat to. There she was, looking at me as if my success was wonderful, as if it made up for Dorsey sitting in his room for four years, as if I could do something important just because I had twenty-five or so nice fresh clean books in front of me full of my words. Why did Mrs. Ebbins have to be the one person to come to my autograph party? It broke me up, though I concealed it. It was obvious that she would take me home and be my mother and love me like she loved Dorsey, if I would let her. She was waiting like a cheerful little bird for me to write something in the book. I had no idea what to write. The blue-eyed teenager was holding two glasses of champagne, ready to give them to us as soon as I inscribed the book. Pressure was on. Finally I just wrote: "To my old friend Dorsey Ebbins, with all good wishes. Excelsior. Danny Deck."

"Tell Dorsey I'd love to play tennis sometime," I said to Mrs. Ebbins. I said it with the last of me. I was plummeting.

"I'll tell him, he'll just be thrilled," Mrs. Ebbins said. "It'll be a little while before he's up to much exercise, but we're hoping to have him back in circulation just as soon as we can. He still talks about finishing his degree. I wish you just a wonderful success. We're all just as proud of you as we can be."

She wrapped my book in her raincoat and hurried out, little and fat. I quaffed champagne. I had never wanted to be drunk worse. I think in five minutes I was drunk. The blue-eyed teenager watched appalled. Mr. Stay was as bad as me. It was long past the time when he was usually drunk. We went through the four bottles of champagne in less than an hour. The pile of books wavered in front of me. Two other people came in, but neither of them bought my book. One bought a cookbook and the other just wandered vaguely through the store and then walked out.

I asked Mr. Stay if he still wrote sonnets. I don't remember what he said. I got very vague. I sat behind my pile of books, drinking. I began to hate the pile. I wanted to carry it out and dump it in the first puddle that was big enough to hold twenty-five books. I was very glad no one else came in to get an autographed book. There was no telling what I might have written. The party waned, Mr. Stay and I dull. The champagne was gone. The phone rang. A lady asked Mr. Stay how many copies of my book we had. He said fifty. She said I was to sign them and he was to send them to the first fifty people in the Houston phone book. He didn't believe it. I followed the conversation vaguely, through my drunkenness. It was a beautiful bookshop, with excellent books in it. Mr. Stay had very good taste. Part of him was an art-for-art's-sake poet and the rest of him was an old-time self-educated bread-for-the-masses-IWW type Communist. He kept good books on his shelves and no one bought them. Dimly I realized that some lady had just bought fifty copies of my book over the phone. When it dawned on me what was happening I knew who it was. It was the only rich lady I knew who liked me. I got up and took the phone. Mr. Stay was glad to let me have it—the whole experience had bewildered him.

"Hi," I said. "You didn't have to do that."

"You're drunk," Jenny said. "I better come and get you. If I don't you'll marry some new slut and get put in jail for bigamy."

"I'm stone sober," I said. "Can you afford that kind of gesture?"

"Of course I can," she said. "Get on over here."

"I have to go to the hospital first," I said. "Then I have to see a friend. Don't wait up. Just leave a door unlocked, so I can get in. I'll be there eventually."

"Promise me you won't marry anyone," she said. "I know how dumb you are. Just don't marry anyone at all."

"I promise," I said.

Mr. Stay and I shook hands very emotionally. It was probably the strangest autograph party he had ever hosted. He had bought a copy of my book too. I wrote the same thing in it I had written in Dorsey's. My ability to think up inscriptions was very weak. We shook hands five or six times. He was an emotional old Communist sonneteer.

"You write them, son. I'll sell them," he said. "It's all I'm fit for. You need a job, just come to me. I'd be proud to have a real writer working for me."

I sloshed away. I hated to be called a real writer, especially by nice old failed writers who had never got to think of themselves as real writers at all.

Only the year before I had wanted nothing more in life than to be a real writer. It had seemed worth any effort. Something had happened. Mr. Stay couldn't get his sonnets published. The high point of his career was getting one published in the *New Republic*, in the thirties. For all I knew Mr. Stay was as good as Petrarch. But I knew that Mr. Stay would always feel that he had missed it, because he wasn't a real writer. Almost everybody seemed to miss it. I probably *was* a real writer. If I kept at it I could probably write as good as anybody but the geniuses. I could be better than average. I could probably even be minor. With great luck I might, by accident mostly, write something fine, sometime in my life, particularly if I kept myself in shape by writing books that were decently good for twenty years or so. But probably I'd miss it too. I felt like I was already missing it. My life was no life. It was sort of a long confused drive. I would have given all my talent to Mr. Stay in a second, if it would make him happy. Or to Dorsey Ebbins. I drove straight to the Methodist Hospital, feeling a great desire to give my talent to someone who would be made happy by it.

Mr. and Mrs. Bynum were there. Sally's parents. It was one of the many times when it would have been better for me not to be drunk.

Unfortunately I had no choice. We spotted one another in the lobby of the Methodist Hospital, immediately after I walked in. I guess they had seen the picture of me on my book. I knew them because they were frightening. They were both tall, taller than Sally. Their faces blotched with anger the minute they saw me and they both got up from their seats and came toward me. Their looks were every bit as hot and insolent as Sally's had been that afternoon. She had her mother's cheekbones. Her father had hands like small hams. When I held out my hand to shake with them Mrs. Bynum glared down at me.

"We won't shake your filthy hand," she said. "You're hog drunk, for everybody to see."

"Boy, you been in a whorehouse all afternoon or where you been?" Mr. Bynum asked. He leaned over me threateningly.

"Is Sally here?" I asked. I was needing all my strength just to face them. I had no immediate strength available with which to argue.

"She's named Lorena, after my momma," Mr. Bynum said. "We'll see the last name's changed. Two hours old, precious little baby girl. That's all you'll ever need to know about her. You just get back to your whores. Me and Mrs. Bynum have had a gutful of you."

"She was right about him, Lloyd," Mrs. Bynum said. "Look at that hair."

"I see it," Mr. Bynum said. "He don't even have a decent suit of clothes. He's just a goddamn young whoremonger."

I was trying to dig in, but the hospital floor was awfully slick. They were ugly people. They couldn't have my daughter. They could have Sally, but not my daughter. I had to fight my way up. I couldn't see one good quality in their ugly, angry faces. Mrs. Bynum looked like the kind of woman who would tear off a dead foe's genitals after a battle. Mr. Bynum kept leaning over me. Their knuckles were white with the need to hit.

"I want to see my child," I said.

"Don't call it yours, you little sonofabitch," Mrs. Bynum said, in a guttural voice. "My daughter had it. You ruined her name. You and your goddamn book talk. My daddy was alive he'd have seen you dead by now."

It was blood fury in her face. Mr. Bynum was the same.

"I married her decently," I said.

"We know all about you," Mr. Bynum said. "We know about your Hollywood whore. Tried to drown our daughter. I oughta lay you out, right here in this hospital."

I wasn't going to be able to hold against them. Not then. They had been waiting, building up fury, and I had stumbled in, unprepared. I was slipping on the floor. I would have to retreat, back away, take a fresh run at them some other day.

I quit talking. I turned and left. They followed me, arguing about whether or not to have me arrested.

"Get the police, Lloyd," Mrs. Bynum said. "They're apt to never find him if we let him get away now. His filthy friends will hide him out."

"Naw. It'd get in the papers if I do," Mr. Bynum said. They were three steps behind me on the hospital sidewalk, too furious to let me out of their sight. It was drizzling rain.

"He ever comes near that little child I'll fix him myself," he said. He had a thick, slurred East Texas voice, made raw and ugly with anger. Finally his voice burned me too deeply. I didn't want to fight, really. I just didn't want to hear either of their voices again. I was pretty tired. I stopped and faced them.

"If you two awful people don't stop following me I'll have *you* arrested," I said. I knew it was a vain boast, but it shut them up for five seconds.

"What's that?" Mr. Bynum said.

"I don't want you following me," I said. "I don't like you. No wonder Sally's so cheap. I feel sorry for her. Maybe that's why I married her. You two shouldn't be allowed to raise chickens, much less children."

Mr. Bynum couldn't believe his ears, but Mrs. Bynum believed hers. Her face contorted with anger. It had been ugly enough before it contorted. "Hit him, Lloyd!" she said. "Hit the little sonofabitch."

He certainly hit me. I saw his arm move, but I didn't feel anything. It knocked me into the wet grass. I didn't feel my left ear until it really began to hurt, about an hour later. As soon as I realized I was down I sat up, holding my ringing head. The Bynums stood over me. For a moment things were almost comic.

"You're calling *our* daughter cheap?" Mrs. Bynum said. "You! The way you look?"

"Yes ma'am," I said. "She's pretty cheap. You ought to meet some of her acquaintances."

Mr. Bynum was dying to hit me again. He was clenching and unclenching his fists, waiting for me to get up. Mrs. Bynum waited too.

"Yank him up from there, Lloyd," she said. "He's too big a coward to stand up and fight."

I was ready to fight them, all right. The comedy of it all had worn off. But then it occurred to me I shouldn't. Probably I would have to make peace with them sooner or later, if I was ever to see the baby that had just been born. I looked at the vast hospital and tried to imagine the tiny creature in it. She was a girl. She might need me. I had better try discretion, for the sake of whatever future there was. Without speaking I scooted back on the grass and got to my feet. I tried to walk away in the squishy grass but Mr. Bynum was immediately after me and hit me again, this time from behind, on the neck. It wasn't a square hit, but it put me off my feet again. I was very wet and muddy. I sat up again. Mrs. Bynum had followed us onto the wet grass, hoping to see more of the massacre. I looked at Mr. Bynum and saw it was no use. He still had his fists clenched. He would probably knock me down three or four more times before I could get to my car.

"Ruined our daughter for life," Mr. Bynum said heavily. Maybe he really believed it. If he hadn't been so awful I might have felt sorry for him. But I couldn't feel sorry for him.

"Cunt and prick and fuck and shit," I said, looking at Mrs. Bynum.

It startled her. "What's that?" Mr. Bynum said. He leaned over me, fists doubled up.

"Vagina, fallopian tube, penis, scrotum," I said.

It took them both aback. I meant for it to.

"That ain't what you said," Mr. Bynum said. But I had him slightly off guard.

"No sir," I said. "What I said to Mrs. Bynum was cunt and prick and fuck and shit." I pronounced each word very distinctly. The

Bynums were silent. The encounter had taken a bewildering turn. I gave them no time to regroup.

"I'm telling you all my favorite words," I said. "Anus, penis, semen, nipple, clitoris, pubic hair. I can say them louder," I said. "I can say them faster. Fuck screw ball. Fuck—screw—ball. Fuck screw ball fuck screw ball."

I got to my knees. I spoke louder. "Lick suck lick suck lick suck," I said. The Bynums were staring. My hair was wild, I was wet and muddy, I was rising from the grass chanting terrible words. I rose, I chanted.

"Titillate, masturbate, cunnilingus," I said. "Cunt prick fuck shit."

I got a little louder as I walked toward Mrs. Bynum. "Cunt vagina cunt vagina cunt vagina cunt," I said. I turned toward Mr. Bynum. "Nipple nipple nipple nipple," I said. I was chanting. I was getting louder. They looked scared. I had them backing up.

"You maniac!" Mrs. Bynum said. Her voice wasn't steady anymore. "I want to go in, Lloyd."

They turned and left, but I didn't stop. I followed them up the sidewalk, weaving from side to side and chanting "Cunt vagina cunt vagina cunt vagina cunt" as if it were a football cheer. Mr. Bynum took Mrs. Bynum's arm and hurried her on. They stopped at the hospital door and looked back at me with expressions of complete confusion on their faces. We looked at one another. I stopped the obscenities. "Sexual intercourse," I said quietly. They knew my weapons. They merely stared. Finally they went inside.

It had worked. For maybe a minute it had been fun. For maybe a minute I felt some little triumph in it. I enjoyed the expressions on their faces. They could not believe what they were hearing. But my sense of triumph vanished quickly. By the time I got back to El Chevy the triumph was gone, and I was desperately depressed. It had been a cheap victory, and I was aware of it. I should have chosen the expensive victory, which would have been to let Mr. Bynum knock me down three or four times. As it was I had really beaten myself. I looked at the windows of the big hospital and felt more hopeless than I had ever felt. I could barely find the hope to start the car. Probably now they could convince anybody that I was a maniac. I couldn't imagine the baby as my daughter. I didn't know what father and

[184]

daughter meant, for us. But I could imagine her as a tiny creature and I knew I had probably just failed her in some major way. How many years would it take me to fight my way to her now? It might not even be possible, or good for her even if it was possible. I had no idea. I sat for a moment, wondering if there was any way I could sneak in past the Bynums and get a look at her. If I could see her I might have more of an idea what to do. But I didn't try. I knew I was too tired. I had no strength left for subterfuge. Hope was draining out of me too fast. I had to get a tourniquet somewhere. I knew I had to. I couldn't afford to lose too much more hope.

A kind of emergency had come, after all. My head rang and the rest of me felt numb. I drove to Emma's and managed to walk up her driveway. She was there. She opened the door. She didn't rush out and hug me, as she might have in former days. I was not returning in triumph. I was limping home.

Emma was still round. Her face was a little thinner, but the rest of her was still chubby. I was really at a loss for introductory words, and I don't think Emma was prepared for me to look the way I looked.

"Hi," I said. "I made it back."

"Good," she said simply. "You better come in and eat."

16.

I WENT IN. The moments of the evening were spaced very far apart. Emma and I couldn't talk. My life had gotten that awry. Even Emma, I couldn't talk to. She stayed over by the stove cooking for what seemed like a long time. I sat in a daze, and ate in a daze, when she brought me the steak. It embarrassed me, that I couldn't talk. It meant I was totally cut apart from people. Emma didn't try very hard to talk to me. She looked at me with big eyes. At some point she said she couldn't stand me in suits. My suit was awful anyway. It was wet and muddy and the crotch was badly pinned. I went to the car and got some Levi's and changed into them. Then I sat on a couch in the living room and Emma bathed my ear. I think I told her it was hurting. She bathed it in warm water. She put a towel on my shoulder so my T-shirt wouldn't get wet. I just sat on the couch. A lot of hope had drained away. I was not thinking ahead at all. Emma's house was kind of messy, lots of newspapers and books strewn around. We were not talking at all. I was trying to think where to go when Emma finished bathing my ear.

But Emma put herself in front of me. It was a moment. Her round serious face was in front of me. She was across my lap. I held her. Then her face disappeared. She was nestled in my arms. Her face was out of sight.

"I was going to stay completely away from you, but I just can't," she said, her voice very meek.

I was a long time doing anything but holding her. We were a long time saying anything. Maybe it was an hour that we sat, hugging.

We were just silent. Finally we looked at each other and I kissed her.

"I think about you a lot, Danny," Emma said. Another moment. We were on her bed undressing. Our making love was full of catches. Not so much physical catches, but some kind of catches. Being together didn't really enable us to escape our lives. We both wanted a lot more than to make love. I don't know what Emma wanted, or even what I wanted. We wallowed in the dark, straining for something more than could be gotten from two bodies. Emma was very fervent—she seemed to feel she had to get me quick or she wouldn't be able to let herself get me at all. A lot of guilt was in the bed. Emma made a strange sound, coming. We didn't talk. We lay all night, now just inside sleep, now just outside it. There was a sense of tiredness, guilt, bodies not used to each other, feeling not really expressed. Houston hummed around us—cars passed, planes flew over our heads, ambulances wailed in the distance. It was hot and quiet. In the first of the light we were awake. We could see each other dimly. We needed to try again. In the murky, drizzling dawn, we tried again. It was not night, not day, not past, not future. A little more delight was possible. "Don't come, don't come," Emma said. Her eyes were squeezed shut, and one of her hands gripped my shoulder. The sound she made was almost scary, part squeal, part sob. We slid back a little ways inside sleep.

When we came awake again it was a bright sunny morning and everything was different. The wallowing and strain of night, sex, guilt, apprehension, need and desire—all those were over. Emma and I were lying in bed, quite friendly. We were resigned, but calm, not downcast. I had betrayed a friend, she had betrayed a husband. Apparently we had wanted to. Undoubtedly we had. We didn't feel like talking about it, or excusing ourselves. We felt like criminals, but like criminals who were resigned, not only to their criminality, but to their sentence. We hadn't heard our sentence yet, whatever it was, but we could accept it. It couldn't make us not like each other. We held hands. For a chubby girl Emma had surprisingly tiny breasts. They were almost all nipple. She was a little embarrassed by them.

"I've always wanted to grow my hair long enough to cover them," she said, pouting a little. "My damn hair won't grow that long."

Her hair didn't even come to her shoulders. I tried pulling it down. "No chance," she said. She pulled mine down. It was almost as long as hers.

We lay in bed for a while, very quiet, seeing each other's bodies for the first time. My ear was very swollen. Then Emma got hungry and we dressed and went to the kitchen. She wore an old blue dress that I remembered—she never seemed to get new dresses. The kitchen was as nice as ever, sunny and cheerful, and Emma made me everything I could think of that I wanted. She had got some sausage. I ate more than I had eaten in days, and drank a quart of milk. When we finished we sat at the table, playing hands. Emma was quiet and reflective.

"Are you having problems?" I asked. We hadn't even mentioned Flap.

"Me?" she said. "No. I don't have problems."

"You looked like you did, last night."

Emma smiled. "You were in no shape to judge anybody's problems, last night," she said. "My God. They're taking your daughter away from you. That's a problem. I don't have anything like that hanging over me. Flap's bored with me and goes off with his dad fishing every weekend and I resent the hell out of that, but that's not a problem. He doesn't like to fish that much—he's just bored. I don't resent him being bored. I just resent him going off with his dad. His dad's just as boring as me. He ought to stay and be bored with me— he married me. But that's no problem, that's just normal. Two people get married and pretty soon one person is bored. It's just ordinary life. It's certainly no reason to feel sorry for yourself."

"Do you feel sorry for yourself?"

"No. I just resent Flap. I'd feel sorry for myself if I had a baby and somebody was trying to take it from me, though. That would kill me."

"I guess babies always get to stay with mothers, don't they?" I said. "I don't know what to try and do about it."

"There's nothing you can do," Emma said. "You couldn't get her and you couldn't raise her if you could get her, and you can't live with Sally. That's three things you can't do. If you could get her Flap and I could raise her for you, but you can't get her. You've just lost your child."

"I don't have any real idea of her," I said. "I don't even know what I'm losing."

Emma looked out the window. Tears came in her eyes. "You will, someday," she said. "I guess you will, if you ever find out anything about what's normal. I've always known personal things were desperate. Personal troubles. I've always known it. Seeing you last night almost destroyed me. I can't even help you. It's going to be hard for me even to be your friend, now."

"I know," I said.

I guess that was the sentence we had been resigned to, in bed, earlier. That was probably what screwing had done. Taken away our chance for long friendship, of the kind we had had. We might love each other and stay on each other's side forever, but we couldn't have the sociable things of our friendship again, at least not for years. And who could imagine years? I couldn't even imagine the day. I could imagine Emma and I trying to be together in Flap's company, and I knew neither of us wanted to. We hadn't been ashamed of it, in the bed in the quiet morning, but that nice hour of our lives was past forever.

"I'm sure going to have to feel guilty for a long time," Emma said, not self-pityingly, just as an observation. A fly lit on the sugar and she waved it away.

"What about Flap?" I asked. I wasn't clear what I was asking, even. I just said it. I hadn't said it to accuse him of anything, but Emma took it that way.

"No, it's not his fault," she said, looking down at her lap. "A man should be able to go fishing with his father without his wife sleeping with his best friend. Flap's very good to me, usually. I've just always been selfish. I've always wanted you. I bet I would have grabbed you last night even if you hadn't looked so terrible."

I didn't want her to get blue. I scooted around to her side of the table and put my arm around her. It helped a little, but the trouble was that we couldn't linger with each other. We had had our night, and day had come. Flap and his father might come back unexpectedly. They might be bored with fishing. Besides, we had done all we could do. A good time together in the morning, breakfast in her kitchen, a nice hour of talk. We weren't going to go back to bed and screw again. We couldn't solve anything by talking. I put my arm around her and she put her hands on my forearms and we sat for thirty minutes, staring across the breakfast dishes, out the kitchen window, at the bright sun on the trees—we said scarcely a word. For a few minutes we were close, and utterly in accord. We had the same knowledge of everything—if we talked we would have agreed exactly on what was what. We agreed so exactly that we didn't have to talk. We sat together. I rubbed Emma's fat leg. Or rubbed the back of her neck. Her eyes were vacant. She was not thinking. She was just sitting with me. Simply sitting. It was my responsibility to go. When I felt I had to I went and got my awful suit out of the bathroom and wadded it up.

"Going to try and see her?" Emma asked, at the door. She scratched her head.

"Yes," I said. "If I go right now maybe nobody'll be there."

"Call me if they arrest you," she said. "Are you going back to California?"

"Maybe," I said. "Oh. I've got my book in the car. One for you, I mean."

"Good," Emma said.

She came down the driveway with me. I got the book out of El Chevy and stood trying to write something in it. Emma stood near, looking at me oddly. My nose and eyes were hot suddenly—I couldn't think of anything to write and I felt big emotion coming. I wrote "To Emma and Flap with love, Danny," and quickly handed her the book.

"Best I can do," I said.

Emma's round face was changing. We managed an awkward hug. "You ought to throw that suit away," she said. "Please don't marry for a while."

"You mean until I get smarter?"

She had gone to the sidewalk. "Oh, Danny, nobody cares about that," she said, with a crooked smile.

She turned and went up the driveway, a chubby girl. She had always had an awkward walk. Emma only moved gracefully in her kitchen. Otherwise she looked better sitting down. She would never be graceful, or without a large behind, and I would never be smart, or have a normal life. It's no wonder we got on so well.

I drove to Methodist Hospital, to try and see my daughter before I left for wherever I was going. It didn't work at all. A thin tough little East Texas nurse with a mouth like a wire turned me back.

"You can't see that baby," she said. "You've got legal problems. I heard what a fuss you made last night. Your wife's mother nearly had hysterics. I'm calling the police boys right now."

I had been disheartened before I came in and I was much too disheartened to try and fight my way through policemen and up elevators to wherever my daughter was. No one would bring her out of her crib to show her to me anyway, and I would probably get life imprisonment if I broke into the nursery without getting a haircut first.

I tried to imagine her, three stories above me, and it was very hard. I gave up and left and drove to Jenny's house. She was outside, in a pair of shorts and a white blouse, working in her flower beds. She had many flower beds, with great flowers growing in them. She didn't notice me parking and I sat and watched her dig for awhile. Since leaving Emma, my spirits had gone straight down, and they were still dropping. Not only had I screwed up my friendship with the Hortons, but I had knocked myself out of a love affair with Jenny, as well. I couldn't stay in Houston. It was the one thing I knew clearly. The Bynums would just have me arrested, and I was too depressed to go to jail. But even if I didn't get arrested, I couldn't stay. I would just make Emma uncomfortable. We would become one another's problem, instead of one another's friend. We would always be wondering if Flap would find us out—or worse, we would always be wondering if we were going to do it again. I just couldn't stay. It was going to be a big disappointment to Jenny.

I got out and went across the yard. Jenny heard me and turned, standing up.

"Are you mad at me?" I asked. "I didn't mean to be so late."

"No," she said. "I could tell you were too drunk to be dependable. You didn't marry anybody, did you?"

"No."

We went in her kitchen and she made me some iced tea. She was hot from her yard work. I climbed up on the woodblock and squatted on top of it, talking to Jenny while she fixed the tea. I told her about the scene I had had at the hospital. Jenny brought her tea to the woodblock and sat on it with me. She drank iced tea and I kissed her. The tea made her mouth cold. We played delicate little kissing games for a while. Jenny was learning. She was very subtle. She had a kind of tact about it all that was very affecting. I grew hornier and hornier. Horniness had had little to do with what Emma and I had done. It had had something to do with it, but not much. On Jenny's woodblock, lust took over. I would not have thought it could survive so much travel and tiredness and craziness and trouble, but it did. We managed to get nearly undressed, but the woodblock didn't do as much for Jenny as it did for me. It just made her uncomfortable. We ended up on her huge, extremely comfortable living room couch. We crowded into a corner and I worked off a lot of lust, much more than I'd expected I had. Jenny was very surprised. It was largely a new world for her. She wasn't the master of it, but she liked it.

"Boy," she said, when we were resting, cuddled up together in one corner of the couch. We had stopped moving, and the air conditioner was freezing us.

"Boy what?" I said.

"It's strenuous, isn't it?" she said. "I hope I'm not too old for it."

"You're not," I said.

To my dismay and Jenny's irritation, Sammy Salomea walked into the far end of the living room, neatly dressed in seersucker. I couldn't seem to fuck his wife without him showing up. It was indecent of both of us. Jenny and I stayed huddled.

"Will this nastiness never cease?" Sammy asked.

"No, it won't," Jenny said. "Quit looking at us. Go find you a friend."

"Don't forget to shower," Sammy said, and left.

"When you get a place we can do it there and he won't always be interrupting us," Jenny said.

My lust was gone, leaving me with nothing but the sad thing I had to tell her. I didn't want to. She was a generous woman, unhappy in her sex life. I would have liked to spend months on beds and couches with her. She could be having orgasms, pretty soon. It was amazing that she could have stayed so nice, after so many years without them. Anyway, I had to let her down. It made me feel awfully low.

Jenny noticed. "Was something wrong with me?" she asked.

"No," I said. "Stop thinking that way. You're wonderful."

"People are supposed to be happy after sex," she said.

"How often have you been happy after it?" I asked.

Jenny sighed. "You couldn't call Sammy sex," she said. "I'm happy after you."

"I'm happy after you too," I said. "I'm low for other reasons."

"Such as?"

I told her. I told her all about the night and Emma and why I had to leave. She watched my face all the time I was talking. I told it quite straight.

"I guess it's because you're so young," she said quietly.

"What?"

"Oh," she said. "I meant that you could fuck your friend and then come right over the next day and fuck me. Sammy could never do that."

She was silent, her face blank. Then she twisted around and put her face against my chest. I held her tightly. I knew she was crying because I felt her tears on my skin, but she didn't make any sound. She just quivered occasionally. It seemed to me that I had spent a week just saying goodbye to women. I was thankful there were no more people who cared about me.

When Jenny finally looked up she had mastered something. There were tears on her face and pain in her eyes, but the look she gave me was remarkably dignified. "Do you need any money for your trip?" she asked.

"No," I said.

Her look gave me to understand that her problems were not to be discussed. I didn't humiliate her by discussing them. Once again there was no point in lingering. We dressed. "You sure have been nice to me," I said, on my way to the car.

"Don't say nice things to me, right now," she said. "I don't want to hear nice things."

I wanted desperately to think of something to say that might help her, but there was just nothing.

"Thanks, old boy," she said, when I was in the car.

"Thanks yourself," I said. She still had her dignified look. She was crushed, but she wasn't admitting it. She had more guts than Martha, I thought. Out where Martha lived it was easy to be strong, if one survived at all. Where Jenny lived it was easy to be weak. Jenny probably *was* weak. She was probably scared to be alone at night. But she didn't trade on her weakness at all. I was filled with admiration. I wanted to ask her to come and be with me in another city, but I didn't dare. Until I had another city to offer, it would just be false consolation. I couldn't just make her random promises, to ease the moment. The moment didn't get eased. When I left she was standing on her lawn, in the bright noon sun.

17.

WHEN I LEFT Jenny I drove to a drive-in and parked. I ordered a malt, hoping it would distract me. I felt terrible about Jenny. I hadn't hurt Emma. She might feel guilty for a while, she might have some trouble with Flap, but she still had a life to live. She could have kids—she had said she might be pregnant, already. Emma would continue. The night we had spent together would recede and recede and recede, until it didn't loom over her present as it was probably looming over it at the time. What would be visible in five years, or ten? How much of it would her memory just discard? Or mine? What moments would I keep? Sitting with her in the kitchen, hugging. Watching her little female pout as she tried to pull her sloppy blonde hair down over her tiny breasts. There was no knowing what moments Emma might keep, but they wouldn't dislodge her from her life.

But Jenny had no life. I might have dislodged her badly. All she had was a routine—flower beds, drinking, badminton, brassy talk. I had dislodged her into a day and a half of real hope, real touching. Maybe it would give her nerve. Maybe she would find a kind man and sleep with him. On the other hand it might just have cost her her nerve. She had gambled big, and been hurt. The rest of her life would seem just that much emptier. I didn't like being the hurter. I would rather have been on the receiving end.

I didn't want to just drive off, either. I didn't want to go right back to California. While I was drinking the malt I thought of Petey Ximenes. Maybe he would want to take a trip to the border, or somewhere. We had often talked of it. He knew a crazy man he wanted me to meet, a retired actor who ran a filling station in Roma, Texas, the little town where *Viva Zapata* had been filmed. Petey always kept an eye out for crazy people for me to know. He considered me crazy and thought I ought to have friends of my own kind.

I finished my malt and drove deep into North Houston. It was dangerous land. The Mexicans lived there, in little houses. The Negroes lived there, some of them, in horrible squalor. Rednecks lived there, in anger and terror. Anywhere you went, you could get killed. No color of skin was safe, in North Houston. It was all bars and corner groceries, smelly cafes and crummy schools with window-panes out. Kids roamed the streets in search of Coke bottles to turn in. Dogs prowled for scraps. The more violent one's pleasures, the livelier the area could be. Loud jukeboxes blared in the bars. Loud talk rang on street corners. Many knives were carried. At night guns went off, and women were pounced on. The rednecks drank beer, the Negroes drank rotgut and wine, the Mexicans drank beer and tequila. The whole area stayed as drunk as possible.

On Elysian Street, practically the worst street in town, all torn-up pavement, falling-down houses, a freeway overpass cutting off light, an old railroad track with dogs fighting on it, there was a pachuco bar. It was called the Angel. The street to it was so torn up I could hardly force El Chevy down it. Mexican kids huddled in the tall grass by the railroad tracks. A hamburger with onions was frying when I walked into the Angel. I was in luck, for once. My old friend Petey was there, kicking the pinball machine, which had just tilted.

Petey was the same size as ever, about five two, and he still had an unkempt ducktail. He whiled away his mornings with pinball, wait-ing for the fourteen-year-olds to get out of school.

"Hey, man," I said. It was the only greeting that would have been appropriate. Petey had standards in cool.

"Hey, man," he said, giving me a limp handshake. He was glad to see me, I think.

"What's wrong with the pinball machine?" I asked, as an ice-breaker.

"It is full of shit," Petey said simply. "If you got any money buy me some breakfast. I lost all mine in the fucking pinball machine."

We got a booth and Petey dreamily ate two cheeseburgers, hot with grease and mustard and onions. A red-headed waitress sat on a counter stool, swigging from a bottle of Thunderbird wine. Petey seemed a little high, but he was delighted with my suggestion that we go to the border.

"I had this girl," he said. "She was gonna come through, but doesn't matter. She can wait. We might get some ass down there."

"How do you know she was gonna come through?" I asked.

"She's crazy about jellybeans," he said, as if it were elementary.

We drove over to his house, a tiny little shack a few blocks away, where he lived with his mother and six or eight siblings. The only reason we went there was so he could pick up some marijuana he had hidden under a brick in the backyard. His fat mother came out to the car and saw him off, chattering in Spanish a mile a minute. It didn't seem to be a harangue she was delivering, but Petey was a little intimidated by it, anyway. He nodded like a metronome.

"She was jus' telling me some people to see," he said, when we finally got off. "She has many relatives in the Valley. Shit, I can't find those people. I can't even find my brother Roberto and he lives right here in this town. I don't think I can find nobody, in the Valley. They will have to say hello to themselves.

"Anyway, we have to find some ass, right guy?" he said, a little later. "We can always find some ass, in the Valley." At the thought, he smiled his sweet, dreamy smile. He kept smiling it at intervals for the first hundred miles. For April it was really hot. We stopped and got some cold beer and sat the bottles between us in the seat.

Petey wasn't much of a talker. After a beer or two he dozed off. As usual he had a few pills, and he gave me a couple for my tiredness before he went to sleep. I wasn't precisely sure why I had hunted him up for the trip to the border, or even why I was taking a trip to the border. Once I got out of Houston it seemed to me that I hadn't really had to leave. I could have hid out from the cops. There were parts of Houston so obscure that even the cops didn't know they were there—pocket ghettos and old forgotten neighborhoods that had been cut off by the freeways. Such neighborhoods were like giant old folks' homes—the buildings, the smells, and the people all seemed to belong to earlier decades.

I could have hidden in some such neighborhood and seen Jenny and let the Hortons believe I was gone. Jenny and I could have had something. I grew very tired, pills or no pills. I hadn't really slept at Emma's—I had really forgotten when I had slept. I didn't know why I had left, or where I was going, or what to do about my daughter or my wife, or even what to do with Petey, who was smiling and sweating as he slept.

I tried to imagine living in some smelly, obscure part of Houston and just seeing Jenny, and I knew it wouldn't work. I would get lonesome for my part of Houston, for Rice, for the Hortons, for the places I liked to walk. I couldn't live in a town and hide from my best friends. I would just fall in love with Emma and complicate her life in a bad way. It would be impossible not to love her, if I stayed. It would be impossible not to love Jenny, too. My fate seemed to be to meet women it was impossible not to love, but whom it was also impossible to love right. It was impossible not to love Jill, too. At moments her face came into my mind. I would have to call her soon. Perhaps I would leave El Chevy in the Valley and fly to New York. It felt wrong to be driving away from my daughter. It felt irresponsible. But nothing it was in my power to do felt responsible. Other than money, I didn't know what I could put in my daughter's life.

In Kingsville I stopped and had a cheeseburger. I got out and made water for several minutes in a fly-blown John. I had gallons of liquid in me. Petey woke up and looked grumpy. Below us lay the King Ranch, seventy-five uninterrupted miles of it. I didn't particularly want to go through it, and neither did Petey. El Chevy might break down. There was no telling what the overlords of the King Ranch might do to people who looked like us. I decided to skirt it. Petey went back to sleep and I turned toward Falfurrias.

Soon we were in the brush country. The brush was incredibly thick and tangled. Mesquite, chaparral, and prickly pear all joined together. It was new country to me. I had never seen such brush. Apparently animals lived in it, but it was hard to believe. I decided to take a motel when it got night. I was running on my third wind, and my third wind was running out. I knew I would never make it back to California without sleep, if California was where I was going.

As usual, calamity took me off guard. I had given up trying to decide what to do about my life and was just driving dully through the hot brush country, when a patrol car passed me. El Chevy wouldn't run fast enough for a Texas patrol car to bother with, so I paid it no mind. Pretty soon I saw it pulled off to the side of the road, ahead, and I passed it. I still didn't pay it any mind. Suddenly I looked to my left and the patrol car was there, beside me on the highway. Two large men in Stetson hats were in it. They were grinning at me, but not pleasantly. One pointed his finger at the shoulder, indicating that I was to pull over.

I was surprised. I couldn't have been doing much wrong, on a straight highway in a slow car. I pulled over, puzzled. Perhaps El Chevy had revealed itself to the officers as an unsafe car.

The patrol car stopped behind me. I got my billfold out and glanced in the mirror. My first apprehension of calamity came then. One of the officers was in the process of lifting a shotgun out of the back seat of the patrol car. He was casual about it. At that moment I remembered Petey's marijuana and got scared. I had no time to act on my fright, though. The sight of the gun and the memory of the marijuana was like shock. The shock conflicted with my general sleepiness. Before I could even wake Petey two very big men were beside the car. The one outside my window seemed enormous. The one with the gun opened Petey's door and yanked Petey out before he was even awake. The one on my side had blue eyes and a jowly face. He nodded me out but then he grabbed my arm and the way he gripped it and shoved me hurt my shoulder. The next thing I knew Petey and I were bent over the trunk of El Chevy, being searched. Petey gave me a sad, pained look. They had already found the marijuana. My shoulder twinged, but bewilderment was my strongest emotion. Why had they stopped us? We couldn't have been breaking any speed laws.

"All right boys, turn yourselves around," one said.

Petey and I did. Two very large men were facing us. I had never seen such large hands. The one from Petey's side held the shotgun by the grip, in one hand, and it looked as light in his hand as a flyswatter would have looked in mine. One look at him scared me. To him, I was a fly, okay. If he wanted to swat me, nothing was going to stop him. His head looked like it had inches of bone beneath about one sixteenth of an inch of flesh. There was no merriment in his face, only a faint contempt. The other one still smiled. Petey had begun shaking. He was extremely scared. I noticed they weren't just highway patrol. They were Texas Rangers. The one from my side walked up and loomed down at me.

"Are you real?" he said. "I ain't right sure."

"Am I what?"

"Real," he said. "I never seen nothing like you in my whole life. What about you, Luther? You ever see anythang like him?"

"Naw, I ain't," Luther said. "He ain't from Texas, that's for sure."

"I *am* from Texas," I said. "I've lived here all my life. What did we do?"

"The Meskin's carryin' dope," the first Ranger said. "I don't know what you done. Me and Luther been trying to imagine ever since we passed you the first time. We just thought we'd stop and ask you point-blank."

I was beginning to understand. My appearance displeased the Texas Rangers. I was too scared of them and too worried about the mess I had got Petey in to be at all belligerent. I was very humble pie.

"I write books," I said meekly.

"Fuck books?" Luther said. "I bet he writes them fuck books, E. Paul."

"Just novels," I said.

"You put that hair in curlers at night?" E. Paul asked. He smiled a half-smile. I was not sure I liked him any better than I liked Luther.

"No," I said.

"Why not?" he said. "Don't it get mussed up, during the day?"

"I try to keep it combed," I said.

There seemed to be no cars on the road. We were nowhere, faced with two enemies. I felt scared and responsible both. Petey might go to jail. I should have left him to his pinball and his fourteen-year-olds. The Rangers were focused on me, though.

"We're real curious," E. Paul said. "Did your momma get mixed up and raise you to be a girl, or what?"

"No," I said.

"How come you got hair like a girl's, then?" Luther asked. Now and then he flicked the shotgun from side to side, as if he were doing wrist exercises.

"I've been very busy," I said. "I forget to get it cut."

"If we was to drive you into Falfurrias and take you to a barbershop would you get it cut?"

Despite being scared I felt a little resistance.

"Is there a law against hair in Texas?" I asked.

The tiny twist of humor went out of E. Paul's face at once. He stepped closer to me. I felt violence very close to me. He jabbed my stomach with one finger.

"Right here on this road there's a law against anything me and Luther don't like," he said. "And me and Luther don't like you asking questions. You just answer questions if you don't want your goddamn head punched."

"What about that haircut we offered you?" Luther asked.

"I guess I'd take it."

"You guess."

"I'd take it," I said. "I'm not trying to prove anything. I just don't go to the barbershop very often."

"Ain't you what they call a fairy?" E. Paul said. "Me and Luther ain't never seen a real fairy—why we asked. Ain't you a fairy? Don't you suck dicks?"

"No," I said. "I'm married and have a child."

E. Paul didn't move. "I's hoping you was a fairy," he said. "I ain't never seen one, for sure. Maybe you are one and just ain't figured it out yet. I been told that happens. Maybe if you was ever to suck a dick you'd find out you's a little old fairy. Might divorce your wife, break up your happy home. I bet that'd be a nice change for your old lady."

I stood. Petey stood. Luther exercised his wrist. No cars passed. E. Paul looked down on us from beneath his Stetson.

"Maybe you ought to find out, before you get your hair cut," he said. "You keep that hair you might find some other little fairy and you two'd be just as happy as shit. We could take this Mexican over behind one of them piles of prickly pear and you could suck his dick for a while, to see if you liked it. Then you'd know if gettin' a haircut'd be the right thang to do."

I was silent. I knew bad things were coming. I wasn't going to hurry them.

"How about that? You like that idea? Answer up."

"No," I said. "I don't like it."

"You'd do it though, wouldn't you?" E. Paul said. "You'd do it if me and Luther told you to. You wouldn't be wanting to defy the law, would you?"

I didn't answer. I was not too proud to eat shit, exactly, but I knew that was the piece not to eat. He meant it. Not one car came along. I continued not to answer.

"Answer up," Luther said.

"No sir," I said. "I wouldn't do that."

"Sure you would," E. Paul said. "You'd probably take right to it. Once a dog starts sucking eggs they don't never stop."

"How long you been a fairy?" Luther asked, boring at me with his stony gray eyes.

"I'm not homosexual," I said.

"You'd do it though, if we was to tell you to, wouldn't you?" E. Paul said.

I was silent.

"Hey you. Meskin," Luther said. "How long's it been since you fucked your little sister?"

Petey looked down at his feet. For some reason they shifted focus. The focus had been on me. It became on Petey. They both looked at him.

Petey shook his head. "I don' do that," he said.

"Aw hell, you ought to," E. Paul said. "Your sister's probably dying for a little fuckee fuckee."

Luther came closer. I have heard nitroglycerine is jelly. What I felt was that such a jelly was in front of us. It quivered. Any shock could set it off. Or no shock. Violence rippled and quivered around us. I didn't know what would set it off, but I saw it in their jaws and hands. Petey and I were helpless.

Then Luther reached out with his right hand and caught Petey by one of his ears. Petey was white. I didn't know what was happening. Neither did Petey. Then Luther lifted him a foot off the ground and held him there, by his ear. Petey's face contorted. Luther held him off the ground by his ear. Luther wasn't straining and he was only using one hand. Tears ran down Petey's face. It looked like his skin would tear.

"When'd you say you fucked your sister?" Luther said. "Answer up." Luther gave him a little shake, and Petey screamed out. Luther shook him again.

"No, don', don'!" Petey said. "Tonight. Last night."

Luther dropped him and as he came down swung the shotgun against Petey's ribs. It didn't seem to hit hard, but Petey rolled when he hit. Luther sat the gun against my car. He picked Petey up by his collar and his belt and carried him to the patrol car. He dropped him, opened the rear door, then picked Petey up and threw him bodily in. The car shook when Petey hit the opposite door. Luther closed the door and came back. Despite his bullethead he had long legs. He was back in two seconds. They both stood in front of me. Violence still rippled. Petey was gone. Four stone eyes looked at me. I was backed against my car.

"Are you sure you're even a boy?" E. Paul asked.

I could almost feel Luther's iron knuckles closing on my ear.

"Why do you want to talk to me?" I said. "You don't have to play games. If you're going to beat me just do it."

"We ain't got much to do," E. Paul said. "Don't nothing that looks like you drive into our part of the country ever' day. We got to make the most out of it. We ain't gonna take no fairy like you to one of these here nice jails we got in South Texas. We got decent criminals in our jails. We ain't gonna put no pervert in with 'em. You do suck dicks, don't you?"

"No," I said.

"Yes you do," Luther said.

I felt sick and nervous and strangely passive. They were going to hit me sooner or later, no matter what I said. There was no backing any farther than I had already backed. I didn't want to, anyway. Hatred of them was in me. It wasn't dominant. Fear was dominant. But hatred was there.

"No, I don't suck dicks," I said. "I never even heard of such a thing. How'd you officers happen to hear about it?"

E. Paul stiffened. "He's shittin' us, Luther," he said.

"He ain't gonna shit me," Luther said. "I'll ream out his goddamn ass for him."

Luther moved. I started to duck, but instead of grabbing my ear he hit me with the shotgun. Not on the head, on my leg, right at the thigh. It went numb. I saw the gun swinging again and I was down. I could see under El Chevy. Oil was dripping onto the short grass of the shoulder. Then hands grabbed my hair, hands grabbed my feet. I was wrenched, I thought my neck would twist off. I was lifted. Luther had my hair, E. Paul had my feet. I tried to grab Luther's wrist but he hit my hand. He only had one hand in my hair. They were carrying me. My eyes flooded. My scalp was tearing. The sky swung above me. We were in a ditch. They began to swing me. My neck wrenched again. I was swinging. Then flying. I had no idea what to do. My wrist hit something. I was over a fence. I hit the earth and rolled. A huge prickly pear bush was over me. I hit it and stopped. Guns went off. Chunks of prickly pear flew over me. Thorns flew. The Rangers were shooting up the prickly pear. The shots were horribly loud and bullets hit right above me. I was squeezed against the thorns. I looked and saw Luther leveling the shotgun. Whow Whow Whow! Prickly pear flew, showering down. I cowered under the bush. I heard loud laughter. The two Rangers were leaning on the barbed-wire fence. E. Paul had a pistol in his hand. Luther ejected a shell from the shotgun. I was trembling terribly. They were laughing. I saw them stroll to the patrol car, perfectly cheerful and casual and happy, like athletes who have just won a game. They chatted. E. Paul holstered his pistol. They got in the car, turned, drove away. Petey wasn't even visible.

A thorn had gone deep into my elbow. I had hundreds of little fuzz thorns in my neck and they were stinging. The fuzz thorns were all over me. I got up and limped to the fence. I noticed a gash in one arm. It was bleeding a lot. My arm must have hit the fence when they slung me over it. One of my legs would barely work. I got through the fence and across the road. I remembered Petey's face, when it had looked like his skin would rip. Now his life was ripped, because of me. He might be years seeing another fourteen-year-old. It was sickening, the hurts I had caused accidentally, but I was too tired to be sick or even to cry. I drove. My left leg was too sore even to work the brake. I drove with one foot. I couldn't begin to get the thorns out of my arms and neck. They were tiny thorns, and I was shaking. I drove and drove, feeling like a coward. Waves of hatred and regret swept over me. The encounter had taken me by surprise, but even if I had had days to prepare for it I don't know how much more courage I could have managed. I drove. I went past orange groves. I was in the Valley. The sun was lower. In McAllen I stopped and asked an old man about a hospital. He told me where to go and I found it. The Rio Grande was only six miles away. It was a white hospital. The nurse at the desk looked at me as if I was crazy. I think I was, a little. Fortunately she was a kindly nurse.

"Well, we're gonna get the stickers out of you and fix that cut," she said.

"Yes ma'am," I said. I followed the nurse down a hall. There was a room with several nurses in it. They looked shocked to see me.

"What'd you do, fall right in the middle of a patch of prickly pear?" one asked.

"No ma'am. Some Texas Rangers threw me in it, because of my hair."

"My lord," she said. "Stretch out here on this table." She looked at my arm and clicked her tongue.

"How long since you had a tetanus shot?" she asked. I had no idea. I shut my eyes. It was a great relief to find someone with a sense of what to do. My own had left me.

"No need to ask him," an old nurse said. "He can't make good sense, he's too tuckered out. Just give him one."

"Thank you," I said. It seemed like a great blessing, not having to try and talk, or remember, or explain. Hands moved my arm, a palm felt my forehead, but I didn't open my eyes. The nurses knew what to do. I left the world for the darkness behind my eyelids. All I heard was the murmurings of nurses. I didn't have to worry. The thorns were being drawn from me. "Don't them Rangers beat anything?" a voice said. I didn't care. I didn't have to think. I stayed behind my eyelids, in a deep deep peace.

18.

THE PEACE didn't last long. A nurse woke me up to ask me if I could afford a room, or what kind. They had the thorns out and my arm bandaged. It wasn't the nurse's fault about the peace. It hadn't lasted anyway. I began to remember Petey, and to feel worried and nervous. Images flickered in the darkness. I was just as glad to be awakened. Sleep was knotting me up again. I sat up. I didn't want to stay in the hospital. I couldn't really imagine being stopped all night.

When I paid the nurses for what they had done, I noticed my money. I really had plenty. I also had thousands in San Francisco. Money was worth something. Before I left the hospital I went to a pay phone and called Godwin.

"Why Danny," he said. "Nice to hear you, my boy. How is Sally?"

"I don't know," I said. "I need your help."

I told him about Petey. Godwin listened. It seemed to me he would be the best person to help. He had more know-how than Flap or Jenny or anybody I knew.

"I'll send you five thousand dollars," I said. "Do you think you can get him off for that? If not, I'll send you ten thousand."

"Hum," Godwin said. He seemed very calm.

"How's Geoffrey?" I asked.

"You broke his hip," Godwin said. "He swears vengeance. I've had a delicious time nursing him, though. I've an idea you oughtn't to come to Austin."

"I hadn't planned to," I said. "Will you try to help Petey?"

"Of course," he said. "What jail is it? Kingsville?"

"Kingsville."

"Where will you be?"

"I don't know," I said. "I have no plans."

"I do sympathize," Godwin said. "For years I led a planless life."

He wished me good luck. The Valley sky was deep purple. I went to a drugstore and bought some envelopes and stamps and mailed Godwin a check for five thousand dollars. I didn't want to get tired and forget it.

But I had stopped being tired. When I walked back to El Chevy after mailing the letter I wasn't very tired at all. I was more lonely. The Valley night was soft and warm, warmer than the Austin night. I would have liked to be walking in it, with somebody. There just wasn't any prospect of anybody, up any of the roads I might drive. I sat in the car on the street of McAllen, watching the other cars go by. I didn't know why I was so alone. I had never really felt quite so alone. The one hope in all the world was Jill, and she was hard to predict. Conceivably she might want to see me. If she did I could start looking for an airplane. I would have somewhere to go.

I went to a phone booth and called New York. Maybe she wasn't still there. But she was. She was still registered at the Hotel Pierre. She was even in her room. When I heard her soft quick voice my heart pounded. My chest filled. I could hardly speak I was so relieved. I said hello.

"Danny," she said. "Where are you?"

"On the Mexican border. I've been meaning to call for days."

"Why is your voice cracked?"

"I'm pretty tired," I said. "I haven't been sleeping well."

"Tell me," she said. "I've been worried."

She sounded like she had been worried. She sounded right, like she knew me and liked me. For a minute I had been afraid she would just be wary.

I told her. She listened. Across the thousands of miles I could imagine her face as she was listening. It was a great relief to talk to her. I told her so several times.

"Stop saying that," she said.

When I had told her everything, we were silent. Jill sighed.

"I've never known anybody who could screw up as bad as you do," she said.

I had no answer for that. "What are you doing?" I asked. I had said enough about me.

Jill sighed again. "Oh, Danny," she said. "I don't want to say it."

"Why? Say what?"

"I'm going to Europe next week," she said, very low. "Carl was in New York when I got here. I may marry him. I think I may be what he needs."

I felt horribly, terribly awkward. What I really wanted was to be off the phone.

"So you see I can't save you," she said. "I know exactly how lonely you are. I know exactly how wonderful you are, too. But I can't even try and help you. I've promised to go try and help Carl."

"Okay," I said.

"I'm going to hang up," she said. "I can't stand to hear you. I'm sorry. I'm just not strong enough to try and talk."

"It's all right," I said. "Thanks for everything."

"I didn't do anything," she said.

The silence after the call was a new condition. There had been silence, and then there had been Jill's voice for a few minutes, and now there was silence again. Only there wouldn't ever be any more of Jill's voice. There would only be silence. People were dropping away from me. I might as well have been in space. I felt like I was in space. I was walking on the earth, but I wasn't walking on it like the other people on the streets of McAllen. I was somewhere else, in a silence.

I decided to go to Reynosa. It was a whorehouse town, just across the river. I didn't feel like driving very far. I didn't feel like whoring, either, but I could sit in Reynosa and drink, or something. There would be a lot of college kids around, whoring. The Valley had beautiful night skies. Purple sky, stars over the palm trees, soft, warm air. Ordinarily I would have been happy just being in the Valley.

At the border I parked El Chevy and got a Mexican taxi. My taxi driver was a fat Mexican who talked about Stan Musial. He wanted to know if I had seen him play. I was forced to admit I hadn't.

"Stan the Man," he said. "He is great ball player. I have seen him play. You should see him play sometimes."

"I'll try," I said.

I sat in the same whorehouse for two hours. I drank enough tequila that the whores even quit pushing it. Every girl in the house came over to feel me up—or all but one. Most of them were young and many of them had their hair dyed red. I didn't want to screw anybody. I just drank and listened to the jukebox. Lots of Anglo college kids were there, bragging about their cocksmanship. They looked at me askance. I looked at them askance right back. The one whore who didn't feel me up was the only one I would have been interested in, if I had been there to whore. She was an older woman, for a whore—dark-haired and maybe twenty-five. Lots of kids were pestering her. She looked half-contemptuous and half-sorrowful. She didn't play the usual games. She didn't giggle and feel boys up. I came to like her. She only went off with boys who dropped all pretense and insisted. She came and went several times, and I got drunk.

Finally a gang of Aggies came in and began to pester the dark-haired whore. About six of them clustered around her. She sneered at them. They pestered. She was very attractive. I had watched her long enough to want her. Besides, I was feeling chivalric. I didn't like Aggies. They would just grow up to be Texas Rangers, probably. I got up and went over. When the woman looked at me I smiled and held up some money. I had a good bit in my hand. I smiled again and nodded. She looked at me again, solemnly, and then got off her bar stool. The Aggies all looked around. They didn't like my looks at all.

"What the fuck," one said. "We seen her first."

I merely waited for the woman to thread her way through them.

"What the fuck," the lead Aggie said again. He had short sandy hair and he looked belligerent. I didn't care. I had had lots of tequila and besides I had already had my scare for the day. No Aggie or combination of Aggies was going to scare me.

"Big idea?" another one said. He had just realized what was happening. He was drunk and didn't enunciate very clearly.

"Why don't you farm boys go fuck a tractor," I said, and walked off with the whore. The Aggies were nonplused. I think they considered me insane.

The whore took me behind the bar, to an open courtyard. Rooms opened off the courtyard. Hers was an ordinary little whore's room. Cheap bed, cheap dresser, two or three dresses hanging on a nail. A color picture of two grinning Mexican children, undoubtedly hers. A pitcher and a basin. A dressing table with a cheap mirror. I was wondering why I had done it. I had seen such rooms before, and I didn't need the depression I usually took away from them.

The woman was friendly enough, but reserved. We made no small talk. Her reserve was part sadness and part dignity. It was the dignity of her face that had made her stand out among the teenage whores. Most of the others were not even old enough to have been disappointed. The woman I was with had been. But there was no bitterness in her reserve. She was just keeping something of herself for herself. Her underwear was cheap. She had a lovely body still, just beginning to show in the abdomen and thighs the falling off there would be in the next few years. Her breasts were beautiful, neither nubile nor fallen, and her skin was a little olive, only faintly. It made me think I might like Italy, where I had been told women were that way. I passed my examination and we got on the bed. The lady composed herself and I felt odd. I wanted to screw her but at the same time I felt wrong about it. Not wrong enough to stop but wrong enough to make me enter as gently as I could. I knew it would have to be depressing, having the hard organs of strangers jammed into one, time after time, day after day, week after week. She seemed a nice woman and though I wanted her I didn't want to increase the difficulties of her life. I entered gently and came quickly. Soon I withdrew. I sat on the edge of the cheap bed. The dark-haired whore sat beside me a moment. She looked at me.

"You gotta wife?" she asked.

I shook my head no. I didn't have a wife.

The bed squeaked when she got up. She went over to the little basin and squatted to wash herself. "Too bad," she said, looking at me for a moment as she was cleaning herself. "You are a good man."

"Thank you," I said.

I could not have told her how grateful I was. She wasn't my friend, she didn't love me, she wasn't the whore-with-the-heart-of-gold pouring out sympathy. There had been no sympathy in her remark. A woman of some experience had passed a practical judgment, while cleaning herself. Someone appreciated something about me. In my whole life I had never felt so certain that I was more or less a good man. She cleaned me and got into her cheap underwear and cheap dress and we walked back through the warm Valley night, without saying much more. Her name was Juanita. The Aggies were still in the bar, at a table with several young whores. They left us both alone. Juanita and I parted with respectful looks.

But I couldn't leave it at that. I tried. I meant to. I just couldn't. I got a taxi and went back across the border to El Chevy and drove to McAllen. Then I got very lonely again. I had it vaguely in mind that I would drive to Roma and look up the old actor that Petey knew. He ran an all-night filling station, so he would probably be up. But while I was driving through McAllen I changed my mind. I was too lonesome to go see an eccentric. I knew too many eccentrics as it was. I needed someone normal, for a while. If I didn't get someone normal for a little while I knew I would never get anyone normal, for any length of while. I was right on an edge. I couldn't get lonelier and stranger than I was or I would never stand a chance of getting back where the normal people were.

Juanita was my best hope. I would go see her again. It would only cost twenty bucks, and it might change everything. Maybe she didn't have anything going in her life. Maybe she wanted to quit whoring and come to America. It wouldn't hurt to see. I went back to the border and got the same taxi and had the same conversation about Stan Musial. It didn't bother me. Inside I was imagining how Jill and Emma and Jenny would all scream and tear their hair with vexation if they knew I was about to ask a Mexican whore I had just met to come to America and live with me. It would confirm their worst fears about my impulsiveness. I couldn't help it. Jill and Emma and Jenny weren't going to help me. I would have to help myself. I liked Juanita. There was no one else who might want to live with me.

She was a little surprised to see me back so soon. The Aggies had left the young whores and were clustered around her again. They were dumfounded to see me. I held up my money again. Juanita smiled a little. She raised an eyebrow, not sure I was serious. I kept the money up. She shrugged and got off the bar stool.

"Fucked any tractors yet?" I asked the Aggies.

They didn't say a word. Perhaps they thought I was a holy man.

I asked Juanita how much for the night and she said fifty dollars. I gave it to her. She seemed surprised and friendly, but she kept her reserve. I didn't care. I was not out to rob her of her reserve. Sex didn't work, the second time. I was too tired, or too empty. I didn't want to go on and on, trying. I hadn't come back for sex, anyway. It worried Juanita a little. She wanted me to try harder. Instead, I withdrew.

Juanita sat up. She looked at me and frowned.

"What's the matter?" she said. "You got somebody you love?"

"I love two or three people," I said. "It just doesn't seem to work out."

Juanita smiled and patted me on the shoulder. "Pussy's pussy, honey," she said. "You might as well get it from me. Come on. We can do it. I'll help you."

"No thank you," I said. "I'm really too tired."

I had come back for company—sex was what Juanita had to sell. In another few minutes we weren't going to know what to do with each other unless we quit being whore and customer. I told her I had a lot of money and asked her if she would like to come to America with me. She was smart enough to know I was serious and it flattered her slightly. But she shook her head. "Couldn't get no papers," she said. "Besides, my children. They live in Morelia. I go see them. I couldn't go see them from the U.S.

"You can come see me, when you get horny," she said. "That's easier. I make you a good price." She lay back with a long easy yawn. She had a wonderful body. I decided to go on. She probably wanted to sleep. By morning I might be in love with her, if I didn't go. I told her I had to go and refused to let her refund me any of the money. It bothered her a little. She didn't think she'd given me anywhere near fifty dollars' worth. I think she decided I was a little crazy, but it didn't make her stop liking me. Naturally she got up and went in when I left, to whore some more. She was a practical woman, with children to think of, and she wasn't lazy. She held my arm as we were walking across the courtyard. She knew she had a satisfied customer and I think she thought I'd probably be back tomorrow. I left her with the impression that I'd certainly be back sometime. It wasn't insincere. I liked Juanita. I would have liked to see her again. It was just that the odds were against it. If I did ever get back to Reynosa, Juanita would be somewhere down the line. She was sitting in the bar when I left, a little reserved, a little melancholy, a little proud. The men around the room were getting up their nerve. Maybe she would escape them, finally. Maybe she would turn into a fat Mexican grandmother, with sleepy sons like Petey.

In any case I wouldn't see her again, probably.

I got another taxi, rode to El Chevy, and this time made it through McAllen. I pointed up the river, toward Roma. El Chevy was rattling a bit. He was old. He had taken me more than a hundred thousand miles. Perhaps it was time I retired him, gave him his freedom, let him rest. I was so tired I was a little high. I had stopped feeling sorry for myself. No more feeling sorry for myself. Why should I? None of my models in life felt sorry for themselves. Not Emma, not Jenny, not Jill. Not Juanita. It was odd that all my models in life were women, but no odder than a lot of things. Wu was a sort of model. He didn't feel sorry for himself.

I saw two hitchhikers, standing at a little crossroads. A man and a woman. I stopped and backed up to them. They were an old couple. The man carried a large paper sack. When they got in the car it immediately filled with their smell, which was the smell of sweat and old clothes.

"Where you folks headed?" I asked.

"Del Rio," the old man said. "We're sure grateful to you. Ma's momma's taken sick. We ain't had no car these last few years."

"Momma's been poorly for six months now," the old woman said. "I'm afraid this time it's apt to be the end. She's eighty-five years old."

"Gentleman might not want to talk, Ma," the old man said politely. "Some people just like to drive along quiet."

"Oh no," I said. "I like to talk."

"Well, we don't need to be talkin' about death and such, nohow," the old woman said. She had false teeth, not fitted too well. Her cheeks pooched a little.

They were silent for a while. Their faces were grave, but in different ways. The old man's was thin, the old woman's fat. The paper sack held their funeral clothes. The old woman held it in her lap and from time to time smoothed the collar of a dress that was uppermost in the sack. The old man reached in the pocket of his worn coat and brought out a bottle.

"Mind if I nip oncet or twicet?" he asked. "I've had the nerves these last few days."

"Put that up, Haskell," the old woman said. "Don't be a-drinking in front of this young boy, you're apt to get him started."

The old man took one nip anyway and then obediently screwed the cap back on the bottle.

"I was always opposed to alcohol," the old woman said. "Three of my brothers went to the bad and alcohol was what started it—ever' single one of them drank."

"Aw, peedoodle," the old man said. "They'd have been sorry even if they hadn't drank, and you know it. I've been nipping all my life and I ain't gone to the bad."

"No, but you'd be a better man if you was to stop it," she said. "Course I don't expect you ever will."

"Son, this Valley's a fine place to live," the old man said, to change the subject.

In Roma, to their great surprise, I gave them El Chevy. I had decided to do it almost as soon as I picked them up. I didn't want to drive on to Del Rio that night. I was too tired. I didn't want to put the old couple out on the road again, either. It was late and there was no traffic. The thought of them standing there with their sack was too sad. They might have to stand all night. The old woman's name was Merle Lou.

I didn't feel like driving any farther anyway. Despite the pills I had taken, and the shot they had given me, and the tequila I had drunk, and all the miles I had driven, my head was very clear. I felt almost light. I was tired of driving. It had stopped being fun. I wanted to walk for a while. El Chevy could carry the old couple to the dying woman, and then he could be free. I wouldn't need him again.

On the outskirts of Roma I stopped. It was as good a place as any to start walking. The back seat was a jumble of possessions. Everything I owned was in it—typewriter, clothes, blankets. The old couple were a little surprised at my stopping, but they politely said nothing.

I let El Chevy idle, trying to decide if I wanted to take anything with me. I didn't—not really. I never liked to walk and carry things. I got my novel, in case I ever wanted to rewrite it, and my parka, in case I ran into cold weather, somewhere along the way. That was enough.

"You folks listen," I said, turning to the old couple. "I won't be needing my car for a day or two. You folks just take it on to Del Rio and leave it where I can find it. Park it down by the bridge somewhere and throw the keys in the trunk. I've got an extra trunk key. I have a friend here in town I'm going to visit. He'll drive me up when I get ready."

They were very surprised. They had thought I was stopping to put them out. Instead, I got out, my novel in one hand and my parka in the other. The old woman accepted it at once. She was too grateful even to make a token protest.

"Why that's mighty nice of you," she said. "Haskell, you'll have to drive."

The old man got out, a little puzzled, and came around the car. There was a good moon. We could see far back down the pale pavement.

"You sure you ain't scared I'll wreck it up?" he asked.

"I'm sure you won't wreck it," I said. He shook my hand and said they were much obliged and got under the wheel and drove slowly off, El Chevy rattling just a little. For a time I heard the motor, for a time I saw the lights, then my faithful car was gone.

I walked into Roma on the pale pavement. It was a tiny town, but beautiful. The buildings were old, and most of them Spanish. It was on a bluff. The river was very near. Mexico was very near. No one was stirring in Roma. Even the dogs were asleep. My neck was sore, from Luther having swung me by the hair, but as long as I looked straight ahead I was all right. I walked right down the middle of the highway, past the low silent houses. Most of the few streetlights were burned out.

But the all-night gas station was there. I saw it long before I came to it. It was on the other side of Roma and was much the brightest place in town. Two strings of naked bulbs were strung around it.

I walked all the way through Roma, to get to it. It was the town of *Zapata*, all right. Walking through it was ghostly. It seemed to me I could hear Mexican laughter, and the sound of goat bells. I imagined a ghost cantina, full of Zapatistas. I imagined Jean Peters, walking to the church with her duenna. I remembered watching the movie with Jill, the first night we were together. Now I was there, in the place we had watched. Nobody else was there, though, only the old, low buildings and the pale street. All I had was in my head—images, and the memory of images. That was really what I needed not to have to carry any farther, so many images of people who were lost to me.

I was glad when I got to the station. It was tiny, but well lit. The naked light bulbs drew a nimbus of bugs. It was a nice little station, though. A couple of potted cactus sat by the gas pumps. The pumps were clean, and the driveway too. Two bushel baskets sat outside the door to the office, one full of peppers, one full of yellow squash. There was a washtub full of pink grapefruit sitting by the air hose. The door of the office was open and a man with a black beard sat in it, reading a newspaper. He wore a plaid shirt and Levi's and high-top motorcycle boots. He looked up at me, obviously friendly. His beard was very black and bushy. A bottle of Cabin Stills sat on the step beside him, but he didn't seem to be drinking.

"Hi, son," he said. "How far'd you have to walk?"

"Not far," I said.

"You ought to get you a Honda," he said. "I haven't walked eight steps since I got mine. Do you drink whiskey?"

"Sure," I said.

He picked up the bottle and immediately broke the seal on it.

"A friend of mine who grew up here told me about you," I said. "Didn't you used to be in the movies?"

"Sure," he said. He went in the office and came out with two clean whiskey glasses. He poured each one of them half full.

"Hope you don't take ice," he said. "If you take water just get you some out of the hose."

He folded up his newspaper, which was the St. Louis *Post-Dispatch*. Then he reached inside the door and flipped a switch. All the filling station lights went off.

"I'd rather drink by moonlight," he said.

We drank by moonlight. The man's name was Peter Paul Neville.

He talked while we drank. He had quit the movies in 1933. He had known Clark Gable, and many other stars. When he quit the movies he went in the oil business. He quit the oil business in 1945. He had enough money to last him. St. Louis was his home town. The *Post-Dispatch* took three days getting to him. Peter Paul didn't care. He was a slow reader. He wasn't a slow drinker, though. Neither was I. When I emptied my glass he filled it right up to the brim. He said the Texas Rangers were mean sonsofbitches. I agreed, though I only knew two. He had a deep voice and a deep laugh. When he paused in his talk the town was very quiet. I kept hearing ghostly goat bells. I asked Peter Paul about them.

"The river's just a hundred yards away," he said. "Little Mexican town right on the other side. They don't never go to sleep in Mexico. Even if the people do, the animals don't."

We listened to the goat bells. Dogs howled. The sounds seemed louder, once I knew they were real. Peter Paul liked my parka. He had been in Alaska. He had been all over the world. I was feeling strange, and getting very drunk. Peter Paul found some mushrooms in the pocket of my parka—they were the ones the New Americans had given me.

"They induce visions," I said.

"Aw," he said.

"They really do," I said.

"You sure it ain't a toadstool? I'd hate to die of eating a toadstool."

"They aren't toadstools," I said.

Peter Paul ate a mushroom or two. There were only five or six in the sack. I ate three. I was a little hungry. I needed something in my stomach besides whiskey. I also ate two Peanut Planks, from Peter Paul's candy machine. He asked me what I did and I told him I was a writer. I gave him my novel, by way of proof. He went in the office and got a flashlight and another bottle of Cabin Stills. I heard the crackle the seal made when he broke it. I was swirling drunk again— tired and drunk. I saw Peter Paul reading my novel by flashlight. I rested. He kept drinking. I don't think he read much. After a while he handed me the box. I took the flashlight from him and looked at a page or two myself.

"I wrote a couple of novels when I was young," he said. "I guess pretty near everybody writes a novel or two. Nobody would publish mine."

I looked at my pages under the flashlight. They looked odd. Pages. Words. Black marks on paper. They didn't have eyes, or bodies. They weren't people. I didn't know why I put marks on paper. It was a dull thing to do. There must be livelier things to do. I remembered the river books I had read. There must be thousands of rivers to see. Seeing the flowing of rivers would be more interesting than making black marks on paper. The marks didn't have faces, and I had forgotten the faces that had been in my mind when I wrote them. Jill had a face. Emma had a face. My words didn't. They didn't flow like rivers, either. They had no little towns on their banks—little towns full of whores, people, goats. I didn't know what I was doing, spending so much time with paper. Looking at my novel by flashlight made me unhappy. Undoubtedly it was no good. It didn't look at all good. Probably I had just written it to take my mind off my various problems. I remembered Jill's anger when she said I had been doing what I really wanted to do, when I wrote. Writing instead of coping. Maybe she was right. It was an awful thought. On the other hand, she was wrong. I would rather have had her with me than to write all the books I would ever write if I lived to be as old as Uncle L and won every prize there was to win and became even more serious than Thomas Mann, if such a thing were possible. I would rather have Jill.

She had won, anyway. Her little sketch of people fucking under the baby bed had had more life in it than my words. It was her story. I had been a fool to think I could steal it. I shined the flashlight on fifteen or twenty pages and didn't like any of them. What a waste of me. Jill was gone, too. Who could blame her?

I felt terrible, and I was swirling drunk. I saw Peter Paul get up. I had almost forgotten him. He went over to the washtub and came back with two grapefruit.

"Here. Eat some citrus fruit," he said. "It's good for what ails you."

"Nothing ails me," I said. "This is just the way I am."

"Did you run away from the woman or did the woman run away from you?" he asked.

"Both," I said. "Everything." I didn't feel like talking to him, really. He gave me a grapefruit but I didn't peel it. I felt like I had several of them crammed inside me. All my insides seemed to be bunched in my chest. The rest of me was light but my chest felt like it was packed with sandbags.

"There's always a woman in the story," Peter Paul said.

I really wanted to go away. Peter Paul, charming as he probably was, had begun to pall on me. He was just a smoother version of Henry. If he happened to write screenplays about the Seventh Cavalry they would be better than Henry's, but not so hilarious. Henry was pure. Peter Paul was just charming. He knew he was eccentric. Also, he sounded like a sage. I didn't need a sage. I was just looking for a friend.

"I've lost five women myself," he said, peeling his grapefruit.

"It don't really kill you," he said, a little later.

"Why not?" I asked.

"Oh, after you've done it two or three times you get some style," he said. "A little style helps, my boy."

"No," I said.

"Sure. Losing women ain't the worst thing in life. You'll learn to handle it."

"No thank you," I said. "How far is the river?"

"Here, son," he said. "None of that talk. Get you some pride. You're too young to drown yourself."

"I'm not going to drown myself," I said. "I'm just going."

I stood up and got my parka and my manuscript. Peter Paul wasn't going to help me. He was a happy man. He liked to keep an all-night gas station. He liked to read the *Post-Dispatch*. He liked having been in the movies. That was all right. He was very good-looking. He had beautiful even white teeth. He had probably looked good in movies. I had nothing against him. I just didn't want his advice.

"Now don't go off feeling sorry for yourself," he said, standing up. "That won't do no good."

"Thank you, I won't," I said.

My head was swirling, but I didn't feel sorry for myself. I had no grounds for being mad at life. Everything that had happened had served me right. I knew that a lot better than Peter Paul would ever know it. I just wanted to be away from all the people who didn't know the things I knew.

"Thank you for the drinks, sir," I said. "I think I'm going to visit Mexico."

Peter Paul was a little shaken up. He didn't know what to make of me, really.

"Listen, son, keeping your pride's the important thing," he said, following me across the driveway. "Don't let no woman take your pride away."

He patted me on the shoulder and looked me in the eye. I think he was used to hitchhikers who were eager to take his advice. He hadn't realized I was independent.

"You're crazy drunk," he said. "You're all confused. Dignity. Everybody's got to have dignity."

"I don't," I said. "Fuck dignity. I'll be who I am without it.

Peter Paul was flabbergasted. I hadn't meant to be so blunt. I was just tired of sententious talk. I was tired of words like dignity, concepts like pride. I walked around the filling station, past a pile of tires, swirling a little. Peter Paul followed me, talking. I could barely hear him. I wasn't too steady on my feet, but inside my head I was clear. My fatigue high had come. I felt like I could walk forever.

I walked past a couple of sheds, past a low stucco house. I was on some kind of trail, maybe some very old trail. Soon I came to the bluff. In the moonlight I saw the shining river. I could see it curving out of the west, see it curving on toward the sea. It wasn't very wide, but it was the Great River—the Rio Grande. At last I was somewhere. I had read about it for years, along with other rivers. I was full of its name, full of all sorts of names, of people I knew, people I didn't know. Everything was coming in on me.

I went on down the bluff, on the little trail. Peter Paul was talking, somewhere behind me. He was on the bluff. I didn't answer. I wasn't going back. I would never turn around. People didn't want such feelings as I had. I didn't blame them. Neither did I. I just had them. I could see the Mexican village, just a few yellow lights. I didn't want to go there. I knew I would never learn. People were right. If I lived to be a hundred I would still be just as stupid. I would still do all the wrong things, with whatever people blundered into my path. Something was just wrong. I had missed some door. It would never open now. My chest felt tight.

The door to the ordinary places was the door that I had missed. The door to Emma's kitchen, or to all such places. There would never be an Emma's kitchen for me. There was no point in being maudlin. Such things were just true. It was as clear as the stars above the Rio Grande, as clear as the sound of goat bells from the village. Okay. My heart would just have to accept it. I would live in the other places, among the exiled ping-pong players and the old ladies with dogs on their arms, and my true companions would be Godwin and Jenny and all those who had missed the same door. Okay. I was tired of trying to make things different than they could be. I wanted to go away. I wanted some empty distance. Voices rose from the village, human laughter, liquid in the liquid night.

Not the village. I turned up the river, walking close to the water. Peter Paul had come down the bluff. He was shouting about Mexico. He didn't like it. He thought I was crazy. I wasn't crazy, though. Just swirling a little, from liquor and feeling.

"You ain't gonna catch no ride, over there," he yelled.

"I don't want a ride," I said. "Ambrose Bierce is there."

Or was it Jack London? Or O. Henry? I couldn't remember. I crossed the sand to the edge of the water. The water was quiet. I could see far up the river. The moon made the water shine. Spaces filled me. I was not close to anyone, not even myself. Parts of me were drifting. Water filled my shoes. Peter Paul was still following me. I thought I heard Godwin's voice. I remembered Odysseus, standing by the ditch of blood, keeping back spirits. Those were dead spirits, though. I had living spirits to keep back. I imagined Jill, flying in an airplane across an ocean. I imagined Jenny, working in her flower beds. And my daughter, a completely unknown spirit, one more girl to love, if I ever met her. Too many spirits. I looked up the river. It came out of Colorado, out of New Mexico.

The only space left in me was in my head. All the rest of me was full, wet, a pulp of feeling, squishy as a grapefruit. I noticed my novel. I was carrying it. What stupidity. The clear part of my head knew that much. I didn't have to write anymore. Knowing things was bad enough.

But then there was Emma. She had liked that about me. Maybe she was right, a little bit. Maybe I had forgotten to tell her I loved her.

I couldn't remember what I had told her, or what I hadn't. I waded out of the river. Peter Paul was still following me. I knelt in the sand. He might as well be some help. I opened the box of manuscript. Fortunately I had a pen. I got out the old prologue, and the old epilogue. Granny and Old Man Goodnight were the only good things in the box. Emma might like them. I couldn't write anything on them, it might upset Flap, but I could send them. I sat down in the sand and scrawled Emma's name and address on top of the prologue. Peter Paul came walking up.

"Well, you come to your senses," he said. "You worried the shit out of me."

I got a ten-dollar bill out of my billfold. I handed Peter Paul the bill. Then I handed him Granny in the flapping tent, I handed him the Old Man, riding. Emma might like them. She had always liked it that I was a writer. If she had understood it, she wouldn't, but there was no reason for Emma to understand things. She had her roundness, her family that would come.

"Would you mail these for me?" I said, handing the pages to Peter Paul. "I wrote down the address."

"Sure," he said. "You're not really going to Mexico, are you?"

I missed impossible things. I had to stop it. I didn't answer Peter Paul. I got up and waded into the river. I almost drowned, but not in water, just in regrets. The banks of the river were dark. Thousands of pale stars swirled over my head. Peter Paul yelled. He thought I was drowning. He yelled that he couldn't swim. He was a nice man. He just wasn't my companion. I was alone again. I noticed my novel. I still had it. It made me furious, tagging me everywhere. It was like it was tied to me. No wonder I felt weighted down.

I began to beat the box on the water. Peter Paul stood in the edge of the river. "You're crazy," he yelled. "Ain't that your book? What do you think you're doing?"

"Beating the pages," I said. "Let me alone! They're just words, don't you understand? I hate them! They're just pages! I'll never forgive them."

It was true. I had never felt such black, unforgiving hatred of anything as I felt for the pages in my hands. The box was soaked, but the novel was still there. Godwin had tried to drown Sally. I had tried too. I could at least drown a novel. I ripped up the box and drowned it first. I shoved it under. Then I only had the book. My head was pounding. I would drown it or die. It must have been funny. Some clear part of me even thought it was funny. But my head hurt so from blood that I couldn't laugh. Peter Paul should have laughed. A boy drowning a manuscript. I would have laughed, if I could have been the one watching. I was never the one watching, though. I was always the one the hilarious things were happening to. I picked off chapters and held them under. They didn't want to drown. The paper I used was too good. It wanted to float. Pages got loose and floated. I caught them and swatted them down. I shoved them under. No mercy for pages. It was a deadly battle. Part of a chapter slipped loose and floated. I splashed after it and forced it under. Finally it squished. The words gave up. I picked off another chapter, but killing the chapters was too slow. I had hundreds of pages left. Finally I grappled the novel in both hands and dove. I would carry it to the bottom. Only one of us would come up. I was Gary Cooper, in *Distant Drums*. My novel was the Seminole chief. We were fighting under water. The current turned me over, swirled me over. Even drunk I could swim well. The depths of the river were black. My head was pounding. I kicked and kicked, going deeper. The book in my hands was hundred-headed, like Grendel. Parts of it nearly slipped loose in the fast current. I wadded them. My superb condition began to tell on the novel—my superior strength began to prevail. The novel got squishier and squishier, deep in the channel of the Rio Grande. Finally it got completely squishy, and I knew it was dead. I let it go and came up. My head was still pounding but the river was clear. No pages floated on it, only moonlight and the reflection of stars.

Peter Paul was yelling, but I was too far from him. He couldn't see me. It wasn't safe to swim at night, he said.

I didn't answer. My feet were on the bottom and the river flowed beneath my arms. Jill Peel would be proud of me, if she could know. I had killed it in honorable battle and given it to the sea, as she had wished. I remembered her little drawing, my pages floating down into the bay, a studious sea gull reading them. My face was hot from the fight I had just had. It was always a borderland I had lived on, it seemed to me, a thin little strip between the country of the normal and the country of the strange. Perhaps my true country was the borderland, anyway.

I looked up the river, north and west, to where the Sorrows lay beneath the same pale stars. A hole opened in the night, but I didn't see the great scenes anymore, the Old Man riding, the Old Woman standing on the ridge, the wild scenes from the past that I usually saw when I was walking some border of my own at night. Maybe all that was over. All I saw through the hole in the night were the bright windows of the hospital, yellow in the Houston drizzle. But I didn't want to see the windows, I wanted to see the tiny person. My face was very hot. I looked up the river again and saw it coming down to me, shining in a beautiful cold flow. It came from the mountains, like the Ganges, came through the desert, like the Nile. I waded up it. It was cool beneath my arms. All sorts of names and faces troubled me. Emma, Jenny, Wu—also Jill. I turned south. Many famous names lay south of my days. The Amazon. The Rio Negro. Zapata in the hills. Balboa and Peter Martyr and the great Juan de la Cosa.

I had read of those rivers, and those people. I knew all the great names of the south, all the way from the Rio Grande to the Straits of Magellan. I waded that way and the river flowed down to me. I was so glad. It was one thing I could have. I waded deeper. Such a wonderful thing, to flow. I wanted to so badly. It was all I had ever wanted to learn. I put my face in the water, to cool it. Stars swirled near me, and swirled above me, too, so high, so pale, such distances away. On the bank I was just leaving, the dim bank of Texas, Peter Paul kept yelling for me to come back.

"I had rather go see the rivers," I said, but I don't know if he heard me and if he did he wouldn't have understood, he was too normal to understand, if my friends came and asked him why I had left he wouldn't know, he had never stood in the river, I don't think he swirled as I was swirling, he didn't seem to yearn to flow, he didn't much want to be undertaken, he didn't remember Zapata and hadn't even read of the great Juan de la Cosa, and if they came, my friends, if Wu came, for some reason, or Godwin, or Jenny, they wouldn't get it from him, he wouldn't know why I loved the river, why I loved any of the people I loved, they wouldn't get it from him and none of them could guess, only maybe Jill could, I knew only Jill could, if I had stayed, if she had stayed, I could tell her, she might guess, she had the clearest eyes, the straightest look, the most honest face, I missed it so—but ah no, no chance, better just to want rivers—Jill was gone.

picador.com

blog
videos
interviews
extracts